DYING BREEDS

KIRK JONES

JOURNALSTONE
YOUR LINK TO ARTIST TALENT

ISBN: 978-1-68510-076-6 (sc)
ISBN: 978-1-68510-077-3 (ebook)
Library of Congress Catalog Number: 2022949601

First printing edition: November 25, 2022
Printed by JournalStone Publishing in the United States of America.
Cover Design by Mikio Murakami
Edited by Sean Leonard
Proofreading and Cover/Interior Layout by Scarlett R. Algee

JournalStone Publishing
3205 Sassafras Trail
Carbondale, Illinois 62901

JournalStone books may be ordered through booksellers or by contacting:
JournalStone | www.journalstone.com

For my wife, Amanda. Thanks for riding along through this series of pipe dreams, even when it was in a '98 Toyota so rusted out the entire rear bumper exploded when we had it towed. If only all the kids on the school bus that morning could see us now...

I think we're finally hitting the open waters.

DYING BREEDS

CHAPTER ONE

MOLLY

SHE NEVER LOOKED in the mirror on April 21st. It was the first of many rituals Molly used to stave off the flood of memories that would inevitably spill over into the present. Getting past what had happened had proven impossible. The next best thing, she resolved, was to avoid even the smallest of triggers. It had been six years, and even that never got easier.

Six years since Pheta Xi burned on Oakland Avenue.

Six years since her grandfather's camera had disappeared somewhere between the house and the hospital.

The worst part was, she didn't just think about that day each April 21st. She relived it every year.

The technical term lobbed at her by her doctor was *hyperthymesia,* sort of like photographic memory, except your mind latches onto the mundane daily activities spanning as far back as memory reaches. Sometimes the memories were so strong it felt as if she were living in two moments at once. On good days, she dredged memories up at will. On bad days, memories were recalled involuntarily through various triggers.

April 21st was *always* a bad day, so she prepared the night before to avoid any and every act that might recall memories from the day of the fire, an endeavor she already knew was in vain.

She remembered eating cereal the morning of the fire—corn flakes—so she always emptied the box of corn flakes, broke down the cardboard, and tucked it into a small stack of kindling in the basement.

Rummaging through her drawers for clothing was another trigger, so she laid her clothes out the night before, always on the dining room table instead of the edge of the bed.

As a student, her favorite spring attire had always been a sweater and jeans. Since the fire, even in the chill of early spring, she opted for a dress.

She always avoided the attic. She'd avoid the house altogether if she could, but being her grandfather's, and being unoccupied when she withdrew from college, her mother secured it for a more than fair price. Molly agreed to live there until she could get on her feet.

Still, as she looked at the calendar to confirm the date, everything came rushing back to her again. The heat seeping through the attic door smelled of dust and drying wood, reminding her of the accordion camera her grandfather had left for her in a tomb of newspaper clippings and mouse shit. The warped threshold to her bedroom reminded her of the camera's awkward construction, the fact that the pictures were dispensed from the bottom of the camera rather than the front.

She knew it was futile to try and stop the salvo of memories from overlapping her morning ritual.

As she fumbled with her water flosser, her mind was also six years in the past, pulling her grandfather's camera away from her face, checking for an opening, somewhere to insert film. She remembered tapping the camera against her palm. It sprang to life, pushing a grainy photograph out of its innards. She reached for the photo as it fell to the floor, but it slid through her fingers and then through one of the cracks between the floorboards.

As she surreptitiously dropped a butter knife onto the countertop, she remembered—relived—waking up to the sound of metal tablespoons clanging against aluminum buckets. One of her classmates from high school, Samantha Ohst, had convinced her to pledge for PXO at Johnstown College. Rush week was a goddamned nightmare. Waking up to the cacophony of inductees being herded from bed was just the beginning. Once roused from bed, Samantha and the other sisters rummaged through the pledges' bags, taking whatever they wanted.

Of course they wanted Molly's camera.

Molly walked to the fridge to grab a stick of butter, wishing she'd switched to margarine. You could leave that stuff out for days and it never went bad. She opened the fridge door and remembered opening the door to her room at PXO. She remembered the flash of her camera as Sam took her picture. They didn't just take her camera. They were using it. Molly wrenched it from Sam's hands, noticing another pledge on the bed, sparsely clothed, skin scrawled with magic marker obscenities. She still didn't understand why the sisters were so intent on humiliating the pledges, or documenting their humiliation.

And she never had the chance to ask.

She remembered turning the camera on Sam, snapping as many photos as she could before running for the front porch. She'd intended to report them. That was all.

The toast Molly had been preparing popped into view, black as ash. Her daughter Jolie had been toying with the knobs again. She made a mental note to talk to her later when the smell of smoke wafted into her nose. She pulled back. Not smoke. Not today.

It was too late. As she inhaled, she remembered Sam holding her lighter over the photos Molly had taken. As they caught fire, Sam dropped the photos onto the cement walkway. She watched the fire scatter across the collection. The pictures curled upward and began to bubble, and Sam's hair erupted in flame. She scratched at her back, tore her shirt off and threw it on the ground, stomping on the sweater. But the sweater was unscathed. The smoke exuding from Sam's back came from within, from beneath the flesh.

Molly closed her eyes as the smoke alarm blared. But she could still see Sam—six years earlier—writhing in the dirt to put out the flames that had consumed her entire body.

She woke to the smallest of hands shaking her. "Mom! Mommy, you okay?!"

Jolie.

"I'm fine, honey."

"You made toast for me?"

Molly tried to sit up, but felt immobilized by the memories still being force-fed to her. She was being slid into the back of an ambulance.

No. That was six years ago. She was on the kitchen floor now with her daughter by her side. She had that much sorted out. Now she just had to let the memories run their course.

Six years in the past, an EMT hovered over her. "Did anyone else make it out of the house?"

Molly looked out the back of the ambulance, watched the smoke exude from the ashes of the sorority house superimposed over...a toaster?

Get ahold of yourself, Molly.

An officer wiped the sweat from Molly's brow. "Do you remember what happened?"

Molly shot up. "My camera!" she moaned.

"What camera?" Jolie's brows furrowed. "Can I have my toast now?"

She lay back down, a hand from the past gently pushing her onto a stretcher. It was the police officer. "Your camera's fine. Hold still."

What was his name again?

Spearance.

SPEARANCE

Since the first year of the Burning Fields Festival in Hastings, Pennsylvania, spring had been ushered in by a combination of fire and thick smoke. Save a handful of residents who complained about the smell, the festival was generally a time for celebration—one last hurrah before the farmers hunkered down in the fields to plant the season's crops. John Spearance had shared the demeanor of other Hastings residents. He'd been at the festival almost every year until he took his oath of office as a village trooper. Since then, smoke signified the funeral pyre of smoldering bodies upon which his marriage and half-extinguished career rested. In his short tenure he'd seen two fires. Both unrelated to the festival. Both bearing casualties. It seemed that no matter how many years life put between him and those damned fires, the smoke was always there to remind him of his failures.

In 1982, John Spearance had only been on the force for two years, and in his late 30s, he was already twenty years late to the profession. As such, he always got the crap calls: noise complaints, bonfires during burn bans, the small stuff that didn't make for good bar-stool stories down at the American Legion, which was fine with him. He'd hated drinking at the Legion anyway.

April of that year was no different. He was called to a bonfire. For the second time in his short tenure, he'd been the first officer to arrive to thick plumes of smoke billowing into the night sky, and flames bright enough to light the smoke's trajectory into the heavens above. The first time...the first time he tried not to think about. But his subconscious still qualified the tragedy such that the urge to flee this second scene overwhelmed him. He trudged on regardless, down the driveway, through the fence opening, and around the house.

In the back yard, Danielle Ohst stood before her gazebo, lit ablaze. She was in her bathrobe, which had been seared in parts by her proximity to the fire. She had a pile of something behind her—photo albums, it looked like—and she had just tossed another stack into the gazebo as Spearance came from around the corner. "Danielle, you need to step away from the fire. That bathrobe isn't long for this world, and I fear you won't be either if you stand so close."

"They burned my baby!" she shouted, reaching for another album on the ground. She tossed it into the gazebo, her robe fluttering in the wind toward the flames.

"They?" Spearance asked. Samantha had been killed the year prior in that first fire Spearance tried in vain to forget, a sorority fire in Indiana, Pennsylvania. After months of investigation, it was determined accidental. Truth is, nobody knew what the hell had caused the fire, but anyone you talked to would agree, no "they" figured into it.

Spearance took another step toward her. "I know you're still grieving, but I need you to step away from the fire. You're going to hurt yourself."

She reached for another album and threw it in the fire. "Every picture..." She threw another in. The pile of albums and loose photos was growing smaller now.

"Please. Danielle. Come with me."

She stepped toward the fire. "Take another step and I'll throw myself in."

"Danielle."

She stepped closer to the flames. Only a few feet away, she threw another album into the fire. She shook her head. "Burned. On every page." She opened the album and ran her fingers down one of the inner pages. "Every picture. She's gone."

Spearance reached out for her hand, turning his face away from the fire. How could she even stand that close? It was unbearably hot. "Please."

She closed the last album, held it firmly to her chest, took a deep breath, and dove into the flames.

She died silently. He remembered that. But every time he dreamed about it over the years that followed—Every. Damned. Time—she screamed. God, that scream, that scream he'd conjured up in his imagination to fill that silence as her body contorted and fell to a lifeless heap of black ash, just as her daughter's had only one year before. That scream that always transitioned into some sound in the waking world—the alarm clock, the snow plows every winter, and this time, the phone.

He rolled over, the pain in his lower back the one thing reminding him it wasn't '82 anymore—he sure as hell wasn't 37 anymore either—and picked the phone up. "Yeah?" He put on his glasses and threw the blankets back. Putting a phone on his nightstand was one of the worst decisions he'd ever made. But with a crew best characterized by its lack of manpower, it was an important decision he felt obligated to make. "I'll be right there."

He sat up and turned his wedding photo toward the bed. He'd made a point to remember his wife after her passing, but she'd told him not to dwell too heavily upon it. These brief interludes between sleep and work were his best compromise. During these moments of trivial tasks—putting on his slippers, brushing his teeth, double-checking the lock on the door—he allowed himself to grieve. But once he got in the car, he had to keep living. That's what Tammy had wanted.

***

Spearance pulled into Tiernan's Self-Storage at half past 11:00pm. It was the first Monday in April, and he was already narrating the incident internally in quintessential police report fashion. But the looming deskwork hadn't fully distracted him from the non-substantive details. The sky roiled in grayscale, clouds so thick and low he swore he might be able to reach up and run his hands through them. Spring was in the air, and by "spring," everyone in Hastings meant the pervasive scent of mud and limestone.

Spearance returned to the template in his head, continued filling it out as he drove through the lot. 0500, Burglary. Intruder already fled the scene, according to the phone call that came in at 10:45pm at his residence. Scratch that. Better say it came in at the station.

He turned into row three and Blaine Norton's limestone truck was parked at the far end, just as it was every spring. Nathan Tiernan stood nearby, bolt cutters in hand.

Spearance stepped out of the car. "Limestone again, Nate?"

"Every year now." Nathan waved with his free hand. "Fred kicks up all the gravel or limestone through the winter when he plows the lanes. Blaine comes in the spring, fills it in." He looked at Blaine. "Starting to think those two have some kind of deal worked out."

Blaine smiled. "A favorable coincidence, I assure you."

Spearance shook his head, laughing. "So what happened?"

Nathan pointed to one of the 8x10 storage units. "Blaine saw someone prodding around Lola's storage unit on his last run through the lot, so he called me over. At first, I thought she must have given the key to someone. She's getting up there in years, and she's got that hired hand, the tall boy there." He scratched the back of his head. "Anyway, I walked over to see if I could help. That's when I noticed the bolt cutters." He held them up.

Spearance looked them over. "Aren't those yours?"

"He must have got them out of the shed next to the office. Anyway, I asked him to turn around." He sighed. "The damned Singleton kid again. Miles. Just can't stay out of trouble, you know? I told him to leave before I called the cops, mulled it over in my mind a bit and decided to call anyway. If the unit would have been someone local, I would have just slapped another lock on there and been done with it. But I only know Lola well enough to know brushing it off might mean the end of the library's endowment, and I'm not ready for that tax hike. I've got two rental properties in the village."

"We can't have that now, can we?" Spearance ducked into the unit. "You think he took anything?"

Nathan shook his head. "It's so cluttered in here, and I'm usually not with customers when they come and go. Probably should get Lola down here, just to see if everything's in order?" he asked.

"I'll stop by her place, try to arrange a time to come down with her for inventory. If you have any spare locks in that eight-by-eight you call an office, throw one on and keep an eye on the unit until then."

Nathan nodded and jogged for the office.

Spearance drew his flashlight across the unit's floor, catching an outcropping of photo albums. At the bottom of the stack, a photo of Lola, i.e. Mama Hastings, the benefactor of half the town. "How long was he in there?"

Blaine shrugged. "Twenty minutes, maybe. I didn't think he was up to anything fishy until he pulled the unit door down to about a foot from the ground. Then when I drove around the lot I noticed he didn't have a car."

Spearance picked up the photo. One of her nudes from the 30s, barely recognizable through a series of cuts and abrasions.

Blaine pointed to the bolt cutters. "Dropped those on the ground and headed for the front entrance." He smiled. "What'd you find there?" He glanced up, raised his eyebrows.

Spearance turned to face him. "It's what you think it is." Spearance turned it toward him.

He nodded. "I've seen that one. Not all diced up like that, though." He leaned in to steal another glance. "You think she knows how many people have seen her in the buff?"

Spearance shook his head. "Not sure I'd want to risk finding out. Best to keep Mama Hastings happy."

Nathan grinned. "She paying your salary now too, John?"

"She owns half the town. She's paying a bit of everything in some measure, I'm sure." Spearance walked back to his car. "I'll go check in with Miles."

***

As he drove, Spearance deliberated about how he was going to approach this offense. Miles had never done anything particularly problematic, but he'd seen this pattern before. Boy from a family so poor he had no prospects and nothing to lose starts off on the wrong foot. A small criminal record keeps that foot greased, keeps the kid poised for worse trouble as he gets older, culminating in a life behind bars.

Miles Singleton was Spearance's first pickup on the job. Petty theft. He stole one of the middle school history teacher's Holocaust photos and an anatomy book from the biology department. Strange combination, looking back, but at the time Spearance just saw it as a low-stakes way to break into his late-start career. Escort the kid home and call it a day.

He found Miles about three blocks from his house, photo tucked under his arm. He pulled up beside him. "Where'd you get those pictures, son?"

Miles pointed back toward the school.

"Those are Mr. O'Reilly's."

Miles froze.

Spearance reached out. "I need Nagle's anatomy reference book too."

Miles handed the glossy 8x10 to Spearance, dropped his backpack onto the ground, and reached in for the anatomy book.

Spearance stared at the image—a mass grave in Bergen-Belsen; some guy, cigarette dangling from his lips, nonchalantly bulldozing corpses into a modest pile. Was O'Reilly really showing the middle school kids this shit? "What d'you want with this?"

Miles shrugged, handed Spearance the anatomy book.

"You ever ride in a police car, son?"

Miles shook his head.

"You'll be fine. We'll just take you home to your folks."

Miles stared out the window, eyes wide and unblinking.

When Spearance pulled up at the address, he couldn't believe the house. Six apartments packed into what appeared to be a small barn cobbled together in parts with chipboard and plywood. It barely qualified as livable.

Spearance turned to face the back seat. "You want me to walk you up?"

Again, Miles shook his head. He opened the door and walked past the apartment into the back yard, plopped down on a wooden swing set and kicked at the ground.

Spearance reluctantly pulled away.

He never filed the report.

As he pulled back up to the same building, Spearance noted that in a strange way, they had christened one another's careers that day.

He hoped that today the cycle would come full circle. That today would be Miles' last day as a criminal. One more pep talk. One more "off the hook," and maybe he'd learn his lesson. He'd hoped, anyway. If Miles didn't turn it around, Spearance wouldn't be able to shake this sense of accountability.

Then of course there was the issue of this hacked-up photo to contend with. It reeked of sexual frustration coupled with violent tendencies, at best. Spearance didn't want to think what it might mean at its worst. Besides, he had no proof Miles had left it behind. He was jumping to conclusions prematurely.

Maybe the kids at the station were right. Maybe he was too goddamned old for this job. Maybe it was time to clock in for early retirement, just settle into teaching night classes in Johnstown until he could collect Social Security.

He stepped out of the car and approached apartment three, the room Miles moved into after he turned 18, just two doors down from his parents.

Spearance knocked on the door. "Miles?"

No answer, so he tried the handle. It turned, but the way the door gave suggested a bolt lock near the top. *I could just about fit my foot in through the bottom of the door.* He gave it another push.

No luck.

He muttered to himself, hoping Miles was on the other side of the door. "We'll come back later."

MILES

Miles listened as Spearance stepped into his vehicle and drove away.

He should have stopped months ago. He'd told himself that.

Hadn't he told himself that?

It started innocent enough. When Miles was a child his grandmother had let him rummage through the Hastings Museum photograph collection. That's where he'd first seen Bridgette Louise. Lola. She was the first objectively beautiful woman he'd seen, and he'd grown fascinated with her, even moreso as he grew older.

He just wanted to see if he could dredge up something interesting on her. He'd heard the rumors. That Lola had come to Hastings to store films presumed destroyed. Films she'd wanted forgotten. He suspected it was all bullshit, that the real reason she came to Hastings was to be revered with a relative degree of solitude. Still, the rumors were enough to draw his interest, but he found nothing to corroborate local hearsay in Lola's storage unit. No rusted reel canisters. No relics of Hollywood's bygone era that hadn't already been replicated and sold through mass marketing.

But even when he suspected he wasn't going to find anything of sentimental or monetary value, he couldn't stop. After everything else, he went for the pictures. Perhaps it had always been about the pictures.

The first time he ventured into Tiernan's Self-Storage, he'd systematically gone unit-by-unit with a Coke-can padlock pick until he found Lola's. That night, he told himself he'd break in just to prove to himself he could do it.

He promised himself he wouldn't look, and he made good on that promise. But a week later he went back in and spent an hour rummaging through the topmost boxes, finding mostly clothes Lola had grown out of in middle age. Clothes so old they'd have likely cycled out of thrift stores and into dumpsters, had they been donated. He had hoped to find costumes, set pieces. Instead he found only the mundane. Slacks and sweaters she wore to hide her figure. Ratty gowns to traipse about the house in private.

After that, he didn't go back for two months.

He watched the place, though. He stalked it as nonchalantly as possible, driving past it on his way to and from work. On his way to grab a six pack at the store, or to the movies in Johnstown. Every time he'd pass to an empty lot. And every time he'd get a sinking feeling in his stomach. Some part of him was glad he'd never seen her there, but another wanted to see her car parked next to the unit. He tired of waiting for the other shoe to drop.

It never did.

So after another month, he broke in again, this time shifting boxes, *hoping* she'd notice. And when she didn't—when her onset of dementia became the talk of the town—he replaced the padlock with his own. Same design; different combination. He figured this'd buy him some time if she ever got wise to his tampering.

Several months passed, and Miles found himself spending most evenings in the unit, scouring the boxes with his father's old lamplight, unit door shut.

He'd learned so much about her and the art form she had been steeped in. He'd read about her lover and the only man to break Lola's heart, the inimitable David Rothman, who co-starred in several of her films.

He'd studied the creations of her companion, Eric Tigerstedt, a Finnish inventor who was responsible for breathing new life into the film industry with a series of inventions streamlining recording and reproduction processes. He'd read stories about G.H. Maier, the famed director of small stature and only modest good looks, who could allegedly cause women to swoon simply by holding a photo of them.

He learned the philosophy that had allowed the patrons of dead art to sustain their egos. That the quality of a medium can be best judged by its ability to make itself obsolete. That the shorter the amount of time it takes to render itself obsolete, the greater the quality of the medium. That silent film expressed itself in the purest form: as a transitory element between the cliché and tomorrow. The genre outpaced itself, and Lola and her contemporaries hated the medium for it.

Only in retrospect—when others began to note the value of their contributions—did actresses like Lola begin excavating the relics of their past. By then, almost everything had been lost, excepting a few films that had been forgotten or misplaced—*Sherlock Holmes Baffled* comes to mind. Some films were lost entirely. Many were destroyed simply because their value was considered only in terms of their marketability in theatres, not the fact that they represented one of the earliest reproducible and potentially immortal forms of entertainment.

The music for these films was even rarer, often one-time performances. The positive: the film, each time viewed, generated a different audience experience relative to the music. The negative: the most efficient representations—the best nights—were forever lost.

Historians blamed the death of the industry on the disconnect between advances in technology and the film industry at the time. The ability to capture sound on film was such a monumental jump forward, that the silent industry's corner on the market was swept out from under them.

Over time, the series of innovations that had led to the industry's death had been boiled down to a single mythic innovation, a single Pandora's Box that had unleashed the plague of sound: the camera that destroyed the industry. Some hypothesized this camera was Denes Mihaly's "Projectofon." Others attributed the development to those who had tried to perfect the synchronization of sound and film. But in Lola's notes, in the photo-album liners, on the backs of what appeared to be aging Polaroids, she had implied the camera wasn't symbolic. Moreover, her liner notes seemed to suggest the camera had been gifted to her by Tigerstedt, a relic that had inadvertently been cursed, and could bring harm to anyone captured in the photos. Through this camera Lola believed she had somehow been responsible for not only the death of a few of her friends, but the entire silent film industry. When first asked about her unfounded beliefs, she'd pointed back to a fire at Fox Studios. When asked again the subsequent year: radio silence. She never spoke of it again.

Many of the stars from that era met the same fate as their medium. But their death was more gradual. The actors and actresses outlived their medium, died in obscurity, only to be resurrected and exalted to immortality after their deaths. Lola's biographer, Louis Stinson, hypothesized this belated celebration merely signified the pace of civilization. We seem arranged in time such that we're afraid to look too far into the future because we're wrapped up in the pain of the present. To complicate matters, most are too afraid to look into the past and find a remedy. We're afraid to look to the past for solutions until we can qualify it as history distant enough not to frighten us. The immediate old is cliché; the distant old is classic. Between the two extremes lies history in which man gravitates toward dissection and understanding, a safe distance from contemporary results. Silent film has finally achieved that safe distance. People are now looking back, dissecting and re-writing. Now is the perfect opportunity to re-write dead history.

But even Lola—as insightful as she seemed about silent film in her autobiography—had no idea how important her forgotten work could be, were it found. The storage unit consisted of vestiges chronicling her life, her film taking up only a tangential space: co-stars trying to capture the memory of a gathering rather than scenes on set, gifts sent to her by admirers...but nothing from the films.

Even though Miles never found what he initially sought, he couldn't stop returning to that storage unit. Even after he'd combed through everything twice, he kept poring over the books, overturning photos for clues about her life, putting everything therein together like a jigsaw puzzle. As the puzzle became clearer, the search no longer was about her life. It became about the art. This—forgotten art which once played a pivotal role in society and existed solely because of its historical importance—was the crux of innovation, and he couldn't help but feel that therein, various segues and trajectories were left unexplored in an art form's declared obsolescence. He felt this was more so the case for mediums that died untimely deaths.

Finally, the search became about this fabled camera. In Lola's albums, he had found one rugged-edged photo of Lola and three others: her director, G.H. Maier; her companion, David Rothman; and the inventor, Tigerstedt. The album liner dated the photo at 1931. According to the liner notes, the photo had been taken in Germany, where Lola had finished up her career before advents in technology made their way across the ocean to Europe.

If there had been a camera, this photo—unlike any other in her albums—had likely come from it.

Miles used that photo as a divining rod, combing through the other boxes to find like productions. He finally came upon a rusted Prince Albert tin. Inside, he found a near-perfect copy of the photo in the album, the only difference being a thick slice in the photo across Tigerstedt's throat.

According to public record, Tigerstedt had been found in his manor, decapitated, in the summer of '33.

Miles continued poring over the photos, looking for evidence of other minor injuries the photos had sustained. What he found was more unsettling than he'd initially suspected.

Every photo of Tigerstedt he found—excepting the ones where his neck was covered—featured the light intimation of scarification across Tigerstedt's throat.

And it wasn't just the pictures in Lola's storage unit. He found pictures in her autobiography, at the museum, all of which featured the faint trace of Tigerstedt's untimely demise.

What's more, in an interview, David Rothman had indicated that he had left Lola when she descended into a sort of self-loathing madness after Tigerstedt's death. She blamed herself for it, for the fire at the studio, for everything bad that had incidentally happened in their lives. She had taken the weight of everything upon herself, and meant to answer for it.

Perhaps she was mad.

Perhaps there was some legitimacy to holding herself accountable.

Miles took the tin and both of the photos of Lola and her friends, the copy and what appeared to be the original. He restored everything in the unit to its original place, and vowed to never return to the unit again.

But he had, and wouldn't you know it, that other shoe finally dropped. Nathan Tiernan had caught him with a pair of bolt cutters, bolt cutters he'd needed because he'd been away so long he'd forgotten the combination on his own lock.

There was no going back there now. They were going to get a warrant. They were going to search the place. They'd find the tin, and that'd be enough to take Miles into custody.

But as long as they didn't find him, he'd be safe.

CHAPTER TWO

SPEARANCE

HASTINGS POLICE STATION, like the rest of Hastings, was only a few rungs up from the apartment building Spearance had just visited. The drywall was discolored near the floor where water leaked in every winter and spring. They'd abandoned the carpet after waterproofing efforts proved futile, leaving them with laminate that tried desperately—and failed spectacularly—to emulate hardwood. Accentuating the spotted drywall and bubbling laminate were the light-blue blinds, highlighted by a thin layer of tobacco tar and discoloration from Bo Durham's fingers prying the slats open every time he saw a car pulling in.

This morning was no different. When Spearance pulled in the driveway, Bo swiveled from his desk, thumbed the rungs open at eye level, and looked out. "John's back."

Jim Craig leaned back into his chair, unfolded the paperback on his lap. "Look busy."

Bo turned back to his desk and started tearing open the mail retrieved from the station mailbox earlier in the morning. Junk mail. All of it. It was a welcome change to the stack of bills he hadn't dared open on his dining room table at home for the past two weeks.

Spearance opened the front door. "What's good, gentlemen?"

Bo waved a Publisher's Clearing House envelope above his head. "We've just won one million dollars." He looked at the address. "Well, you have anyway. Care to split?"

"One million dollars." Spearance took the envelope, shuffled it into the stack of mail on the desk, and headed for his office. "Might just be enough for a new squad car. Maybe, the way prices are these days."

Bo crossed his fingers on his empty desk. "Or retirement."

Spearance laughed. "Don't hold your breath."

Jim turned the page in his book, dutifully pretending to focus more than he actually was.

"What you reading?" Bo asked.

Jim held the book cover up for Bo to see.

Bo leaned in. "*The Cellar.*"

Jim nodded and pulled the book back up to his chest.

Bo watched him, scanned his desk for something, anything. He found a pencil, picked it up, and tapped the eraser against the particle board. "Any good?"

"Helps pass the time."

Spearance opened his door. "Bo, you want to call around, see where that Singleton kid's working this month?"

Bo sat up. "Sure thing." He picked up the phone, dialed the local IGA, and held the phone to his ear. "Yeah. This Beth?" he asked, a little too eager. Always too eager when his work involved a woman. "Oh. Hi, Molly." He frowned. "That Singleton kid still working there?" Pause. "Oh. Okay. Thanks!" Bo hung up the phone and picked it up again. "She thinks he's at the hospital now. Conemaugh Memorial."

"Probably thinks she's the alien Virgin Mary too." Jim rocked in his chair. "That woman's spent one too many days staring down paranormal tabloids by the register, you ask me."

"She's a strange one." Bo laughed. "Pretty, though."

"You aren't the first to notice."

Bo sighed. "And yet, she remains a rose unplucked amongst the chaff."

"Not for lack of trying, I'm sure." Jim lowered his book, cocked his head. "Don't quit your day job, Shakespeare."

"I only asked her out on Tuesdays." Bo pulled the phone book out of his desk and worked through the thin transfer-paper pages in the back. "Sometimes Fridays, when we were in high school." He dragged his finger down the page. "Conemaugh." He dialed. "Hi, Bo Durham speaking. I'm with the Hastings Police Department. Just calling to inquire as to one of your employees." He twisted the cord around his finger. He hated talking to people he didn't know on the phone. "Miles Singleton?" He pointed at Jim, eyebrows raised. "All right. Thanks." Bo hung up the phone. "He's not on the clock, but he still works there." He pushed himself up from his desk and headed for Spearance's office. He pushed the door open slowly. "Conemaugh Memorial."

"He there now?" Spearance asked.

Bo shook his head. "Should be, but didn't show up today."

Spearance rose from his desk and headed for the door.

"Can I go?" Bo followed behind him. "Things are moving a little slow around here."

Spearance nodded. "Sure."

Jim laughed from behind his book.

Bo shrugged. "What?"

"It was a woman on the other line, wasn't it? You're not going because it's slow around here. You're fishing for numbers again."

"I'm not going for that purpose solely." Bo put on his hat. "But if it happens, I'm not going to impede." He ran to his desk and grabbed his coat. "See you."

Jim gave a half-efforted, two-finger wave from behind his book. "Don't have too much fun."

Spearance stared down at the puddles in the department driveway. "It's muddy as hell. Going to have to get Blaine to put a fresh layer of gravel on the drive, like we can afford that."

Bo opened the passenger-side door and stepped in. "There's always Publisher's Clearing House."

"Yeah." Spearance sat down opposite Bo and turned the key over. "Your dream, my dollars."

***

The drive between Hastings and Johnstown was a stretch of pine-crested hills masquerading as mountains, with the faint scent of liquid manure punctuating the town lines. Spearance preferred the drive to both Hastings and Johnstown, a sterile colosseum of sandstone with mountain-forged seating. Nothing towered above the mountains, through which a system of vein-like roadways had been carved such that anyone who wanted to hide on the periphery could. But if you were in the city, you were center stage, and yet invisible at the same time.

In Hastings you were always the foil, but everyone was watching to see when you'd break a leg. Everyone did eventually. All the hedgerows and flowerbeds in the state couldn't save you from getting shat upon at least once during your tenure in the dilapidated town, and that's what separated the insiders from the outsiders. If you stuck around with your stains, you were an insider. If you moved to Johnstown to enjoy the relative obscurity, you didn't belong in

Hastings to begin with. And Hastings was a worse place for that general predisposition, in Spearance's opinion.

Spearance had always enjoyed Johnstown. A little. It was one of the only places where you could feel like you were a part of nothing, like dwelling at the eye of a tornado. Bo, on the other hand, was a Hastings boy, through and through. As they pulled into Conemaugh Memorial Hospital, Bo cracked his window and sniffed at the air. "Smells like formaldehyde and bed pans."

"That's the chemical plant." Spearance parked the vehicle and unbuckled himself. "Beats cow shit, right?"

Bo stepped out of the car and closed his door. "At least that's natural."

"So's radiation."

"Touché." Bo took a deep breath, looked up at the building.

Spearance closed his door and headed for the entrance.

Inside, Spearance walked to the small reception desk just past the doorway. The woman—her nametag read "Tanya," but neither of them recognized her—slid open the glass panel. "Can I help you boys?"

Spearance placed his hands on the counter, tried to peer in at the flickering computer monitor perpendicular to his vision. "We're here to talk to the shift manager, or the administrative equivalent."

She turned to the monitor. "Mr. Drowne is in. You want to talk to him?"

Bo peered in. "He in charge of hiring or scheduling?"

Tanya nodded. "Both."

"That's our man," Bo replied.

Spearance edged Bo out of the window. "We just want to speak to him about one of your employees."

Tanya closed the glass divider and dialed her boss. "Two officers here to see you." She eyed them carefully. She'd watched enough crime dramas to be wary of everyone, including men in uniform. "You want to come down or should I send them in?"

She hung up the phone and opened the divider. "He's in 106."

Spearance smiled. "Thank you."

She nodded meekly.

"I think you made her uncomfortable," Bo chided.

"Me? You practically crawled in there with her."

"Did I?"

"I thought you were going to slither right across that counter and onto her lap, the way you were lurching over her."

"I kept it casual, didn't I?" Bo's face reddened. "Damn it."

"I'm just busting your chops." Spearance put a hand on his shoulder and squeezed. "Let's get this over with. You want to do the talking?"

They stopped at room 106. Bo knocked. "You know Miles better than I do. You talk."

A short man, around 5'6" with a balding crown, opened the door. He pushed his glasses against his face.

"Mr. Drowne?"

"Yes?"

Spearance took the lead. "We just have a few questions about Miles Singleton. He works for you."

"Come on in." Mr. Drowne turned for his desk. "Is everything okay?" He sat comically low to the ground then boosted his chair a few inches. "He didn't show up for work today."

"How long has he been here?"

Drowne sorted through a small stack of papers on his desk. "Just a few weeks. He hasn't missed any days yet, save today."

Bo and Spearance looked at one another.

"He missing?"

Spearance sat down in one of the metal folding chairs opposite Mr. Drowne. "You might see him again. Might not. That's his modus operandi. Peter out or pull out completely."

"His references were good."

Spearance nodded. "It'd be unfair of us to speculate any further about his prospects. We're just trying to contact him."

Mr. Drowne crossed his hands. "I can call you if he shows up. Maybe he'll come in late."

"Do you have a copy of his schedule?"

He picked up the phone. "I'll get Tanya to make a copy. You can pick it up on your way out."

Bo took his hand off the chair he had seemed to be claiming. "He have a locker or a cubby, something for personal effects?"

Mr. Drowne placed the phone back on the hook. "He has a closet. He's custodial."

"Mind if we take a look?" Spearance asked.

"Wouldn't you need a warrant for that?"

"You're the boss here. We'll defer to your authority."

"What about liability? If you guys find anything, I mean, is there any way it could get me or the hospital in trouble?"

"We're not going to give you a hard time for cooperating," Bo said.

"We're not going to give you a hard time if you don't either," Spearance jumped in. "We're just curious, is all."

"I'll let you take a quick look." Mr. Drowne stood, fumbling through his keys. "We make all employees sign a waiver when they're hired. Any personal effects left on the premises are subject to inspection. Medication theft is too common to do otherwise."

He walked to the door and held it open. "Go ahead."

Spearance and Bo walked into the hallway. Mr. Drowne followed behind them, locking his door as they left. "It's down here." He waved them on.

On the other end of the hallway, Drowne unlocked a door marked "Facilities" and led Spearance and Bo into a room of winding pipes and antiquated medical equipment. In the right corner of the room, Drowne unlocked the custodial closet and pulled the drawstring to turn on the light. "There you are." He stepped back and did his best Vanna White impression.

There was barely room for Spearance and Bo to stand back to back, let alone crouch to look through the lower shelves.

Bo knelt on the floor. "I'll start at the bottom. You start at the top."

Shelf-by-shelf, they looked through the unmarked cleaning agents, disheveled boxes of cleaning gloves, and other items. *OSHA'd have a fucking field day in here*, Bo thought. But he knew better than to say it out loud. "He keeps it pretty clean in here."

"Any personal effects?" Spearance asked.

Bo worked his way up to the top shelf. "Not on this side." He turned. "You?"

Spearance worked his way down the opposite wall: rusted cans of lead paint, a cornucopia of dust-covered chemicals.

One shelf from the bottom, he found a small military ammo box. He pulled it out.

No dust.

He opened it up.

A handkerchief, unused, by the looks of it. Under that: the 1979 yearbook from Hastings' high school, North Cambria. Spearance pulled out the yearbook and flipped through the pages, looking for placeholders. There were none, but at the back of the book, there was an aged glossy of Lola, one of her nudes.

The first time he had seen one of her nudes was when he was twelve. In a ritual as far-reaching across western Pennsylvania as it was across generations, Jim had snuck them out of his house with a wine cooler from his father's mini fridge in the basement. He, Jim, and two other boys from the neighborhood twisted the top off the wine cooler, passed it around once, each taking a sip, and threw it deep into the woods. Then Jim fished the pictures out of his pocket. Modest by today's standards, Bridgette Louise—Lola—stood, arms outstretched, revealing herself entirely. Her eyes were warm and inviting. That's what he remembered the most. Warm, inviting eyes.

In the other he remembered, she lay on a couch, legs parted ever so slightly.

The third picture—the one he now held in his hand—had never made it into public circulation. Louise lay on a crush velvet couch, arms resting above her head, mouth agape.

She was covered in gashes from head to toe. Some looked dried and scabbed. Others appeared fresh.

... so much blood.

Nobody could have survived that.

It was obviously fake.

Doctored.

A much more meticulous job than the photo he'd found in Lola's storage unit, and between the two it looked like whatever impulse Miles was operating under was escalating. "Kid needs help," he whispered to himself. Spearance closed the yearbook, turning toward the wall so Drowne wouldn't see him tuck the pictures in his breast pocket. "There a possibility Miles has been here today at all?"

"I can ask Tanya." Drowne looked behind him. "You all set?"

"Sure thing." Spearance closed the ammo box and placed it back behind the rusted paint cans. "Thanks for letting us have a look."

On the way out, Spearance stopped at the front desk to collect the schedule. "You see Miles come through here at all today?"

Tanya nodded, handing Spearance a manila envelope. "Schedule's inside. He alternates nights and afternoons."

Spearance took the folder and handed it to Bo. "Thanks."

Bo tucked the folder under his arm and peered in through the glass. "Bye, Tanya."

She waved daintily.

Once outside the door, Bo leaned into Spearance. "I think she likes me."

"You might be right."

"So what'd you find?"

"I'll show you once we get in the car."

"Is it juicy?"

"Juicy?" *Juicy like what?* Spearance thought. He tried to conjure up an inventory of items for which the descriptor "juicy" would be appropriate, coming up with only watermelon. "No, I don't think so."

Spearance turned over the engine, keeping the wipers off. It was only lightly raining, but he wanted the drops to obscure their movements behind the windshield. He reached into his breast pocket and handed the photo to Bo.

"Oh, this is juicy."

Spearance cocked his head. "You telling me you've never seen those pictures of her before?"

He remained fixated on the photo. "No."

"You grow up under a rock?" Spearance laughed.

"My mom would have blistered my ass for looking at these." He flipped the picture over. "What the hell happened to it?!" He handed it back to Spearance. "I've seen enough."

"I should have warned you." Spearance returned them to his pocket, turned on the wipers, and backed out of the parking lot. "I'm heading over to see Lola right now."

Bo turned to him and opened his mouth to speak.

"No. You can't come with. She'll be embarrassed enough as it is."

Bo stared at the wiper blades cascading across the windshield. "Fine."

MOLLY

Jolie sat at the kitchen table, staring down at the toast she'd so vehemently requested. Now that she finally had it in hand, it looked much less appetizing. "It's burnt."

Molly slid the plate to her end of the table and set down two fresh pieces of toast in front of her daughter. "That's because you were playing with the toaster again."

"I didn't touch it!"

Molly rolled her eyes. "Eat your toast." She brought one of the burnt pieces to her mouth, but the smell proved too much. She tossed it back onto the plate and opted for something more palatable. Liquid breakfast, as her mother called it. Only Molly couldn't afford to drink anymore. There were bad memories tied up with that as well. So a cocktail of milk and memory it was.

She'd grown better over the years at controlling the worst of her ailment. She'd found that memories with similar levels of emotional intensity could bring her out of an involuntary lapse. So on the anniversary of the sorority fire, she allowed herself to indulge in the memory of her failed marriage.

The night before, she'd propped up her wedding picture that had sat face down since her husband died, because he was a variable that came into her life after the fire, not that the image didn't carry with it its own baggage. In only a handful of years, she'd accumulated a vast amount of wisdom associated with a loveless marriage. Perhaps not wholly loveless, but a shade of love that wasn't often used to color a lasting relationship in which the love-him-like-a-high-school-crush supplemented the love-him-because-you-know-him-inside-and-out love. For Molly, the first faded fast. When it did, it left forever.

By the third year of her marriage, she supplemented lack of love with something, anything else. Beer, prescriptions, friendships with guys she'd like to sleep with but knew she shouldn't, which by year four turned into guys she'd slept with but knew she shouldn't have. Then, in low moments, she'd read into Tom's downtime outside of the house because her downtime inside the house involved other men. Trust waned, and it became easier to prefigure infidelity with mistrust grounded in guilt, a compelling, albeit paradoxical cycle she was only now willing to take responsibility for.

After the affairs, guilt didn't suffice. Rituals of self-punishment and self-sacrifice proved the quickest and most effective way to forgive oneself, like a hangover that instills in us the notion of karmic balance, of paying for joy. So she paid it forward by placating herself, deadening her ambitions. Benadryl in her herbal tea to help her get back to sleep after putting Julie on the bus to preschool. Toprol to stave off hangover-induced heart palpitations. Antidepressants to curb the psychological effects of alcohol withdrawal. Another cycle, self-initiated. The ups justified as a means to the greater end: the lull of complacency, the pain that necessitated self-care and kept her away from higher aspirations.

Molly kept herself in the proverbial pumpkin shell.

And there she kept herself very well.

In their fifth year—last year—Tom died. Car accident. She told herself this was that karmic balance she had waited to be restored. But shouldn't it have been her? She'd been left with a modest sum of money and a monthly check from his years of employment. He was eight years her senior and had been working since she was in middle school. Their daughter was safe, taken care of. They had a roof over their heads, and Tom's compulsive renovations meant nothing—barring natural disaster—would need major overhaul for at least another decade.

Though she'd never admit it to herself, in some ways Tom's death was a blessing. But any sense of relief she felt exacerbated her fear of some intangible, impending doom. Tom's death was a shoe drop, and from that day forward she kept waiting for the next one to drop, one that would collect on any sense of joy the world had paid forward to her.

But she had to keep moving forward. There were bills to pay, and Jolie wasn't going to feed herself. She couldn't think of anyone who could take care of her in her absence—certainly not her mother—so she signed up for another shot at college, a small extension site that offered night courses well-away from campus. Even with the courses she'd already taken, it'd take over a year to earn a two-year in criminal justice, something to get a leg up in applying for civil service jobs.

Wouldn't you know it, the course started April 21st.

The phone rang, tearing Molly away from the calendar. She picked up. "Hello?"

Her mother sighed before answering. "How are you?"

Molly's eyes glided back up to the calendar. "Fine."

"So, school today." She breathed in quickly, trying not to give Molly time to respond. "What are the odds, you know?"

Molly pulled a chair out from her particle board breakfast nook—something Tom picked up on the side of the road and would not let go of—and sat down. "I'm not sure I'm going to go."

"First day's the most important. People only have the capacity to let a few others imprint on them in a new setting. You have to establish rapport with the professor day one."

"Imprint?" Molly rolled her eyes. "Christ, he's not a duckling, Mom."

"Some things are universal, Molly."

"And yet no one's quite as 'new age' as you."

"I think that Gary Zukav fellow could give me a run for my money. You read that book I gave you?"

"Haven't had a chance yet."

"It'd give you a chance to clear your head for a while."

"Yeah, then next year and every year after I'll have these horrible flashbacks of reading the psychotic ramblings of some hack masquerading as a spiritual guru. It's bad enough I have flashbacks about listening to one," Molly chided.

A timer blared on the other end of the phone. "Hang on a second. Blue-green algae bites are done."

"Holy shit."

"What?!"

"Green algae bites? That for your tofu salad? I swear, Mom. You're a white, middle-class Californian stereotype. How'd Dad ever manage to drag you across the country to the back woods of Pennsylvania?"

"He was handsome."

"Not as handsome as Gary Zukav though."

Her mother set the phone down. "Handsomer," she shouted.

"Mommy?"

Molly peered around the edge of the dining room door to see her daughter, Jolie—the one good thing that came out of her marriage—rubbing the sleep from her eyes. Even though she was only five, for her sake alone Molly wished she could slow time down. "Hi, honey."

"What's for breakfast?" she demanded, stepping into the room.

"Excuse me?"

Jolie plopped down on the chair opposite Molly and opened the phone book to the Yellow Pages, doing her best Mommy impersonation. "What's for breakfast, *please*?" She yawned.

"I wasn't looking for the magic word." Molly picked up the phone and tucked it between chin and shoulder. "I was hoping more for—"

"—no words," Jolie interrupted. "Hungry."

Molly untucked the phone and held it against her face. "The monster's awake. I better let you go."

"Put her on."

Molly handed the phone to Jolie. "Want to talk to Grandma?"

Jolie took the phone, placing it against her ear. "Hi, G-ma."

"Is that Mommy giving you a hard time about breakfast?"

Jolie nodded. "Yeah."

"You want me to bring over some of my blue-green algae bites? They have maple in them."

"No." Jolie continued flipping through the Yellow Pages. "Mommy's making pancakes."

Molly turned from the fridge with a cup of yogurt in hand. She tore the aluminum top back, stuck a spoon in the cup. "Here's your 'pancakes.'"

Jolie stirred the yogurt. "I gotta eat, G-ma."

"All right, honey. Put your mother back on."

Molly waved the phone off silently.

Jolie took a bite of the yogurt. "She's pooping."

Molly could hear her mother on the other end of the phone from the sink. "At least she's regular again. Tell her I said bye."

"Bye, G-ma." Jolie handed the phone to Molly, who promptly hung it up.

"Really? Pooping?"

Jolie laughed. "It was all I could think of!"

"Makes sense, you being such a little turd."

"Hey!"

Molly knelt down for a hug. "A cute little turd, though."

Jolie brought another heaping spoon to her lips, spilling blueberry yogurt across the phone book. "What are we doing today?"

Molly glanced up at the calendar and decided, despite her mother's insistence, that she couldn't muster the strength to go in today. "Ice cream?"

"Yay!"

CHAPTER THREE

MILES

HE SHOULD HAVE stepped onto the porch and talked to Spearance when he had the chance. He should have tried to redirect him. If they found out about his research, about the camera. Oh god, if they actually found the camera before him...

He shook the thought of it off.

If he would have just talked to Spearance, it would have ended with another slap on the wrist. He just wanted to delay the discussion a bit. Now Spearance had already been to Conemaugh rummaging through his stuff, according to Tanya, so Miles was out of luck on that front. By now Spearance had probably secured a warrant, or at the very least had someone watching his place, so he wasn't getting back in there either. He was running out of options, and the one he had remaining was the least plausible and most risky. There were still too many unanswered questions, so he took inventory of what he did know.

He thought back to the first time he had felt the sinking feeling. Soulfalling. That's the word that came to mind. He had no idea what a soul felt like, hadn't even been sure if the soul even existed, but when he touched the Bergen-Belsen photo—the one with the soldier bulldozing dead bodies into a small pile—he felt like he was slipping outside of himself. Backward. Except instead of falling backward, he fell *in*. When he opened his eyes he was inside the photo.

It reminded him of the old stereo viewer his grandmother used to let him play with when he was a child. She had run the museum in Hastings, and let him sort through the stereo viewer collection when he was only five years old. Most of the photographs were drab—street views, pictures of the first hotel, the trains, anything that brought people to and from the area—but every now and then he'd stumble upon Lola. Lola with the deep brown eyes. Lola with the elegant bob that revealed her thin neck and subtle chin. She was the first woman he'd found beautiful. He'd wanted that photo, that memory, to be the first time he felt that soulfall. But he hadn't touched that picture the same way he'd touched the Bergen-Belsen photo.

He'd run his fingers across the bodies. A shock coursed through him, and his mind split, two trajectories so close that they segued into one another: Sympathy, then something else.

Hatred? No.

Disgust, maybe. Not disgust over the scene itself, but with the vulnerability of mankind. Disgust with himself, with everyone. His classmates, scurrying like rats to the lunchroom, leaving him behind, blocking the remaining open spaces until he was exiled to a table that remained empty save one girl who sat there alone because of a peanut allergy. He sat with her most days, eating flavorless soup just so he had someone to talk to.

He didn't eat lunch the day he touched the Bergen-Belsen photo. He couldn't after what had happened. After the soulfall, he'd opened his eyes to the scene. There he was, frozen in time inside the image. He turned away from it to find only blackness. He turned back to the scene. The soldier bulldozing the bodies was there, frozen in place.

He stepped forward, the brittle ground crumbling under his feet. Another step, and the bodies grew closer. Somehow, he was *inside* the photo. He bent down to look at the body closest to him, the skin stretched like tissue paper over protruding ribs. He reached out to find the skin tight, sun-bleached like leather. The smell was overpowering. How was this happening? Would he be able to get out? He stood, panicked suddenly, turning again to the blackness behind him. The image remained where he had initially stood, but beyond that everything transitioned to nothingness. He reached out, and his arm disappeared into it. The air on the other side was cool and damp.

He stepped into the blackness and found himself back in the classroom. He took in the familiar surroundings as his heart settled. The room was empty, all of his classmates now gone to lunch.

He looked over at his teacher's desk.

Empty.

He'd thought it was the picture. For years, he thought it had been the picture. He'd slipped it under his arm and adjusted the remaining photos so the missing photo would be less noticeable. He wanted to go in again, at home, when he had more time to explore the bodies.

Even then, he knew that eventually he'd run out of things to explore in that inner-space. Eventually, he'd want to see how far the parallels to reality went. He'd want to go inside the bodies, to see if what rested inside was true flesh and blood, or some strange facsimile that only partially emulated the real world.

Had his teacher known about this? Had he, too, ventured inside the images?

For years he thought that might be the case as well.

But that day, the first day he fell into that image, the only thing that mattered to him was getting that picture to his bedroom. There he could hide it between mattress and box-spring with his pictures of Lola from the museum. He would have made it home too, but he'd grown too bold. He'd taken an anatomy book from the biology teacher, a large, expensive edition with real pictures of cadavers. He should have waited. He'd told himself to wait. Hadn't he told himself that? To wait. Always to wait. To be patient.

***

A few years went by, and the girl with the peanut allergy had moved up to the high school lunch period, leaving Miles alone again. The history teacher had resigned, presumably taking his photographs with him. Miles had tried to touch other photos the way he'd touched the Bergen-Belsen picture, but to no avail. He'd never felt that sensation of sliding outside himself until his freshman year in high school. He'd been looking through the newspaper for images to soulfall into, hoping one might someday pique his interest or work the way the Bergen-Belsen photo had. He'd always suspected that the phenomenon had something to do with death, that when pictured, the dead somehow broke some seal between image and reality. He'd spent years scouring the newspapers for images of car crashes, pictures in the obituaries. So Miles was surprised when the next photo he felt close to falling into was a wedding photo.

It was the peanut allergy girl. Molly Richards. He ran his hands across the photo, not to enter, but just to spark his memory. She looked so beautiful in her white gown, waist cradled by some guy Miles had never seen, not even in the school. Probably some Johnstown junky. Tom was his name. He'd hated him without even knowing him. Hate came so easy; love less so. But he felt intimations of both in this moment. Again he became torn between conflicting emotions. That's when he started slipping out of himself. When the soulfalling began.

Then he was there with them, in this tightly packed space. He turned his head to find the unending black behind him. He worked his way around her, standing behind the couple. He touched Molly's face. Then her neck. He took Tom's arm from her waist and let it drop to his side. Miles placed his arm where Tom's had been. Why hadn't he asked her out when they sat together?

He posed with her for a moment, resting her head on his shoulder. Then his hands went to the zipper on her dress. He pulled it gently downward, then wondered if the image would change—if all of the images would change—if he undressed her. He paused, ruminating on the consequence. They'd never catch him, but she'd be embarrassed. Terribly so. But he might also never enter the image again. He still didn't understand how soulfalling worked.

He couldn't risk her being hurt out there. He lowered the shoulder strap on her dress to the side of her arm and let it hang there and turned to the blackness.

Again he found himself sitting in his room, newspaper in hand. He looked at the photo, at the shoulder strap, now hanging around her upper arm.

The photo had changed.

He remembered frantically trying to re-enter the image then, to put the strap back where it had been. He couldn't get back in.

He'd run that day to the corner store to check the papers, fearing that someone would notice. Someone would find out and somehow trace it back to him.

Someone, somehow.

His father would take the piss out of him.

He'd say it just like that, belt in hand. "I'm going to take the piss out of you, boy."

Miles ran faster until he saw the store in the distance. He held his pace all the way to the front door and stormed in. "You have the paper?!" he asked.

Mr. Kellerman pointed to the rack near the counter.

Miles grabbed the top paper and opened it. He turned to the last two pages, where the obituaries and wedding announcements were.

The photo was fine. Unmarked. Just the way it had been.

He was safe.

He re-folded the paper and headed home, to the image that remained altered.

For two weeks he tried to re-enter the image so he could fix that one as well. He wanted no evidence that he'd been in the image.

He'd felt himself slip a handful of times, but always opened his eyes before the process was complete.

Again he reminded himself to wait. To be patient.

The next time he felt himself slip into the image, he kept his eyes closed. Instead, he waited for the smell. He'd remembered that in the photo there'd been a distinct smell, like an old wardrobe. Dust and dry air hung around him the first time. Once that scent returned, he opened his eyes and found himself standing before the couple again. He circled them once, taking in the dimensions.

He reached for Tom's arm and pushed it away from Molly. He remained lopsided, leaning into nothingness as Miles pulled Molly away from him. He unzipped the dress, letting it fall open, revealing her back. Miles pulled the straps down from her shoulders and let the dress fall to her waist.

She was beautiful.

He continued, pulling the dress to the floor, and took in her naked body.

Two weeks. It had taken two weeks to find himself back in the image with her. But he knew now that he'd be back again, many times over the years. He decided then that he'd take her. He'd take her today, and at every opportunity he had in the photograph. He'd lie with her, his chest against her still heart, and make love to this young facsimile of her as she aged in the real world.

He laid her on the floor then, gently pulled her eyelids down, and entered her.

It was his first time, and even though this wasn't her—not really her—he treated her delicately. She was so beautiful, so warm to the touch. But she was so much more. They were so much more. Their two bodies together in this liminal space, this moment, seemingly outside of time, was art.

SPEARANCE

Bridgette Louise—Lola to most of the folks in and out of town—kept to herself in the top apartment in one of her duplexes. She kept the bottom apartment empty for her guests, which rarely, if ever, came.

She lived with a younger man, no relation, who ran errands in town and wheeled her into mass every Sunday.

She spoke to no one, save through checks surreptitiously delivered via the U.S. Postal Service.

Spearance pulled into her driveway, noted the thick gravel settling into place under his tires. He'd taken to small details like that over the years. Though superficial, his attention to the minutiae of experience had transcended investigative curiosity. It had become a compulsion, thinking every piece of loose data might right a wronged world. The data now beneath his feet told him nobody had pulled into this driveway for a long time. The ground, ripe with weeks of autumn rain, enveloped his boots, soaking into his socks.

Waterproof, my ass, he thought.

He kicked the mud from his shoes at the base of the outdoor stairs and walked up, wondering how the hell Lola managed such a steep incline when he could barely manage it himself. Each step introduced him to another row of trees on the horizon, with few still donning their fall colors. The spindly fingered birch etched empty trails across the clouds.

Lack of sleep had led Spearance to see the world in fewer frames per second than he was used to. His sleepy disposition rendered Hastings in the vein of a late Van Gogh. The wind stirred morning's fog cauldron into a backdrop for *Starry Night*, and the navy sky hung before a black backdrop a la *Wheatfield with Crows*.

Christ above, he needed sleep badly.

Spearance topped the stairs, photo in hand. He rang the doorbell and held the picture closely, noted her bobbed cut, her jet-black hair, and her deep brown eyes as vast and foreboding as the darkness in the distance. Everything below the neck was cut beyond recognition in the picture, intimations of wounds—actual wounds, if Spearance hadn't known better—covering her from throat to toe. Still, beyond the scars he could make out the ivory contours and the sweater-like mat of fur between her legs. Behind the curtain of horror remained something capable of inducing arousal.

He rang the doorbell again.

A small hand delicately parted the curtains.

Deep brown eyes peered out cautiously.

Spearance smiled.

The curtains fell closed, and there was an uncomfortable silence as if Lola deliberated opening the door.

Finally, he heard a single chain lock slide out of place and a bolt lock slide away from its casing.

Only two locks: she couldn't have been as cautious as he had heard.

The door opened and Lola stared out at him. "Can I help you?"

Her voice was strong, not indicative of the frail countenance and posture that carried it. She wore her hair pulled back in a hair band, and traces of her historic beauty shone through her scowl.

"You come to stare? This is why I don't go out much, you know?" she said.

"I—uh. I'm here to return something I think may have been taken from you. Had a few questions, if you'd be so kind to—"

"—I suppose you want to come in then." She pushed the door open and waved him into the living room. "I'm not making tea or coffee for you. Hastings water is shit and the dishes are dirty, but you're free to wash a mug and fill it if you're thirsty."

Spearance took off his hat and stepped inside, closing the door behind him. "I'm fine, thanks." Again he stared at her, taking in the periphery. The room was draped in inspirational cat pictures, all glowing in Bob Barker's flickering image emanating from the television.

"You did come to stare," she muttered. She gestured toward a small recliner. "Have a seat."

Spearance sank into the chair. "Sorry."

"You expected an aging actress surrounded by relics of her past, maybe one of her own films on the TV?"

"Something like that."

Her hands quivered as she brought the coffee to her lips. "I don't have a single film in this house, can you believe that?"

"Why not?"

"Life's too short to experience the same thing twice. It's bad enough I had to look back twice for biographers. At least they paid me to look back." She set her cup down on a stained doily, the only thing remotely reminiscent of her past. "It helps that my career died while I was still in my prime. I had no choice but to look forward for the longest time. I'm not a big fan of looking back. That's what you're here for though, I presume." She smiled. "I hope you're willing to pay."

"I don't have money, but I have something you might be interested in." Spearance unfolded his hands, revealing the picture. "Did you misplace this?"

"If I had a dollar for every copy of these... You know the pastor asked me to sign a copy last year?"

"Did he now?"

"No." She shook her head. "You would have fit right in with the guys I worked with fifty years ago. Believed anything you told them. I always wondered what would have happened to them if the film industry collapsed. Now I know. They'd be in law enforcement."

Spearance brushed the comment off. "We found it in a resident's work space at the hospital over in Johnstown. Does it look familiar?"

She fumbled over the items on her Pembroke table, finally landing on the glasses. Spearance watched her tremble as she lifted them to her eyes. She adjusted as her eyes dipped into the lower half of the bifocals. "Sweet Jesus."

Spearance, hand still outstretched to take the picture back, continued. "They must have spent a lot of time painting you up like that."

She raised her hand to her mouth. "Nobody...I never took pictures like that."

"Have you ever seen anything of that nature, in film perhaps? Any photographic manipulation, colorization, anything that might produce such a result?"

She stared at the photo, mouth agape. "No. No, I don't think so." Her hands shook as she placed it, face down on the table.

"I'm sorry." Spearance slid the photo to his side of the table. "I thought it might have been a staged photo or something. I'll dispose of it." Spearance smiled. "Wouldn't want the pastor to catch wind of it."

Again the world went quiet as she looked at the black backing on the photo. "Where'd you find it?"

Spearance deliberated as to whether or not he should tell her about the break in yet, deciding finally on saving that information for her aide. She didn't recognize the image. It had likely been in Miles' locker before he broke into her storage shed. The photo provided a tangential connection at best, for now, and he didn't want to disturb her any more than he already had. "I can't say just yet. We're still investigating, but as soon as we've wrapped things up I'll tell you everything I can." Spearance braced the armrests on the old recliner and stood. "I can come back later."

"Could you stay, actually? My help should be here shortly. He went into town to get more coffee."

"Sure." Spearance let himself sink into the recliner once more.

Plumes of dust shot through the air. These roiling clouds were no *Starry Night*, and the silence was stagnant. Spearance watched Lola's eyes shift from the television to the table.

After a few minutes she turned to him. "Who are you again?"

"Detective Spearance. I came to drop off one of your possessions. A photo. I thought it was yours."

"A photo?" She looked genuinely curious. "May I see it?"

He handed the photo to her again.

She reached for it, pulling it close to inspect her younger self. "Oh gosh, where did you find...?" She stopped short, brought her hand to her mouth, and gasped. She dropped the photo and struggled to pull up her sleeves. "Am I okay?"

"You're fine."

She ran her hands up and down her arms, watching intently as if she expected some marked reaction. "You scared the shit out of me, Officer."

"I'm sorry."

A knock at the door prefigured Lola's aide gently sliding the door open. "Everything okay?" he asked, setting down a small bag of groceries on the kitchen counter.

"I'm fine." Lola waved her help over to the living area. "This is Officer—"

"—Spearance." Spearance stood and extended his hand.

Lola's help clasped his hand tightly and shook once vigorously. "Mike."

"I just stopped by to return a photo of hers that we dredged up in a recent case."

Mike glanced at Lola, brows raised.

"Yes," she said. "One of *those* photos."

Mike rolled his eyes. "I think every kid in Hastings sees those pictures before they turn fourteen. It's a damned rite of passage around here."

Lola stripped her glasses from her face. "If it brings them joy, who are we to stop them?"

Spearance leaned in to Mike. "You mind if I talk to you for a minute?"

Mike nodded and followed the detective to the front porch. "I'll be right back."

They shut the door behind them.

Mike put his hands in his jacket pocket and stared into the distance. "She says those pictures don't bother her, but they do."

"The one I showed her, it's pretty banged up. We're still trying to track down the guy who had it. He must have manipulated it somehow, made it look like she'd been mutilated."

"Really?"

Spearance flashed the photo at Mike. "I shouldn't have shown her. I thought it was something she agreed to, makeup for a death scene maybe. It really distressed her. I'm going to keep my hands on it throughout the investigation."

Mike held the corner of the photo steady, shook his head. "I've never seen that one."

"Neither have I." Spearance tucked the photo back in his coat. "Not the effect, nor the pose, which makes what I'm about to tell you all the more disconcerting."

"All right."

"The guy who had the photo, we caught him rummaging through her storage unit last night. We're still trying to track him down for questioning, but if you could get her to go down and inspect the unit...if anything's missing we can try to track it down for her."

"Sure thing." Mike extended his hand. "Thanks."

"I could come, or send a deputy."

Mike shook his head. "I'll get her there, but she's not going to want anyone hovering over her while she looks. She'll probably make me wait in the car as it is." He smiled. "I'm practically paparazzi, as far as she's concerned."

Spearance nodded, and with another vigorous shake he was heading down the stairs. He felt guilty for feigning altruism. He'd paid for it though. Now he had to go on second-hand testimony, which might not be enough to warrant a probable cause search of Miles' apartment.

LOLA

Inside, Lola watched Spearance pull out of the driveway.

Mike entered, locking the door behind him.

"What was he trying to protect this delicate flower from, Mike?" She let the curtains fall into place.

"Someone broke into your storage unit. Owner thinks he chased them off before anything was taken, but the police still want you to take a look. He thought maybe the kid had stolen the photo he showed you."

Lola sighed. "Do they really fancy me so petty? That I'd pack my bags and withdraw my support over a few stolen items?"

"I don't think they can afford to take any chances." Mike plucked the coffee from his bag and tossed it into the cupboard. "Mother Hastings has to be kept happy, so they say."

"My god." Lola rolled her eyes. "Bring me my coat."

"Will do."

CHAPTER FOUR

MILES

EVEN AFTER SEVERAL years, Miles never got fully comfortable with the disparity between what happened in the photos and his relative powerlessness in the real world. He'd concocted a series of rituals to abate his anxieties. After leaving a photograph, he'd always scrutinize the surface to make sure no evidence of his time within had transferred to the picture. Then he'd go back in, to make sure everything was as it had been before his tampering. He'd grown used to the disappointment of unchanging images. Part of him wanted his work to remain intact. Each time he re-entered the photos, he felt a combination of relief that the evidence was gone and regret that his work had been lost.

Then there was the matter of Tigerstedt to contend with. The fact that, somehow, either something had happened to him in reality that triggered a domino effect in all of his pictures, or something had happened to his pictures that resulted in his death. At first he thought it had been the camera. But then he saw the same phenomenon again in his yearbook. Samantha Ohst, who had died in the sorority fire at IUP, had the same faint traces of scarification running across her face in her yearbook photo. At the library, her newspaper image from T-ball dating back a decade or more featured the same light scarring. He'd double-checked in other copies to be sure. The scars were barely visible, but they were in every copy he'd managed to get his hands on. Pictures that pre-dated the fire. Pictures taken by multiple cameras, all featuring the same traces of her death. Just like Tigerstedt.

Again he felt that cognitive dissonance, a resonant fear that there might be someone out there like him coupled with the excitement of knowing he might someday evolve into someone who could carry traces of his work across all reproductions of a person's photos.

If there was someone out there like him, perhaps they were inextricably linked and someday he'd run into them in that timeless void on the other side of photographs. Perhaps they'd want that space, that power, all to themselves.

That was only a minor worry though. What plagued him most nights was the fear that one day he'd exit one of his favorite photos to find that all photos of Molly had been tarnished. Or worse, that he'd wake to find that what he'd done to her in the image had been done to her in some remote location, wherever she was.

So each day, he'd pass her house on the way to the library so he could read the day's paper for potential emergencies. Scouring the pages for any evidence that what he'd done in pictures had somehow shifted into reality.

Over time he'd started work on others in town. The winners of a local trap shoot contest. One of the VPs of a local bank branch that had won branch of the year. Anyone above the fold in the Hastings paper, he'd go in, do whatever struck him, and then follow up throughout the week to see if there'd been any impact on them.

But there was nothing.

Soon he craved more immediate results. He spent a summer mowing lawns, trimming hedges, until he could afford a scanner. Then he'd leave the pictures, turn on the scanner, and let it lull him to sleep.

The lawn job led to references, which led to janitorial positions around town. First at an Ames, a pizza joint, and finally at the local grocery store, where Molly worked. Had he unconsciously applied, seeing her there on some occasion? He had no recollection of seeing her there before. Yet there she was, plain as day, beautiful as she had been in the picture. As if she hadn't aged a single moment. As if she was encased in a timeless slip of cellulose acetate. Being so close to her, having her there each day as direct evidence of her safety, gave him the freedom to try even more with her in the photo. He bound her, slapped her lifeless body, took pleasure in knowing that she'd unwittingly treat him kindly the next evening as they crossed paths before her shift ended.

He told himself he'd never treat the real Molly so cruelly.

Several weeks later, the scanner roused Miles from sleep.

Molly's husband, Tom.

He'd been in an accident.

Miles had performed on him only a few hours earlier.

The eyes. He could never stand his eyes. It wasn't enough to turn Tom away when he made love to Molly. That was sacred, between him and Molly. He had to remove all possibility that Tom would watch.

Miles learned two days later that Tom had died from a high-impact car crash.

A sigh of relief and disappointment.

It had not been him.

He was innocent.

He was innocent, and Molly was alone.

He was of a gentler position with the young woman in the photograph over the following months. Caressing her, treating her as he had when he had first touched her, when he'd yet to learn what repercussions might exist outside of the photo. He apologized to her, wiped away tears that never threatened to fall from her still eyes.

He resolved to leave the photo and never come back.

He resolved to apologize to her at work for her loss, and then leave it at that. He wouldn't pursue her in the real world, because the rejection would send him hurtling back toward the photograph.

He needed to break himself of this addiction.

He'd told himself that too.

But he never listened.

The next evening, he walked up to the checkout counter with a bottle of iced tea and a candy bar. He hated buying food from her. Food made him feel...vulnerable? Human? He couldn't put his finger on it, but he needed something, some excuse to talk to her.

He dropped the candy bar onto the counter, set the tea down, and looked up.

"You liking the job so far?" She held the tea up, typed the price into the register without looking at the keys.

He nodded, noting the acrid smell of—was it brandy or cough syrup?—on her breath. "It's a living."

It's a living, one of the most repeated lines from Lola and David Rothman's headline film, *Everyman*. It was also twenty years out of circulation, and cliché as hell. Still she laughed.

"That it is." She picked up the candy bar. "Got a bit of a sweet tooth, do you?" She typed in the price. "50 cents."

He could feel himself blushing. "I suppose." Miles dug the cash out of his pocket and handed it to her.

She cradled the money, letting her fingers run across his. "How sweet?"

He looked at her.

She handed him back his change and kept eye contact. "You're kind of cute. Don't remember you much in school."

"I was a bit younger." Their point of connection struck him. "The table!"

She leaned back quickly. "Excited about furniture too. Noted." She laughed.

"You used to sit with me at the peanut-free table."

"You have an allergy too?"

He lied. "Yeah."

She chewed on his memory for just a second before conjuring up her early days in school. There he was. A look of recognition crossed her face. "Yeah. I remember. You were quiet then too."

Miles took the candy bar and stuffed it awkwardly in his pocket.

"When you off?"

Miles took the tea into his hand. "Hm?"

"When do you get off work tonight?"

"Eleven."

She looked down the front aisle and toward the exit. Nobody in sight. She took a flask out from under the desk, took a drink, and offered it to him.

Against his better judgment, he took it. It tasted terrible. His face caved toward the center. "What is that?!"

"Elderberry brandy." She reached out for the bottle. "I've got a bit of a cold."

"Wow."

She screwed the cap on the flask and set it back under the counter. "So what do you think?"

"About what?" he asked. *This can't be real.*

"Hanging out when you get off work."

"Where?" *This is definitely not real.*

She lifted her pointer finger and drove it playfully into his chest, tilting off balance as she did so. "Your place."

"I—uh."

"You'll—uh, see me there?" she mocked.

He nodded.

"All right." She turned to the register. "I'm cashing out. See you later."

This can't be real, he thought again as he headed toward the back of the store. Yet here he was, about to...was she going to let him fuck her? Would it even be appropriate, given her obvious state of intoxication that would only progress as the night wore on?

Was he somehow responsible for this? For her reception to him? Was it his time with her in the photo? He wanted to believe it was, that she too had felt the cumulative buildup of emotion inside of him, that it had somehow led to their chemistry here, in this world outside of the photos.

He stopped midway through the dairy aisle and ran back to the front. He'd forgotten to get her number!

She was gone.

***

Hours later, he opened the door to his apartment and headed straight for Molly's photo. He carried it with him to the door, locked it, and lay down on his bed.

He closed his eyes.

11:15pm

The phone rang.

He dropped the photo, ran to the phone, and picked it up. "Hello?"

"I forgot to ask for your address." Molly, her voice now considerably slurred.

"How did you get my number?"

"Contacts, under the checkout counter." She laughed.

"How about I pick you up?" Miles suggested, eyeing the photo on the bed.

"Sure. I'm at Boo's."

"Booze?"

"The little bar on the highway heading out of town."

Miles sighed. "All right."

***

An hour later, Miles rolled off Molly, disillusioned. He'd rehearsed this so many times, how could he fail now?

Molly ran her hand down his back. "Don't worry about it. S'just whiskey dick. You'll be fine tomorrow."

Miles fell back into his pillow. "I'm sorry."

She fell beside him, almost smashing her head off the sheetrock behind them. "I'm just here for the company." She raised her arm and let it fall onto his chest, laughing. "So, regale me with your wisdom."

He turned to her, imagined clasping her hair and pulling her to him, rolling her onto her stomach and having his way with her. "I—um. Do you like photography?"

She smiled. "I used to. Now it just reminds me of the past. Hurts more than helps, you know?"

He nodded. "You ever hear that some cultures believe photographs capture a piece of your soul?"

She slid her arm under his neck. "Uh oh. He's going deep."

He leaned into her arm, reluctant to say anything else.

"I'm just teasing." She let him settle into her and threw a leg over his. "Beats talking about water tables."

"How about those water tables?" He managed a modest smile, trying to hide his crooked teeth.

"Ugh." She slapped his chest again playfully. "Topic change."

"Do you think photos capture a part of our soul?"

She thought about it for a minute, trying to avoid the torrent of memories coming back. Cameras...Photographs...maybe the water table was a preferred thread of conversation after all. "I don't know. I can kind of see where people who believe that are coming from. I mean, I'm not going to go as far as to shun photography and keep a box full of nail clippings under my bed because I'm afraid of losing some part of myself or anything. But I can see where people might feel like photographs, gravestones, relics of the past leave behind some element of vulnerability. My grandfather's gravestone has been knocked over twice since he passed. Each time it is like feeling a dulled version of that loss all over again. If we live on in memories, and photos and other mementos are meant to keep our memory alive, then in some way we live in or through them or something."

Miles listened intently to the slurred words that came out of her, carrying more wisdom than he had expected. He hadn't expected much, admittedly. He'd always thought her shallow, but he'd grown enough since high school to know that was just his bias as one of the unpopular kids on the outside looking in. "Figuratively, sure. But I mean literally."

She paused for a moment. "Why are you asking me about this?"

For a moment they shared a mutual paranoia, her fearing Miles had caught wind of her camera, him fearing she had maybe seen the picture he had of her. Had he put that away? He scanned the room quickly, checking the far side, the floor, and his nightstand.

In the nightstand.

She hadn't seen anything. He was fine.

"Just curious is all."

Molly sat up. "You got anything to drink around here?"

Miles shook his head. "Sorry."

She fished the floor for her clothes. Miles watched her naked body in the moonlight. Her body was the same, save the small tuft of hair that sprouted from between her legs. It was thicker now, a difference he savored as she pulled her panties around her waist. "I better head out."

"You're not going to stay?" Miles asked.

"Bar's open another hour. Want to come with?"

He shook his head. "I shouldn't. Do you want a ride?"

Molly pulled her shirt over her head, slipped on her shoes, and headed for the door. "I'll be all right." She came back to the edge of the bed and kissed him. "You're a nice guy," she said.

Then she was gone.

Miles waited until she closed the door, then took the photo out of his nightstand. He walked to the door and locked it behind her. Once he returned to the bed, he felt that slipping sensation take over his body before he lay down again. He wanted her so badly. She had been his for the taking. Why couldn't he have her then?

Inside the photograph, Miles took in her beauty again, comparing the living, breathing Molly to the silent, doll-like version in the photo. He took her hair into his hand and pulled it tight behind her. Her head jerked back and remained in place. Her face remained expressionless. No indication of pleasure or pain. He began to tear her dress from her body, wishing she felt it now, like some inverse of Dorian Gray's image. He put his hands around her throat, wishing she felt his hands now. He imagined her clasping her throat as she walked, gasping for air in the street.

Now he was ready to take her.

But when he left the photo that night, Molly only smiled back at him, just as she always had.

The next day at work, the same.

She smiled, as she always had.

For months she remained silent, just like the photograph. Did she remember? Was she ashamed?

She'd become more like the photo after the night they'd spent together.

But in the cold air, he could see her breath. He could see her chest heave with what he imagined was unbearable guilt. He wanted to snuff that out, end the warmth of her breath as he passed the checkout counter.

Instead they both waved, as they did every night until he finally lost hope, and found a job at Conemaugh in Johnstown.

LOLA

It had been two years since they visited the storage unit together. Mike had made solo runs since then, picking up an item here, depositing a few safe keepings there. Then there were other times when she'd tell him to drop something off that she had scolded him for moving the week prior. Those items he surreptitiously tucked away in the trunk of his car or the back of the guest room closet for quick retrieval in the event that she remembered their importance.

As he helped her into the car, he remembered the items in his trunk. An old lamp she'd been gifted after her time in Germany. A cardboard box filled with composition notebooks, half-remembered stories from her youth and incomplete poems from after the silent era. A knot tightened slowly in the pit of his stomach at the thought of her seeing them there, should she decide to pack the vehicle full of items in the unit now deemed too important to risk losing.

And when they got there...when they got there, he knew the plethora of relics from her past would unlock a mental repository of items lost over the years far more vast than what remained in the unit. And it would be his fault that they were gone.

When he agreed to be her aide several years ago, her mind was just beginning to turn. One of the first tasks he was given was taking inventory of the possessions she was finally settled enough to revisit.

When she first blamed him for lost or misplaced items, he began to doubt his own memory. This doubt eventually worked to his advantage. He began taking inventory of everything sorted between the apartment, the unit, and eventually his car. That's when he noticed that certain items conjured up memories of other items she no longer had in her possession, and perhaps never had. He wondered how many of those items would evoke false memories today, and how much trouble he'd get in for it.

Eventually, he gave up on the task. No matter how meticulous he was, he was destined to fail in her eyes.

Mike pulled up to the front office of Tiernan's storage units and stepped out of the car. "Be right back."

Lola did not respond.

He could feel the tension building already.

When Mike entered the building, Nathan Tiernan peered around the edge of his desk. "That Lola?" he asked.

Mike nodded.

"She know?"

Mike nodded again. "Police just notified us, asked if we could come down and see what's missing, if anything."

Nathan kept staring out at the parked car. "I don't think he got anything. He dropped a pair of bolt cutters and ran as fast as he could." He reached for the keys and waved Mike toward the door. "I'll open her up for you. He cut the old lock."

Mike got back into the car and crawled behind Nathan to the unit.

Lola crossed her arms. "Couldn't he just give you the keys?"

"He's just trying to be nice."

Nathan waved them into the next aisle.

"He should." Lola rolled her eyes. "Why is he waving us on? We know where it is."

"He feels bad," Mike whispered. "He wants to help."

"Please ask him to leave once he lets us in."

Mike gripped the steering wheel. Lola was generally of a bearable disposition, but the closer you got to her unit, or any conversation pertaining to her possessions or, more notably, the memory of her possessions, she became increasingly belligerent. "Fine."

Mike parked the car and stepped out.

Nathan toggled with the lock, staring at Lola. The lock popped and he pulled it off. He slid the key off his holder and handed both lock and key to Mike.

Mike stuffed them into his pocket and lifted the unit door. "Thanks for helping out."

"She coming?" Nathan asked. He waved at her.

She looked away.

"She's pretty upset."

Nathan looked genuinely hurt.

"Not at you." He smiled and dipped under the door into the unit. "Just at the circumstance."

Nathan followed. "Maybe I ought to talk to her."

Mike shook his head. "Just leave her be. She's in one of her moods."

Nathan nodded understandingly. "Actresses."

Mike took in the perimeter of the unit. Everything looked in order. "Yeah."

Once Nathan headed back to the main office, waving once more in a failed attempt to console both Lola and his bruised ego, Mike went to the passenger side and helped Lola out.

She stumbled over the gravel stones. "When is he going to pave this hellhole?"

"Shh." Mike guided her to the concrete floor of the unit.

Her shoulders dropped. "That's it?" she asked. The question reverberated through the small room, answering in kind. "I was expecting a warzone, the way that officer stuttered his way through our conversation."

Mike started for a box and opened it. He knew her mind was stuck on the physical representation of the room rather than the meaning of the objects contained within. He had to get her past the point of despondence quickly. "Your mother's silverware. It all here?" he asked, handing her the box.

She countered with a question. "What about her bone china teapot?"

Mike rummaged through the boxes. The one small mercy of Lola's mind is that it was predictable in that it almost always thought in a chronologically linear pattern. As such, most of the room was organized similarly.

He opened another box. Doilies. Tablecloth.

Another box. Coffee mugs, highball glasses.

Another. The bone china teapot.

He lifted it. "Here it is."

She stared blankly into the box, like she was waiting for her mind to take her somewhere else.

He set the teapot down and reached for a box on the rear wall. They needed to focus. "Let's take a look at the photographs."

Lola looked at the floor. "It'd be nice to sit somewhere."

Mike stacked several of the sturdier boxes into a makeshift chair, helped her sit, then went back to the photos. He held the box up. "Red, brown, blue albums." *From Hollywood*, he thought.

She reached for the box.

As she looked through each album, Mike sped up the inventory check. He knew which album, which box, the nudes were in. If any pictures were missing, they'd likely be from that album.

Third box down, orange 8x10 album.

He opened the box and grabbed the album, thumbing through the pages slowly, looking for white squares cradled by nicotine tar and dust.

Everything was in place.

"My Prince Albert tin," Lola muttered.

Mike closed the orange album and slid it back into its box. "What?"

"My old tin. Had a few photos."

Mike combed his memory. Prince Albert tin?

"Red," she said. "Rectangular with rounded edges."

He saw it in his mind. But where had he put it? Not with the photos. He'd remember that. They were important to her. "It had photos in it?"

"Yes!" she shouted.

He dug through the neighboring boxes. It had to be stored somewhere near the photos. He organized everything in the order she had it organized—thematically—first, and then chronologically second.

"Where is it?" she asked.

"I'm looking. It's not with the photos. We must have stored it in another box."

We.

This time he was responsible.

Two hours later, Mike had checked and re-checked every box in the unit. "It's not here." He closed his eyes, almost wincing in anticipation of her reaction.

Nothing.

He opened his eyes.

Lola was crying. "We have to find it," she said.

"It's not here. I've checked everything."

"It must be at home. In the guest closet where you hide things from me, maybe," she said.

He smiled. Even with a mind half gone, she was more attentive than most. He took her observation as an invitation to lock up. "Let's check at home. If it doesn't turn up, we'll call the police and let them know."

Mike re-stacked the boxes to the best of his ability in the order they were originally placed, and headed back to the car. "We'll find it."

She nodded tearfully, placing her hand on her cheek. She pulled her fingers away and stared at them, confused.

Mike recognized the blank stare in her eyes, immediately followed by panic, reorientation to the moment.

"Why am I crying?" she asked.

He held his hand out, helping her to her feet. "We're just reminiscing."

She nodded as he helped her to the car.

CHAPTER FIVE

SPEARANCE

BEFORE GOING BACK to the station, Spearance stopped by the town court to appeal for probable cause with Judge Dashnaw. He ran the judge through his rationale, opting for the short story. Miles Singleton was caught breaking into one of the storage units at Tiernan's earlier in the day. Lola's. Spearance had collected two eye-witness reports and drove to Miles' apartment for questioning. The door was locked. They made a few calls to find out where Miles was working this week, found out he'd taken up a custodial position at the chemical plant. So they took a trip out there to check out his custodial closet, and sure as shit—always good to pepper the dialogue with a touch of universal colloquialisms—there's a picture of Lola in an ammo box.

No, neither the door nor the box had been secured.

No, Lola hadn't had a chance to inventory the contents of the storage unit, but she was down there currently, presumably.

The judge gave Spearance conditional probable cause. He signed the warrant, but said that if Lola didn't get back to him by the end of the day, Spearance was to shred the damned thing and come back the following week when there was a bit more time to spare.

Spearance pulled into the station, warrant in hand. He folded it and placed it in the glove box. Didn't want the boys getting too thirsty before the search.

Before walking in, Spearance donned his best poker face, braced to tell Bo that no, he had not, in fact, heard anything "juicy" while he was at Lola's.

Bo wasn't waiting for him though.

The room was empty, save Jim, sitting in the same position he had been when Spearance left.

Spearance closed the door, eyes still on Jim. "Where's Bo?"

Jim pointed his book toward the door. "Paperwork."

"He's still trudging through that?"

Jim shrugged, face still buried behind his book.

Spearance opened the door to find Bo sitting at his desk. "How long does it take to fill out a police report?" Spearance leaned in over Bo's shoulder.

Publisher's Clearing House.

Spearance rubbed his forehead. "You've got to be kidding me."

"Gotta keep the dream alive." Bo carefully peeled a grand prize sticker from one form, placed it on another. "So, what'd Lola say...about the pictures?"

"She was more disturbed than anything." Spearance picked up the entry forms Bo was working on and flipped through them. The stacks, complete with scratch offs, stickers, and more, reminded him of a children's activity book. He dropped the pile on the table beside him.

"Took you a while, getting back." Bo gathered up the documents and slid them into the envelope. "You stop at the court to get a warrant?"

"Tried." Spearance stared at the phone. "Just waiting for a call from Lola. If anything's missing, we can search Miles'."

"You ask her to fib? I'd be interested in seeing what's in his apartment."

"Her mind is so volatile, anything is liable to send her over the edge. Chances are, she'll think something's missing even if it isn't. We just have to wait for the call."

***

The call came an hour later.

After a four-hour review of the storage unit's contents, nothing appeared out of place. Lola, however, had become visibly agitated, claiming that a small Prince Albert tin was missing from her photography collection. Her aide said he thought he remembered seeing it, but had not dedicated it to memory as he had many of the other items he helped her move from California.

With that, Spearance gathered Jim and Bo and headed to Miles' apartment. If Miles was not present, Jim and Spearance would lead the inspection, with Bo in the vehicle, parked two blocks away. He was to be on the lookout for a light blue Oldsmobile Achieva.

They pulled up just after dark. Spearance had hoped Miles would be home by then so they could question him about his whereabouts earlier in the day, but when he knocked, no one answered.

Spearance toggled the knob. "We should have called the landlord."

"Just break it down," Jim whispered.

Spearance waved Bo down the road.

Bo put the car into gear and reluctantly rolled down the street.

"I don't want to make too much noise." Spearance tried the knob again. "There's a possibility he's in there. If he thinks it's a break-in, he could fire on us." He leaned into the door. "Miles. It's John Spearance, from the police department. I just need to ask you a few questions."

No response.

He knocked. "We have a warrant to inspect your apartment. We're going to force entry."

The door to the neighboring apartment unlocked. An elderly woman stepped onto the porch. "He's not home."

Bo stepped forward. "Have you seen him at all today?"

The woman shook her head. "Rarely do. He's the quietest thing."

Spearance peered around her. "His parents home?"

She turned to their door. "Haven't seen them either."

Spearance edged in front of Bo. "Do you have a spare key, by chance?"

"I don't. Sorry." She looked out to the street. "Is he in trouble?"

Spearance handed her the warrant. "We need to search his house."

"No business of mine." She handed the warrant back. "Sorry to intrude, officers." She walked back inside her house, shut and locked the door.

Spearance fished a pair of rubber gloves out of his pocket. "Gloves. Both of you." Spearance turned to Jim. "Try the side window. I'll take the front one. I'd rather bust a latch than take the door off the hinges."

While Spearance toggled the front window, Jim rounded the edge of the house. Two minutes later, a loud pop echoed from the side of the house. "Got it!" Jim whispered emphatically.

Spearance rounded the corner to find Jim shimmying into the apartment, legs dangling from the sill.

Spearance walked to the edge and pushed Jim's legs through the window haphazardly. Jim fell with a heavy thud onto the living room floor.

Spearance whispered into his walkie-talkie. "We're in. Let us know if you see anything."

Bo's grainy voice echoed through the speaker. "Got it. All clear so far."

Jim turned to the window and reached out. "Thanks, asshole."

Spearance grabbed Jim's arms and braced his feet against the old shingles. As he scrambled up, Jim pulled him in, so his lower half slammed into the side of the house. Spearance tumbled onto the carpet and noted the distinct scent of cat piss—both fresh and stale. He covered his nose. "That's terrible. Open the other window, Bo."

Bo got to his feet, running his hands across the wall to find a switch. He found one near the front door, flipped it on, and bent to open the window.

Upon rising, Spearance stopped and took in the wall opposite him. He let his peripheral vision work the neighboring walls.

They were covered in photographs, most of them black and white, or unusually dark.

Jim holstered his flashlight. "Would you look at that," he whispered. "Those aren't all Lola, are they?"

Spearance got to his feet and approached the wall before him. He shook his head. "All sorts of people." He peeled one of the photos, revealing more beneath. "From all over. Magazine cut outs, Polaroids, newspapers."

Jim walked to the neighboring wall and stared at the photos. "Should we call it in?"

Spearance stared, bemused by the plethora of images stacked tightly together from floor to ceiling. "To who?"

"State boys over in Susquehanna?" Jim mused.

Spearance remained transfixed by the images. "It's just photos."

"You aren't seeing what I'm seeing." Jim waved him over.

Spearance turned slowly, taking in the images from left to right until he reached the far wall, where the pictures transitioned from darkened hues of black and grey to brighter shades of red. He drew his eyes down the wall, trying to determine if the blood trailed uniformly across the images. He expected it to fall down the images in a distinct pattern, assuming something or someone had been murdered here.

But the blood followed no predictable pattern. Each photo was so blood-soaked it created the illusion of uniformity. But each work stood apart upon closer inspection.

Jim ran his hand across the pictures. He pulled his hand away and ran his thumb over his fingers. "It's dry."

Spearance stepped forward. "It's not dry." He pulled a Polaroid off the wall and turned it over. He flipped it face up and held it close. "The blood is in the photos." He handed it to Jim.

Jim took the photo in his hand and rubbed at its surface, confirming what Spearance had observed. The blood wasn't on the pictures. It was *in* the pictures. On the faces of the photographed, pooling out from the wounds on their bodies. Had it been real, it would have dried, coagulated. It wouldn't have been so vibrant.

Just like the photo Spearance had returned to Lola.

Jim turned to Spearance. "What's the plan?"

Spearance shook his head. "Get shots of them as they are on the wall. Then take them down. Bag 'em. See if we can ID anyone on this wall, starting with local people. We'll check missing persons reports. If anyone in these pictures is missing or presumed dead, he'll be going in for more than just attempted burglary."

Jim craned his neck to both sides. "All of them?"

"Start with this wall." Spearance started for the bedroom. "I'm going to look around. See if I can find that tin Lola thinks she lost."

The door gave without resistance. Spearance ran his hand across the wall until he found the light switch, and braced himself for the possibility of more explicit photos adorning the bedroom walls.

There was nothing. Only the cheap, vertical wood paneling from the 70s. The same kind Spearance had in his living room as a kid.

The carpeting underfoot was no different, a green shag carpet that from a distance looked like AstroTurf. It squelched beneath his feet, gurgling as it took in air after each step he made forward. The floor was soaked.

Spearance checked the neighboring bathroom. The faucets were off.

Was it always this damp, just seeping up through the foundation?

He shook his head, checked all of the outlets as he walked back into the bedroom. He unplugged the television on the dresser and the alarm clock on the nightstand, just to be safe. Then he opened the top drawer of the nightstand and rummaged through the contents. There were a few sentimental items in the top drawer. A picture of Miles' mother and father. A few pictures of Miles when he was a child, one of which featured Ed—presumably—drinking beer out of one of those

German boot mugs. He was still in diapers in the picture, but any unnerving quality was abated by the sour look on the boy's face. Besides, pictures like this weren't wholly uncommon.

Spearance tossed the photos on the bed, making a mental note of the organization. The current pile, soon to be the right pile, would be inconsequential material. The left pile would be for potential evidence.

He kept digging. The dresser drawers were well organized. Socks and boxers on the top. Pants in the second drawer. A miscellaneous collection of stained clothes in the third. Undershirts in the fourth. Spearance gutted the third drawer and threw it into the left pile, just in case.

The bottom drawer held a modest stack of books.

A copy of *Goodbye, Mr. Chips*, one of the books middle schoolers suffered through at Hastings Central School: inconsequential to the investigation.

A copy of *The Witch of Blackbird Pond*, another middle school classic: also inconsequential.

Spearance flipped through the pages, checking for photos or letters, finding only an old chewing tobacco stain at the center of *Mr. Chips* and a condom wrapper tucked between the pages of *Blackbird Pond*.

He deliberated as he stared at the wrapper. They had already secured probable cause for search. In a perfect world, the place would have come up clean save the tin, which still hadn't made an appearance and might not. But now—with walls adorned with collages of the dead and the suspect in question missing—it was hard to determine what qualified as evidence. Practically everything in the room could be relevant, depending on what crime had been committed. So, what to take?

Evidence of thievery was a must. But what about the collage? If those people were dead...Spearance shook his head. A serial killer that prolific, that young, and undetected to boot. It'd be impossible. Besides, some of the photos in the neighboring room were local—the subjects still alive—which gave him peace of mind. It was also what unnerved him, and what finally led him to decide on placing anything he thought worthy of consideration into the evidence pile, regardless of whether or not it related to the break-in at Tiernan's Storage.

He folded the pages closed and tossed the book into the evidence pile. The condom wrapper slid out of the side of the book. Spearance tucked it back in, thinking to himself, *This is why we wear the rubber gloves.*

Under the books, old notebooks, the contents of which could be explored in more depth back at the office. Spearance tossed them into the evidence pile and turned back to the drawer to find Prince Albert staring back at him, encompassed by a fading coat of red paint.

Spearance popped the lid carefully and set it down inside the drawer.

Yep. This was *the* Prince Albert tin. No question about it.

Inside, there was one picture of Lola and a few of her companions. Like the photos in the collage, their faces were slashed, bodies cut.

Spearance ran his thumb across the photo.

There were no marks, no abrasions.

Like the nude he'd found in Miles' locker, the cuts seemed to emanate from beneath the surface of the glossy finish, and they looked like actual flesh wounds. He placed the photo back in the tin and closed the lid. "Bedroom's clear. Need a tote though."

Jim pushed the door open, stepping into the wet carpet. He stepped back over the threshold. "Find anything?"

Spearance nodded. "Got the tin. Found some other items of interest as well."

Jim looked at the pile on the bed. "You're taking all of that?"

"Yeah." Spearance looked at the pile, then back at Bo. "Stack up what you've got and call Hometown. Let them know we're going to need a few large coffees. It's going to be a long night."

MILES

He had run. Now he needed to cut his losses and hide. Losing the photos was painful. He'd put so much work into them, surface work on those he couldn't enter. Interior work on those he could. The yearbook...he *wanted* the yearbook. He didn't *need* the yearbook. He'd gleaned from it what he needed, and it had led him nowhere. He knew this much: for some reason, the photos of Samantha Ohst had been altered in *every* copy of the yearbook to match the remains of her body in the sorority fire. The change to the photo was barely noticeable, but in the right light, if you looked closely, you could see the scarring beneath the surface of her face, almost like a double exposure of her face in life and in death. It suggested someone like him, albeit more powerful, was out there. But the yearbook couldn't tell him who that was, or how they'd altered the photos.

Everything the yearbook could offer him he already had, and he had everything else that he needed. He had the picture of Lola and her friends from Germany, presumably taken by the camera that destroyed the industry. He still had the ability to soulfall. And now, he'd finally found a place to hide away for a short while, a six-mile dirt road with a closed bridge at the end. The road was narrow, and hadn't been frequented in ages. He'd been down the road many times over the years and had never seen as much as a soul. The little pockets of solitude like this, just on the outskirts of Hastings, kept his growing social anxieties at bay. No matter how many people he had to nod and smile at throughout the day, a brief five-minute drive out of town could take him down a meandering road to solitude so seemingly absolute it was almost as frightening as the prospect of talking to others.

Miles leaned back in his car seat and took the image of Lola and the others into his hand. He ran his other hand across the image, across Lola's face and body, and closed his eyes. He waited for the sound of trees quaking in the wind to be replaced by a relative silence. That'd tell him he was in. Relying on smell only worked when he re-entered photos. Upon first entry, he had to rely on the silence.

He kept his hand on the picture and began to slip, but the trees continued to quake.

He opened his eyes. He needed to prime himself.

What would he do once he got inside? Lola was too beautiful, too perfect to be tainted by sex. He wanted to build to that slowly. This time he just wanted to get Rothman's hands off of her, so he could enjoy the picture without the accompanying twinge of jealousy.

Jealousy.

He clung to that, that envy coupled with his admiration of Lola. He closed his eyes again and drew his hand across the image, thinking of Rothman's hands on Lola's body. They should be his hands. Lola was his.

The trees rustled to life with another gust of wind. Then silence.

He was in.

Miles opened his eyes to confirm.

Lola stood before him, David Rothman at her side, Maier and Tigerstedt on the far end.

That sense of being trapped tugged at Miles. He turned to find the escape hatch, that black blanket of nothingness that he could fall through when overwhelmed.

It wasn't there.

Instead, he found the other half of the room, the half that wasn't in the photograph. And there, near the wall, was a camera resting on a wooden tripod. Miles walked toward it. Was this it? The camera that destroyed the silent film industry? He took it into his hands and turned it slowly. He held it up and snapped a photo.

The camera did not respond.

Miles tucked it under his arm, hoping he might leave with it, but there was no easy access exit as there had been in previous pictures. He rushed for the nearest door and opened it. Another room. This photo hadn't just preserved the image itself. It had preserved the entire house. Perhaps more.

Miles walked to the next door and found himself in a magnificent hall. He recognized it from photos. This was Tigerstedt's mansion.

Guests gathered below, mid-discourse. Two white-gloved servants circled the crowd, one with thin-stemmed champagne glasses, the other with hors d'oeuvres. The hors d'oeuvres plate was, unsurprisingly, untouched. The champagne glasses disappeared amidst a flurry of guests. Miles descended the stairs to view them up close, when a door slammed behind him.

He'd been inside hundreds of photographs over the years and nothing had moved. Of course, there had never been anything as robust as this within the photos he entered either.

Another door slammed, not shut but open, and Miles could make out the shadow of a person standing at the edge of the door.

He ran.

He ran down the stairs and into the courtyard, looking back to see if anyone was in pursuit.

He saw movement at the front steps, so he continued running. In the distance he saw the ocean. He reached the edge of the yard and thought about jumping over the edge to the beach below. But he could go no further. He had reached the edge of whatever he was encased in. Held by an invisible barrier.

He turned to the approaching figure behind him.

"Who are you?!" It loomed over him. "How did you get here?"

Miles held the camera above his head. "I'll destroy it!"

The figure laughed. "It's a copy. All of this is." He motioned around him. "It means nothing."

He turned to the threshold and tried to reach through. The barrier was solid, like glass.

The figure was fully visible now. It stood upright, draped in black. No discernible features. "How did you get in here?"

"How do I get out?" Miles asked. The figure loomed over him. He closed his eyes.

Then he felt it, felt himself outside of the photo, clutching the photo in his hand. He was both here and there simultaneously, another milestone.

He clenched his fists as the figure blotted out the sun, and in doing so bent the photo in his hand. Out there. Outside of the photo.

The sun returned.

He opened his eyes. Though he could feel the car seat beneath him, and the photo in his hand, the rest of his senses were steeped in the photograph.

The figure had collapsed before him, arm outstretched. It touched Miles, clasping tightly to his pants.

Then he was back in his car.

No camera.

Just the photograph, a new crease across Tigerstedt's body from Miles' grip.

Miles tried to straighten the crease, restore the photo to how he had originally found it.

Was that Tigerstedt in the photograph, in there with him?

Had he somehow harmed Tigerstedt through the photograph?

LOLA

Lola woke in the middle of the night, fighting her memory for the last threads of a dream she thought was real, or was real. Something about a can of tobacco.

Photos. They were photos from Belgium. Or was it California?

She couldn't remember.

She cycled through the piecemeal memories in her mind, a sort of centrifugal approach to separating real memories from false ones. She fell out of bed and pulled herself to her feet. She passed through the kitchen.

Lola made her way to the guest room closet. She pushed open the door and began pulling boxes onto the floor beside her.

Prince Albert-Belgium-photos-still frame, she thought, coaxing her memory to life.

She tore open a shoebox and poured the contents on the floor.

"*Prince Albert-California-or-Belgium-still frame-ph-photos!*" she shouted to herself.

Mike rushed to her side and propped her into a sitting position against him.

Mike-California.

She pushed him off and fell back into the pile of scraps on the floor.

Mike leaned over her. "What's wrong?"

"Prince Albert-Belgium-photos-still frame," she muttered.

"What?"

Louder. "Prince Albert-Belgium-photos-still frame."

He shook her gently, tried to prop her up again.

She shrugged him off and primed her memory again. "Prince Albert-Belgium-photos-still frame." She pounded the floor with her fist. "Remember, goddamn it!"

She scattered the contents of the box, revealing a small, metal lens cap and a photo of herself from her time working on *Everyman.* Who were those men with her? *Prince Albert-Belgium-photos-still frame-lens cap.*

Her co-star, David; the director, Maier; Tigerstedt.

Tigerstedt!

She picked up the photo and clung to it, desperately trying to remember. What was it about Tigerstedt?

Tigerstedt. Lens cap. Lens cap. Come on, damn you. Lens cap. Tigerstedt...camera.

"My camera!" she shouted.

Suddenly, Lola found herself shrouded in blackness. The floor was now cold and hard, like concrete. She ran her hands across the flooring. It *was* concrete. "Michael!"

She patted at the floor, trying to find a clear path to the wall, and then to a door, and finally, safety. She knocked boxes to the floor clumsily as she crawled forward in the darkness. "Michael?!"

Another step forward and she found the wall. No, a door. As she knocked on it, she already knew where she was. The hollow clang of the aluminum door...the concrete floor...

Lola was stuck in her storage shed again.

She pounded her fists against the door, damning herself, until she thought she heard something outside. She backed against the wall and rested her head on her arms and knees.

Sometime later—Lola hadn't been sure how long she'd been there, nor whether or not she had fallen asleep during her wait—headlights pooled in at the bottom of the doorway.

Lola sat up as the first car door opened, then slammed shut.

Keys rattled on the other end of the door.

"Miles?"

She did not answer.

"Tiernan called about a disturbance. We've been looking for you."

The door rolled upward, revealing the officer...Spearance. He shined a flashlight into the unit. "Lola?"

"Don't just stand there," she muttered. "Help me to the car."

He assisted her on her way to her feet. "How'd you get in here?"

She shook her head, but said nothing. "Just take me home. Michael's probably worried."

Spearance opened the back door and waited for her.

"Are you serious?"

"What?"

"I'd prefer to sit up front, thank you." She walked to the front, passenger-side door. "I'm not an animal."

Spearance slammed the door gently, more confused than angry, and let her in.

Lola plopped down on the seat, pulled the lower quarter of her bathrobe onto her lap.

Spearance closed the door and met her on the other side. He looked at her, expecting her to be soaked from head to toe from walking in the rain, but she was completely dry. "You're not going to tell me how you ended up in there, are you?"

"A woman must keep her secrets," she said, staring at her reflection in the window. "And I'd appreciate it if we could keep this between us."

"And Michael," Spearance corrected.

"Obviously." She sighed. "You find my tin yet?"

"We've found some items of interest to aid in our investigation. That's all I can tell you."

"Of course." She folded her hands on her lap. "Your inflated sense of self-importance never ceases to amaze me. You're investigating petty theft with a twist of perversion, for Christ's sake."

"My deepest apologies." Spearance shifted into drive and let the vehicle roll to the front entrance of the lot, bracing for the pervasive silence that would inevitably accompany their trek back to Lola's, then again as he spent the evening sifting through Miles' photographs.

CHAPTER SIX

SPEARANCE

"COMING THROUGH!" BO hoisted his poker table into the air and brought it through the door. "Pull a couple of the legs out, Spearance."

Spearance tugged at the table's underside in vain.

Bo ran his fingers along the bottom and flipped one of the leg locks. "Get this one." He tapped the upper edge of the table.

Spearance pulled the leg out and together they dropped the table into place beside Spearance's desk. As they worked the remaining three legs into place, Spearance began spreading the photos from Miles' apartment across the table. "I want three piles." He continued spreading the photos across his desk and Bo's poker table. "Local pictures on my desk chair. Everything else I want sorted by the abrasions. If the picture looks like it had been cut with something, put those on Bo's desk in the main room." He opened his top drawer and took out the Prince Albert tin. "Any photos you find that look like this." He held the photo of Lola and her companions up. "You put them in this tin. I'll leave the drawer open."

There were 400 in total, mostly Scotch-Taped together two—sometimes three—layers deep. Half way through the search, they'd deemed the bottom layer of newspaper clippings unsalvageable. But they left them intact, attached to the backsides of glossy pictures from magazines and photos that made up the top layers.

400 photos, and not a single one unmarred.

So far, not a single one like the photo in the Prince Albert tin.

The kid had collected everything imaginable. The top layer ranged from magazine cutouts to catalog models, everymen and everywomen from all walks of life. Local faces peeked out from behind the angular clippings. He thought he had recognized himself once even, but didn't want to know until he'd taken a more thorough inventory. It would have been difficult to discern who was who in many cases anyway. The images were obscured by violence—cuts and abrasions, most likely from an X-Acto knife, maybe sandpaper.

In his violence, Miles was indiscriminate. Male. Female. Adult. Child. He didn't seem to have a "type." All of the photos were hacked in the same crosshatch pattern.

In total they ended up with four locals on Spearance's office chair, all cutouts from the Hastings newspaper, *The Gazette.*

Spearance pointed to the modest pile. "We need ID on these. They're out of the local paper, I'm guessing."

Bo picked up the cutouts and shuffled through them. "I know these two." He lifted the first. "That's...Katie something. I can't remember her last name. We went to school together." He shuffled it to the back of the pile. "That's Molly, from the grocery store...Richards."

Spearance took the last two photos and scanned them again, priming his memory. Molly Richards...somewhere down there in the recesses of his memory he tried to forget...Burning Fields Festival. The gazebo...

No...

The first fire.

The fire he tried not to remember.

He handed the photos back to Bo.

"We'll show Jim when he gets back."

Bo set the cutouts back on the desk chair. "You want me to call the newspaper?"

"Not yet." Spearance went back to the remaining unsorted photos. "But the other two?"

"Yeah?"

"Look them up and give them a call, just to confirm they're all right. There was an accident in Johnstown earlier today. Tell them you thought they had the same make and model, and wanted to check in."

Bo headed for his desk. "Sure thing."

The stack slowly diminished as Spearance worked through it, carting the sorted photos stack-by-stack into the main room where Bo was still on the phone.

Bo combed over them carefully as the callers played catch up. "Yup. Yeah, she's off to college now." Bo laughed. "Indiana, where else?" He rolled his eyes at Spearance as he flipped the photos over one by one.

Spearance sorted the last photos into the pile bound for Bo's desk. "That's everything."

Bo hung up the phone. "Everyone's good." He stepped into Spearance's office. "Except these two." He handed two thumbnail photos to Spearance. "You guys must have missed this one."

The photo was glossy, cut from what appeared to be a yearbook. There were off-center partial photos on the backside of the image. The backgrounds were flat blue. Clothing formal. It was Sam, the girl who had died in the sorority fire.

"Good catch. Juicy, even." Spearance eyed it carefully. "You remember her?"

Bo reeled from the image. "Her dad taught physics at the high school. None of the guys would even look at her until they finished their second lab science with him." He tapped the desk. "You were on that case, weren't you?"

Spearance shrugged. "I was there the first night. Collected evidence, accompanied the fire marshal. Then state boys took over. Suspected arson with a body count that high isn't a gig for a town boy."

"That was a strange one."

Spearance looked up from the photos. "Why's that?"

"Two girls. Same town. One dead. One with direct involvement the only survivor."

"IUP's one of the closest state colleges. There's practically a funnel straight from Hastings to Indiana. It's where I went. You?"

Bo nodded. "I went there for a year."

Spearance turned his attention back to the photo. Sliced hatch-marks ran across it. But beneath that, scarification. Blistering from the sun, or from fire.

Spearance ran his thumb over the photo, finding it difficult for his fingers to distinguish between the ridges of the crosshatch cuts and what might be blistering on the photo or on the girl's face in the picture.

What he felt wasn't enough to cast reasonable doubt on his gut reaction.

"We should go back to the hospital in the morning. See if these came out of the yearbook in Miles' closet." He tossed it into the Prince Albert tin. "Radio Jim. See if he's heard anything."

Bo turned to the CB radio and picked up the mic. "How's it going?"

"Nothing yet." Jim's grainy voice echoed through the room.

"Where you parked?" Spearance asked.

"By Mrs. Finch's hedgerow."

Spearance shook his head. There really was nowhere optimal to park on Minor Street. It was one of the reasons they rarely patrolled there, and likely one of the reasons so many people tore down the street on weekends while Bo and Jim ticketed college kids for public urination on Main.

"Boss doesn't look too happy about that," Bo chided.

"If the boss has a better idea, he can share it."

"I'm just frustrated with the circumstance, not your position." Spearance headed for Bo's desk. "Mrs. Finch might take issue with your position if you damage that hedgerow though."

Jim laughed. "It hasn't been trimmed in ages. Pretty sure she's not concerned with aesthetic anymore."

"With what?" Bo asked.

"Never mind. Over and out. I have a job to do, boys."

Bo set down the CB mic. "What's bothering you?"

"I just don't understand why he ran."

"Maybe he thinks he'll get jail time."

"He's had enough brushes with the law—gentle brushes—to know he'd get off lightly. He's up to something."

"Only time will tell." Bo sat up and started pooling the scattered photos together. "Let's clean this up."

Spearance headed for the closet.

Bo continued corralling the photos into a narrow pile. "We're out of Ziploc."

Spearance grabbed a cardboard box from the closet. "This'll do for now." He held the box at the edge of the desk. "Sweep them in."

Bo pushed them to the edge and into the box. "You want me to stay tonight?"

"I can't afford to have two men on the clock tonight. I want Jim on lookout." His eyes went to the clock. How much time did he have before...Spearance sighed. "Shit. Night class." He pointed to his office. "Yeah...I guess you better. Pull out the cot and man the phone."

"Will do." Bo took the box out of Spearance's hands and carried it into his office.

MOLLY

Molly only had five minutes before class started when her mom started circling Lowell Hall for parking in her absurdly large 1979 Buick.

"Mom, just stop the car and I'll get out."

"I'll get a ticket for double parking."

"You won't even be in park. You're just dropping me off."

"Fine." Her mother tapped the brakes. The car squeaked to a stop.

Molly turned to Jolie. "Be good for Grandma, okay?"

Jolie stuffed something between herself and her car seat quickly. "Nokay."

"What is that?" Molly reached into the back seat, fishing for whatever it was Jolie tucked behind her. Finally she wrapped her fingers around a small plastic tube and extracted it from behind her daughter's thigh. "Jelly beans?!" She turned to her mother. "Come on, Mom."

"She asked for them."

Molly spun the plastic tube in her hands. "God. These are from Christmas!" She turned the tube on its side and read the packaging. "Last year?!" She stuffed them into her backpack. "Gross."

Jolie smiled, her teeth dotted with orange and blue.

Molly opened the car door, turning to her mother as she exited.

"I'll make her brush her teeth as soon as we get back to your place," she said, already knowing Molly's next line.

"*You* brush her teeth." She closed the passenger-side door. "Bye, Mom." She knelt in front of the back seat window and waved at Jolie. "Bye, honey."

Jolie waved back with one hand, fishing for loose jellybeans with the other. "Bye, Mommy." She pulled a green jellybean out of her car seat and popped it into her mouth, relishing every second of her mother's look of shock and awe as the car pulled away.

Molly took in a deep breath of the cool air, watched the heat from her lungs dissipate before her as she exhaled. The Buick's taillights cast light trails along the pot-holed pavement to the edge of the road, then crept out of sight.

For the first time in almost a year, she was alone. No child. No overbearing (albeit benignly so) mother.

And she savored every second of it, from the sidewalk to the Lowell Hall's walkway, through the electric wing doors, past the exit sign and up the stairs. She loved everything about this relative solitude. She loved the way her footsteps echoed through the building as she trudged upward to the second floor. She loved the distant sound of lockers slamming and doors closing on open discussions.

Though she hadn't thought about it, or perhaps hadn't allowed herself to think about it, she realized now that she had missed college.

She walked down the hallway toward the opposite end of the building, counting the room numbers down until she found 203. She peered into the sterile space, waiting for someone to notice her and wave her in.

She checked her watch.

7:01.

Shit.

The professor was digging through his bag for something, so Molly turned the knob and entered quietly.

She flinched as he looked up.

"Come on in," he said.

She rushed into the room. "Sorry I'm late."

He continued rummaging through his things. "Don't worry about it. We're all commuters here. You think you're late now, wait until the fall semester."

Molly smiled and worked her way down the far wall of the room to the back and found a seat. By the time she approached, she noticed the large black duffel bag snaked across the seat onto the floor. The guy in the neighboring seat stared down at his book.

Molly cleared her throat.

He looked up. "Oh. Sorry." He dragged the bag onto the floor and toward his seat.

"Thanks," she whispered as she stepped over the bag and sat down.

The professor opened the front door and looked both ways. "Must be this is it," he said as he closed the door behind him. "Well, we have one new student today, but we'll spare her the introductions. We've got a lot to go over, after all." He turned to the board and started writing.

Molly turned to Duffel Bag Boy. "What'd I miss?"

"Course orientation. No actual content." He handed her his syllabus. "You got the book?"

Molly tipped the book toward him.

Duffel Bag Boy gave her a thumbs up and opened his notebook.

She followed suit, opening her notebook and putting pen to paper. Everything started to bleed together, but she got the gist of what's required. Two chapters per class period. Three times per week. A *lot* of reading. Two papers. A midterm. A final.

The lectures were setup in a chronologically linear fashion, exploring criminal justice in the United States.

The professor—she turned over the syllabus and looked for his name. Mr. Spearance. She knew the name, but tried hard not to remember from where. Instead she focused on the moment.

He placed the heading on the board and started.

Crime in the Nineteenth-Century American City

"So, as you may or may not know, prior to the development of larger areas, police weren't needed as much because small communities were self-regulating. Self-righting. But with the advent of cities came the need for structure, systematization, whatever you want to call it.

"Police.

"Cities needed police.

"Long story short, the police forces weren't large enough to fully regulate crime, so officers were relegated to profiling. Who took the brunt of the punishment? The poor and destitute, of course." Spearance smiled. "Which left the rich to whatever criminal inclinations they might have had at the time."

"So nothing's changed, really?" Molly's neighbor inserted.

A few students laughed.

Spearance raised his eyebrows. "Not really, no. But that's what we're here for, right? To rectify the errors of our predecessors." He turned back to the board, writing truncated notes from his lecture. "In smaller areas like the one where I work, it's a bit easier to keep tabs on folks. Everyone knows everyone, and citizens are naturally inclined to...we'll call it 'socially regulate,' but what we're really talking about is gossip. People love to gossip." Again, Spearance punctuated his lecture with what Molly assumed was his best attempt at a disarming smile, but since he often used it after relaying grim facts about abuses of power and unsolved murder, it had the opposite effect. Molly might have referred to it as unsettling, but the word she thought more accurately captured the essence of his smile was "creepy."

Professor Spearance's smile was creepy.

Molly turned to her neighbor. "He's an odd one, isn't he?"

He spoke as he continued writing. "He's all right."

She turned back to the front of the room. Something about her professor's gait, or the setup of the room, took her back to her computer literacy course in freshman year. She remembered her professor telling everyone to look to their left, then to their right. He said the course had a 50% fail rate like he was proud of the fact, and said not to get too attached to the faces in the room, because most of them would be gone by the end of the semester.

Comparatively speaking, she guessed her neighbor was right. Spearance was all right. Anything she found off-putting could probably be traced back to her poor experiences with cops in '81. It was never enough that the place burned down. The officers who interviewed her wanted it to be someone's fault. Her fault, she had to assume, from the way they had questioned her. But Spearance.

Spearance...had been there.

She closed her eyes and shut the chain of thoughts down, searching for other times she had run into him, any time but that night.

The store. She saw him at the store sometimes.

She tuned Professor Spearance back in.

"Once criminals get outside of the purview of small-town dynamics, they become just another face in the crowd, which you'll be reading about tonight." Spearance reached into his bag. "That's right, bonus reading assignment!" He pulled out a stack of papers. "It's short. I want you to read this for next class. Poe's 'Man of the Crowd.'"

"He knows we have lives outside of this class, right?" Molly whispered.

"Nevermore." Her neighbor laughed.

It's only for a few years, she thought to herself as she waited for the stack to reach her. *A few years and we'll finally be on our feet again. Better pay. Better benefits. We got this.*

The girl in front of Molly passed back the last copy of Poe's "Man of the Crowd." Molly scanned it quickly before stuffing it into her bag.

"That's it for tonight, kids. We'll see you Friday."

Molly looked at the clock, then to the board filled with notes she'd somehow missed. Had she really zoned out that long?

She started packing her things up.

"Can I get that back?"

Duffel Bag Boy had his hand extended. "My syllabus."

"Oh." Molly handed it to him. "Sorry."

"No worries." He stuffed the syllabus into his bag and extended his hand again. "Name's Greg."

She reciprocated. "Molly."

"Nice to meet you." He packed his books up. "Hey, ah. You got time for a cup of coffee or something?"

"I have a friend picking me up."

"Tomorrow, maybe?" He smiled. "Daylight. Public setting. I'll let you sit by the door so you can run if I turn out to be a weirdo. Maybe you could help me with the course."

She smiled. "Sure, I—uh—"

"—Morning or afternoon?"

"Afternoon is better." She deliberated. "Six."

"Sounds good." He scrawled something on a piece of paper, handed it to her. "Diner okay?"

His number. She folded it up and slid it into her pocket. "Sure."

"Cool. Cool." Duffel Bag Boy—Greg—walked to the front of the room. "Later, Teach."

Spearance waved, distracted by the contents of his bag. "Bye."

Molly watched him leave and walked to the front of the class. "Do you have an extra copy of the syllabus?"

Spearance stepped behind the desk and dug a copy out of his bag. He handed it to her, noted her reluctance to take it, and looked down at the coffee-stained, wrinkled document. "Sorry it's not more presentable. I assure you the coffee stains are dry."

Molly took the syllabus, eyes darting from the syllabus back to Spearance and back to the syllabus again.

"And also that the brown stains are, indeed, coffee."

"I had no doubt."

"Well, the custodians don't always re-stock the toilet paper, so you can never be too careful."

"Ew." Molly laughed.

Spearance zipped his bag and put his hands in his pockets. "I see you've run into our resident expert back there. Self-proclaimed, of course."

"Greg?"

He nodded. "He used to work EMT. He knows his fair share about police procedures. Just wish he was less prone to sharing."

"He just asked if I could help him with the course."

"Ah, I've given him away then. He ask you to meet him at Monopole for your study date?"

"Monopole?"

"It's a bar downtown where all the first responders hang out. They hold a Christmas party for the fire department there every year."

"Never heard of it." Molly smiled nervously. "You work in Hastings, right?"

"Been there for years." He eyed her, trying to dredge up where he'd seen her. "You're Hastings too, aren't you?"

She nodded. "Grew up there."

"What's your last name?"

"Richards."

He shrugged. "A lot of those in Hastings."

"Yeah." She slung her bag over her shoulder. "No relation," she joked.

He stopped, cocked his head. "You wouldn't be related to Ken Richards, would you?"

"That's my father."

He nodded in recognition. "We've met before then. After—"

"—I remember." She looked out the window, then at the ground. "I had to talk to pretty much every cop in a thirty-mile radius after that."

"I'm sorry."

Awkward silence.

"The good news is, after this course you'll know how many of those meetings were protocol, and how many were folks letting curiosity get the best of them."

"Not sure I want to know."

He shook his head. "Probably not."

"I better go. I have a ride waiting." She headed for the door.

She stopped at the door. "Did I miss anything important last time?"

He held his hand over his heart. "The words a teacher never wants to hear." He laughed. "We had class, so you definitely missed *something*. Whether or not it was important, I guess you'll find out on the first exam."

She stared at him, expression blank, but he recognized the undercurrent of panic.

"Aaaaand those are the words a student never wants to hear." Spearance shuffled a few loose papers on his desk, looked across the desks for extra copies of the handouts he'd distributed. "Now we're even. First two chapters should catch you up."

"I won't miss again."

He waved her off. "You're fine. Show up. Pay attention, and you'll be out of here in no time. Homework's on the syllabus. Greg's got the notes."

She nodded and headed for the door. "Thanks!"

"No problem."

On her way down the hallway, Molly watched the fluorescent lights cascade across the glazed brick walls, intent on avoiding eye contact with anyone else. Almost as soon as she stepped out of the classroom, that sense of general dread struck her. She had actually enjoyed the class. Dread would pay in kind. It'd only be a matter of time.

What she feared most was losing Julie. She was the only thing Molly had found the capacity to love unconditionally in her life. Whenever the dread—what she had come to call "the impending"— loomed over her like some formless specter whose presence could only be felt and never seen, her thoughts went immediately to Jolie. It was only a small consolation that in those moments, Molly slipped out of the past. But while she could rarely control her near perpetual entanglement with the past, the past was easy. It was, for the most part, static. It was the future Molly feared. It was the future that sent her sprinting for the medicine cabinet on sleepless nights. She remembered the bitter taste of everything she'd put inside her. Darvocet, Vicodin; each one struck a different part of her palette.

They were all gone now.

For the longest time she thought that was her penance, the suffering of withdrawal.

The feeling in her as she left Lowell Hall strongly suggested she was wrong.

MILES

The graveyard in Hastings neighbored a small racetrack. Beyond that, railroad tracks separated the graveyard from a modest trailer park where one of his childhood friends had lived. Tim. Whatever happened to Tim?

Due to proximity, Miles and Tim had spent a lot of time in and around the graveyard. The area had become like an old friend itself. First walking through it after pacing around the cracked pavement of the racetrack, puffing on cigarettes he'd stolen from his parents.

They'd camped at the racetrack once. His friend even dragged his parents' push mower up there to clear an area. But even in that small clearing they could see Tim's trailer, the rear porch light casting its glare through the thin web of dying trees in autumn. They had resolved to always hide and drink the cans of beer Miles stole in the graveyard. They just needed a little more distance. A little more darkness to rebel without that looming sense of prying eyes that followed them everywhere.

Those hypothetical prying eyes were with Miles now, but he knew better than to let it hold him back. He drank beer wherever and whenever he wanted to now, which was sparingly. That wild hair had been plucked years ago, when he graduated to more refined tastes. When he discovered alternative modes of escape.

Tim disappeared into a bottle. Miles, into photographs.

He parked his car along the tree line separating the last row of headstones from the race track, which was all but gone now. Small crops of grass had shifted the crumbling pavement, and wheatgrass crept in from the edges, creating lightning streaks of greenery that coursed through the roadway. His old friend was growing old. Forgotten.

Forgotten was good. The floodlight at the back of the trailer park had not been replaced, leaving only the dim glow of the eternal lights dotting the graveyard.

Miles sat in his car, cradling the photo of Lola and her friends. He thumbed the thick slice across Tigerstedt's throat, thought about his headless corpse bleeding out in his mansion so many years ago. Was it just coincidence? Had someone put the slice there afterward, a macabre indication of his removal from this world and the nature of said removal? Or had the small slice on the photograph somehow carried over to Tigerstedt, miles away, a voodoo doll effect of sorts?

Tonight he would find out.

It would be a long walk, but he was ready.

Miles stepped out of his car and gently closed the door. He walked along the dirt path that connected the graveyard to the street and walked along the grass, stepping into the trees every time a car passed, which was rarely.

He skirted around Hastings to Lola's apartment, checking first for a rear window he could face from the pasture in her back yard. The chipboard on the wall opposite the window suggested it was only a porch or a mud room, not likely to have much traffic. So he followed the fence to the edge of her driveway, and settled on a window looking into what appeared to be her kitchen. On the windowsill, an unkempt Chia Pet rested alongside a glass swan barometer and an aloe plant. For an aging woman who didn't get around much, two plants resting immediately above a source of water would make sense, and because the window rested square in the center of the upstairs apartment, it was likely she'd be at least passing through at some point in the night.

He waited for her to pass, photograph in hand.

She passed quickly, catching him off guard.

He'd missed his chance.

He lined the photograph up with his view of the house, lined his thumbnail up with her left arm so he could cut into the picture without breaking the glossy surface, presumably without breaking the skin if what he thought would happen were to happen.

She passed again, cup and saucer cradled against her chest.

He pushed firmly into her arm in the picture.

She tossed the cup and saucer forward and grabbed her arm.

She leaned over the sink.

Her aide came to her side and helped her up.

They both looked outside, their vision beyond the edge of the driveway obscured by the flood lamp overhead. As they watched, Miles drew his thumb over her face and pressed, gently at first, which did not illicit response. So he pressed harder, until he could see the evidence of his touch through the window. She grasped at her throat, the universal sign for choking.

Miles pressed harder, watching her aide turn the faucet and bring a handful of water to her lips. As her eyes widened and the water ran down her chin back into the sink, Miles released his grasp.

She clutched her chest as it expanded finally.

It was real.

The camera was real.

Or had been. It may have been destroyed, lost, or otherwise misplaced.

But of those remaining in the picture, who had the camera now? Lola, Maier, or Rothman? Someone else, perhaps?

He wanted to start right here. Right now. Wanted to snuff her out of existence, drunk with power. But he couldn't keep sniffing around Lola's. Couldn't afford to stay much longer tonight, even. Spearance was already frequenting her place and his. Even if he didn't know what was up, if Lola had noticed the missing photos, she'd at least suspect why they were missing, and why her arm was sore now, which is what Miles wanted. With the stakes of pain or death weighing on Lola and her friends, they'd be willing to dredge it up. Now he needed to make his intentions clear. He'd taken their sense of safety for ransom, and wanted the camera. But leaving the note here or speaking to Lola directly would narrow Spearance's search too much. He needed to reach one of the others.

Rothman was on the other end of the country. Maier, on the other hand, had taken up residence in Buffalo, NY. It was a long drive, but his next best shot. Miles would check with him next, talk to him even, if he could. Coerce him with the photograph, if necessary. He needed that camera. If there was a way to make real the work he did in photographs, he wanted that power. He wasn't sure exactly how he'd use it, but he intended to use it.

And there was still the issue of the girl in the yearbook to sort out. Those photos—he'd seen them in several copies now—suggested someone like him was out there, someone capable of sinking below the photographic veneer to the very essence of images below. What's more, they seemed to be able to spread their alterations across photographic replicas. Was this also somehow the camera's doing? If so, it'd be unlikely they'd relinquish possession of the camera willingly. But he was ready to do whatever it took to get his hands on it.

One thing at a time.

He'd start with Maier.

CHAPTER SEVEN

SPEARANCE

BY THE END of April, Spearance always had to take it easier pulling into the station entrance. The dirt-sodden snowbanks at the edges of the driveway had started to retreat, leaving in their wake veritable sinkholes.

But it wasn't the threat of sinking that inspired Spearance to navigate with caution. It was the grass shoots, poking through the receding snow. Those shoots, with their tenuous grasp on oversaturated ground, would be the only non-dismal sign of spring well into May.

As superficial as it seemed, he needed those bright green tufts of grass greeting him as he wheeled into work, especially today.

Especially since Bo was still parked where he had been the previous night.

"Shit," he muttered to himself.

Since Spearance had quit drinking alcohol, he had started weighing his tolerance for others in cups of coffee. People he enjoyed working with, those were one-cup companions. Bo stood around three cups, and Spearance hadn't even had time for one yet today. Incidentally, nobody was a one-cup companion. Hell, he couldn't even stand himself sans one cup.

Spearance took a deep breath as he stepped out of the car and started for the front door.

Bo lifted the blinds on the door window and opened the door, robbing Spearance of that short but crucial walk he needed to mentally prepare himself for whatever pile of "juicy" bullshit Bo had waiting for him.

Bo extended his arm. "Coffee. A tablespoon of cream, just like you like it."

Spearance picked up his pace and reached for the steaming cup. "Thanks, Bo."

Once Spearance had the cup in hand, Bo jogged toward his office door and opened it. "Already cleaned up the cot."

Spearance nodded and walked into his office.

Bo closed the door behind him. "Let me know when you're ready."

Spearance sunk into his chair and drank deeply from the cup Bo had given him. He closed his eyes. *Ten minutes*, he told himself. *Just ten.* He estimated that'd give him enough time to get about half the cup down.

There was never enough time in the morning. Never enough coffee.

But the silence emanating from the neighboring room, and the cup of coffee cradled in his hands, made him think Bo might someday soon prove himself a half-cup companion anyway. So why not test that hypothesis?

Spearance took another drink. "You planning on coming to Conemaugh Memorial with me, see if there's any update on Miles?"

"Was thinking about it." Bo shuffled through a stack of papers on the neighboring desk. "You think we'll have time to drop by the post office?"

"Why?"

Bo opened the door and waved a handful of envelopes. "Just a few bills."

Spearance hid his mouth behind the steaming mug. "All right. Give me a few."

Bo closed the door again. "Going to take forever for the rest of the snow to melt, isn't it?"

Spearance looked out his window. "Last bit always hangs on forever. I've seen snow in July between here and Johnstown. We seem to get more every year."

Bo laughed. "And yet the water table's always low."

Spearance leaned forward, pushed himself to his feet. "You've been eavesdropping on those old men at the diner again, haven't you?"

Bo grabbed the keys off his desk and headed for the door. "It was either eavesdrop or watch *General Hospital* on the old black and white."

Spearance followed. "Glad to see you picked the lesser of two evils."

"Says the guy who voted for Carter."

"It's too early for politics." Spearance pinched the bridge of his nose as he walked through the door. "You got your envelopes?"

"Oh!" Bo ran back inside, giving Spearance a few moments to gather his thoughts. "Got 'em!" He ran to Spearance's side. "You want me to drive?"

Spearance thought of the grass just beginning to creep above the snowline. He took the driver side. "I got it."

Bo sat down in the passenger seat and tossed the small stack of envelopes on the dash. They scattered, revealing their destinations.

Spearance eyed the stack of envelopes, then Bo. "Really?"

Bo smiled. "What?"

"Publisher's Clearing House?"

"People have won. It's not a scam."

Spearance put the car into gear. "I hope those stamps aren't from the office."

Bo put one hand on his heart and raised the other. "On my life, I swear I did rob the taxpaying citizens of Hastings, Pennsylvania."

"Those old boys at the diner'd have your head for that."

"It'd give them something to talk about, other than water tables."

Spearance backed out, watching the small patch of grass through his rearview. "That it would."

The drive down 219 was generally uneventful, your average spread of modest mountains and tree lines highlighted by budding branches. It'd inspire awe in city goers, sure, but Spearance and Bo had seen it hundreds—if not thousands—of times. As such, once conversation had run dry they'd been relegated to passing the time listening to disco and folk rock die a slow and painful death on the radio until they'd reached Conemaugh Memorial Health Center.

Bo rolled his window up as they pulled into the parking lot. "I still maintain that this place smells much less sterile than it purports to be."

Spearance stepped out, slamming the door behind him. "I think that's the chemical plant."

Bo covered his nose with his shirt as they walked to the front entrance.

"Be a poor move, covering that face of yours," Spearance chided. "Don't you want that receptionist to see that handsome mug in all its glory?"

Bo let the shirt drop. "I forgot about her."

"Sure you did." Spearance laughed. "Looks like she forgot about you too."

On the other side of the glass, Tanya took a stack of papers from a man in a lab coat.

Spearance nudged Bo in the ribs. "She's smiling at that paperwork like its Davy Jones himself."

"She's just being polite."

"Let's see how polite she is to us." Spearance opened the door and waved Bo in. "You take the lead."

Bo walked in, stiff-legged. He leaned over the counter. "Hi there."

She set down the paperwork, bid the lab-coated gentleman farewell, and turned to Bo. While she'd been smiling at the paperwork like it was a late 70s heartthrob, she smiled at Bo like he was a stack of paperwork. "Can I help you?"

"We're here to see Mr. Drowne."

She looked up at Bo like he was vaguely familiar. "You guys were here a few days ago, right?"

Spearance nodded. "Just here for a quick follow up."

Tanya picked up the phone and tucked it between shoulder and face. "I'll let him know you're here."

Bo relaxed on the counter—practically melting—smiling at her like she was an oversized envelope from Publisher's Clearing House.

Tanya spoke through pursed lips. "The officers from Hastings are here to see you again." She hung up the phone. "He said come on up. You guys can find the way, right?"

Bo turned away from the counter as stoically as possible. "We'll be fine."

He waited until she was out of earshot before continuing. "She hates me."

Spearance shrugged. "Maybe she's just shy. Friendly around guys that don't intimidate her."

"You think?"

"Maybe." Spearance put his hand on Bo's shoulder. "What's the harm in trying? She hasn't *told* you no, right?"

Bo perked up. "I suppose you're right."

Mr. Drowne rounded the corner to greet them in front of his office. "Gentlemen."

Spearance reached out to shake his hand. "Mr. Drowne. How have you been?"

Drowne tried to match Spearance's grip this time. "Better, since we found someone new for custodial."

"That's good to hear." Spearance reached into his pocket and extracted the seizure warrant Dashnaw had provided them with after the search of Miles' apartment. "You still have his stuff?"

"We cleaned out his locker. He hasn't been in since we last spoke." Mr. Drowne led them to his office. "Come on in." He opened his closet and bent down.

Bo drew his flashlight and shined it into the closet. "Need a light?"

"I got it." Mr. Drowne came out with a paper box filled with Miles' belongings. He set it down on the edge of his desk. "Technically we're supposed to hold possessions for 90 days, but you're free to take a look."

Spearance stepped forward. "Thanks."

He pushed through the contents until he found the yearbook.

Bo tucked his flashlight away and leaned into Spearance.

Spearance opened the book, flipping to the opening pages, then to the back: no signatures.

He shifted back to the front of the book and thumbed through it slowly.

Mr. Drowne watched them nervously, hands in pockets. "Looking for anything specific?"

"A few cutouts," Spearance said. "Missing pages, maybe."

There were none.

Spearance turned to Bo. "You know what grade she was in?"

Bo took the book and turned it over. "It's '79." He turned to the junior section, pointed. "There's me." He smiled, self-satisfied.

Spearance rolled his eyes. "What about Sam?"

"I'm getting to it." He flipped forward to the seniors, going page by page. "She should be in here."

Spearance stopped him. "There she is."

Bo squinted, moving his face closer to the book. "What'd he do to it?"

Sam's image was scarred, just as it had been in the one on Miles' collage. Except this picture wasn't scratched or torn. The only evidence of tampering was the burn marks on Sam's face. The glossy finish of the book, however, was untarnished. Spearance ran his fingers over the picture until he phased back into the moment, scaring himself as he slammed the book shut. "We need to take this into evidence."

"I—uh." Mr. Drowne jingled the keys in his pocket. "Okay." He reached for the box. "Is that all you need?"

Spearance remained transfixed by the yearbook, staring at the heavy gloss cover reflecting the fluorescent lights above. "Better take it all into evidence to be safe. We've got the paperwork for it."

Mr. Drowne set the box down in his closet and closed the door. "What should I do if he shows up looking for his stuff?"

"Call us immediately," Spearance said, still staring at the yearbook.

Bo grabbed Spearance by the shoulder and steered him toward the door. "We'll let ourselves out."

Mr. Drowne leaned over his desk. "Let me know if you need anything else."

Bo closed the door behind them. "Snap out of it," he whispered. "You can stare at that book all the way back to Hastings if you want, but you're creeping people out, man."

Spearance tucked the book under his arm. "Sorry." He stared ahead.

"I can tell you're racking your brain about it, what do you think?"

"Not sure."

"You must have some kind of idea."

Spearance shook his head. "I'm out of ideas at the moment. A lot of questions, and I don't want to commit to any hypothesis until they're answered."

Together they found their way to reception. Bo all but pushed Spearance out the door. "You go on ahead, I'll check us out."

Spearance ambled out the door, still caught up in reflection. He buckled himself into the passenger seat, green grass be damned, and waited for Bo to work his...well, he wasn't sure if it was magic, per se, but you had to give the kid points for trying.

Five minutes later Bo burst through the doorway, beaming from ear to ear. He popped open the driver side door and sat down. "She's got my number," he said. "In case she hears anything."

"That all?"

"Or if she gets bored or lonely."

"You said that?" Spearance asked.

"Yeah."

Spearance shook his head.

"What?"

"Just wish I had half of your courage when I was your age."

Bo spun the car around and turned out of the parking lot. "You think she'll call?"

Spearance opened the yearbook to the senior photos. "I hope so."

"I bet she will."

Spearance flipped to Sam's photo. "How'd you sleep last night?"

"Not bad. Cot's a little hard, but it works."

"You willing to man the station for a few hours when we get back? I need to see Lola."

"Sure." Bo sighed. "You ever going to let me go out there with you?"

"No." He smiled, eyes still on the tarnished photo. "Give Mike a call, let her know I'm heading down."

"Why?" Bo turned to him. "You get off on showing her those creepy pictures or something?"

"I think she knows more than she's let on. Maybe she's forgotten over the years. Maybe she's hiding something. Doesn't hurt to keep her in the loop about what's happening with the investigation either. Let her know we're not the enemy."

"Will you at least tell me what she says?"

"If I hear anything *juicy*, I'll be sure to relay the information."

LOLA

Lola stood over the sink, scrubbing at coffee residue in the bottom of an old aluminum mug she got from her nephew years ago. Her attention was only half there. The rest of her shuffled between the driveway and the pain that blazed outward from her mid-back. It hadn't quite made its way around her ribcage, which her doctor had told her was good. But the pain wasn't subsiding when she lay down, like it used to. She did everything her doctor told her to. She kept her chin tucked as her eyes went from mug to mud-caked parking area. She crawled down onto the floor every night before bed and tried a few yoga poses—downward dog, lazy river, several others that had equally absurd names and equally meritorious functions. They did little to mitigate the pain.

Still, she tried to ignore it as much as possible. It proved more difficult each day.

If there was one thing she loathed about growing old, it was the increasing attention paid to the body and bodily functions. It took you out of the world, the constant pain a dowsing rod drawing you further and further into yourself until your life boiled down to a system of physical checks and balances. Pop your Monday pills, drink 32 ounces of water, eat your fiber, lament the lack of foods you'd rather be eating in your life, check blood sugar, walk your blood sugar back down to base levels, check blood pressure, sit down and wait for the pain from bad posture to emerge, lie down, fall back asleep. Wash. Rinse. Repeat.

She turned the cup upright on the countertop. "Mike, I'm going to lie down for a few minutes before the police arrive. Can you fix me a cup of the breakfast blend?"

"Milk or cream?" he asked from the neighboring room.

She mulled the options over for a moment. She planned on having a cup full of fat-free, frozen whipped cream later. Best to take it easy now, then. "Skim," she replied.

She lay down on the couch and tried to stay in the moment, relishing the brief interlude of painlessness that accompanied the first few minutes of lying down. But as soon as her body stopped screaming, her mind always took her back, and the more time that separated her from the past, the more painful that too became. Who was it that had said the art of life is the art of avoiding pain? She tried to conjure up the name. Jefferson, was it? She balked at the thought. *Life isn't the art of avoiding pain*, she thought. *Pain is inevitable.*

A knock on the door brought her back.

The police...

His name was...Monteroy.

No.

Spearance.

Monteroy was one of the extras in *The Last Port*, either the actor or character's name.

"Can you get that?" she asked, arms outstretched toward the door as if she had hoped to draw it open from halfway across the room.

She could hear Mike's gentle footsteps approaching the door.

The bolt lock receding into the door.

The door opening.

"Come on in." A brief pause before Mike closed the door again.

"Lola here?"

Lola waved Spearance into the living room. "In here." She lifted her legs and slid up the edge of the couch. "Have a seat."

Spearance sat down at the far end of the couch. "So we found that Prince Albert tin you'd mentioned."

As she reached for it, Mike swept in, grabbing it and easing the top off for her before presenting her with the contents.

"There's a picture, but it's...it's like the other one we found."

She pulled the tin gently out of Mike's hands and took the picture into her hand. "I want to see it."

She looked at the young woman in the picture staring back at her, taking tally of the years that have passed. She still felt like the same person. Still stubborn, full of fire. Qualities she'd once been loved for. Now they were merely tolerated.

Crosshatch scars ran down her and her companions' faces in the picture. Blood ran from the wounds, appearing fresh beneath the veneer. She felt her face with her free hand, feeling those same crosshatch marks, only etched into her by time instead of by a madman.

The photo was a duplicate. It had no effect on her. "There were more pictures."

Spearance sighed. "There's a possibility Miles has them on him. We're having a hard time tracking him down."

Mike brought Lola her breakfast blend, setting it on the table when he saw her hands cradling the Prince Albert tin. "What about the camera?" He looked at Lola. "You said there was a camera missing from the storage unit as well."

"I—"

"We didn't find any cameras at his house," Spearance interrupted.

Mike leaned over her to take in the picture. He flinched.

Spearance sat up. "We can't understand how the photos were altered. Is there any possibility these were damaged *before* Miles got his hands on them?"

She stared at the picture, then handed it to Mike. "No."

Spearance set the yearbook on the coffee table and opened it up. "I found another photo like it in the North Cambria yearbook." He turned to the first photo. "No damage to the gloss. No indication of tampering, but obviously something's happened." He ran his hand over the image to demonstrate. "At first I thought Miles was responsible for this picture. He had a cut-out of it in his house. But we found the same thing in a separate copy of the yearbook."

Mike helped Lola sit up so should could look at the first photo in the yearbook.

"This girl died in that sorority fire out in Indiana about half a decade back. But the picture in the yearbook appears to have changed after the fact, or maybe Miles somehow altered it using photos from the coroner's office."

Lola's breathing became jagged. She brought her hand to her mouth. "You have to find my camera."

"We'll do what we can for you. Any identifying marks or anything that could help us track it down?"

"It's vintage, a folding camera." She turned away from the yearbook. "Please. You have to find it."

Spearance turned to Mike, brows furrowed. "You think your camera had something to do with these photos?"

Lola shook her head, trying desperately to piece it all together. But her back, her knees, everything hurt so damned bad. Every time she tried to step outside of herself the pain brought her back. But there was something off-putting about that camera. She could feel it coursing through her, a reverberation fighting against the pain in her arthritic bones. "I—I don't know."

Spearance picked the yearbook up and tucked it under his arm. "When is the last time you remember having this camera in your possession? Do you know with absolution that it was in the storage shed?"

She combed her memory. The last time she saw the camera...She glanced at the photo in the Prince Albert tin. It was there that day. She tried moving forward, focusing on the camera. There were more photos, taken a few years later. But beyond that, she had no recollection. "I wouldn't have given it away. Couldn't have lost it. It must have been that boy."

"We'll keep our eyes open for it." Spearance grabbed the tin. "We'll need this for evidence until the investigation is over, but you'll get it back soon."

Mike followed Spearance to the door. "I'll see him down."

As soon as the door shut Lola's apartment behind them, Lola reached into the neckline of her shirt and pulled out the locket she had kept nestled therein. She fumbled with the small hook lock and opened it. Inside was an aged picture of her friend David. She took the locket between thumb and forefinger, then slowly curled her thumb around the edge and onto the picture. "Can you still feel me? Please come soon." She closed her eyes and waited.

SPEARANCE

Outside, Spearance tossed the yearbook onto the passenger seat and leaned on the driver side door. "She seems a bit distressed about that camera."

"More than a bit." Mike sat against the front hood. "The other night she woke in a panic. I found her digging around the house for it. I haven't seen her that frantic since I started working with her."

"She ever tell you how she ended up down at Tiernan's Storage?"

Mike shook his head.

"You think someone might have given her a ride?"

"Unlikely. She makes a point not to talk to people. Doesn't even want me around most of the time."

Spearance sat down and slid his key into the ignition. "Try to prime her about the camera when she's lucid...and when she's not. Where she last remembers it...what she thinks it was capable of."

"Sure thing." Mike stepped off the hood and slapped it. "Let us know if you find anything."

Spearance pulled his door shut and backed down the driveway, mulling over the cases he'd worked on, his mental inventory of their evidence room. Somewhere along the lines, he'd run into a camera or two, but never one of the old accordion cameras that predated his lifetime. He would have remembered something like that, but something about the situation hearkened back to a moment in his past. Lola's reaction maybe.

"You have to find my camera," she'd said with some small degree of urgency. It tugged at him, compelled him as if there was more urgency in her voice than she'd led on. Like he'd heard it before.

He thought about the girl in the yearbook, Samantha. Sam for short. The sorority fire in Indiana. That first night, when he was doing day patrol in Hastings and working nights in Indiana. He'd managed to pull a double with no coffee until the state boys showed up and asked him to turn everything over.

Reluctantly he'd handed the keys over to the evidence room, transparency being his primary motivation. He wanted to show them he played by the books. He wanted to be one of them.

Was there a camera in the evidence room that night? He'd inventoried everything out on his old desk, now Bo's desk. He remembered only photos.

***

Spearance half-slept most of the evening until around 8pm, when his wife's goddamned cat had gotten himself trapped in the back room.

He looked over at the ornately framed image of his wife and him on their wedding day. His smile was modest, hiding the subtle asymmetry of his front teeth. But Tammy's smile was pearl white. Everything about her radiated at 11, like the amplifiers in that Rob Reiner mockumentary. What was that? *This is Spinal Tap.* Spearance laughed. He'd wanted to be a rock star once, and that dream was still lingering in the backdrop when he and Tammy met. It's one of the things she'd loved about him most, and while some of his friends would chide him, telling him she Yoko'd the dream, he had woven a different narrative in his mind. Tammy didn't kill that dream. It existed exclusively for her, to draw her toward him. Once its function was complete, the dream died.

They had five years together to build upon a new dream. She'd finally convinced him he wasn't—would not be—like his father should they have children. He'd finally allowed himself to believe they were financially secure enough to do so.

They were ready.

After four months, Tammy was pregnant. Another handful of months went by and the bleeding began. The pregnancy was ectopic. The doctors pushed for surgery. There were no alternatives. The surgery destroyed her, destroyed their dream, but it wasn't what killed Tammy. Her killer was the post-surgery blood transfusion, carrying with it a virus wreaking havoc on the general population. He buried their dream with her, and her memory lived on through a modest, polished plot stone on the outskirts of town and on his nightstand. Most nights he made a point to come home too beat to look over at the photo. Tonight he left it up, but facing away from him. It was a new coping mechanism of his own devising, to turn the photo toward him a little more each night, returning the memory of his wife to him by degrees. Their photo currently faced him ever so slightly.

It wasn't getting any easier.

But at least he managed a spotty night of sleep, punctuated by copper piping and cat calls.

Each time he'd woken up, the only thing that reminded him he had been asleep was his dreams.

In the most unnerving, he'd lost all of his teeth when talking to his wife. They'd started falling out. Then he began plucking them from his bloody maw, more and more until he was standing ankle-deep in a river of blood, mucous, and yellowed teeth.

When he finally fell back asleep, his mind was still mulling through the day's events.

"You have to find my camera," Lola had said.

My camera, he thought, isolating her voice from the image he had of her in his mind.

The world went black. "You have to find my camera!" he heard her whisper, only now with more urgency.

He opened his eyes, or thought he had, and found himself looking out the back of an ambulance, watching smoke billow from the ashes of the sorority house.

He turned to Lola. She was strapped to a stretcher. "You have to find my camera," she whispered.

He blinked, and Lola became one of his back-row students. The back-row students always made him anxious.

He reached for his mouth, sure his teeth would begin falling out if he tried to speak.

His student tried to sit up. "My camera!" she moaned.

Against his better judgment, he opened his mouth and pursed his lips to keep his teeth from pouring out.

Only words came out.

"Your camera's fine. Hold still."

CHAPTER EIGHT

MOLLY

MOLLY HADN'T BEEN in the diner for a long time...one year and thirty-five days. It was one of the few places that felt like community in that small-town, non-foreboding way pitched in film and on television. Everywhere else the reality of small-town living was all too apparent: families and friends broken into smaller factions, subsets of subsets divided first by money, then by blood, then by other less-transparent variables. Who was sleeping with who? Who had divorced or snubbed who and who hung onto those things over the years...over generations.

The diner was the hub of this information, a veritable train station of oral discourse with indecipherable tracks, mostly because the people who harbored Hastings' secrets would tell anyone willing to listen. Loose lips sink ships, and in Hastings, loneliness made for loose lips. Loose lips and poor tips, as the waitstaff would say.

It had changed considerably since her last visit, not in function, but in appearance. The ceiling bulbs had been replaced by low-hanging, stainless-steel lamps to restore the ambiance of 50s diners. But the bulbs were too bright, revealing every blemish and stain on the menus, which had also changed. The prices had jumped up a dollar or two, but that was to be expected. The only thing that remained intact were the red pleather seats, frayed at the edges, torn at the top from the bite marks of anxious children staring over their booth at the neighboring tables.

They were perfect.

She scanned the room, avoiding eye contact with those all-too-willing to sink ships, finding Greg in a two-person booth.

Of course he was facing the rear wall, the seat she had hoped to take.

Molly approached the booth, unslung her purse from her shoulder. "Hey."

He smiled. "What's up?"

She hung her purse on the back of the seat, covering it with her coat. "How long you been here?"

"Just a few minutes." He eyed her seat. "My aunt would have had you know that a lady should always put her purse between her feet."

She looked back at her coat and purse. "Is this unladylike or something?"

"No, she was just paranoid about thieves, swindlers...sexual predators."

"My kind of lady." She sat down. "Keep her away from the devil's lettuce."

"Devil's lettuce. That on the menu?" He smiled. "Now that you mention it, maybe that's why she was so paranoid, actually."

The waitress approached the table. "How you folks doing today?" She shot Molly a quick glance. "Hi, Molly. Haven't seen you in awhile."

Molly took the top menu and forced herself to make eye contact. It was Sarah. Her face dredged up a host of memories automatically. She was a few years ahead of Molly in school. Married, with kids now. She worked at the school during the day, and apparently had started working weekends and other odd hours to pull in a little extra income. "Hi, Sarah." She gave her best disarming smile.

Greg took one of the menus and flipped it over. "Breakfast and lunch all day?"

The waitress nodded. "I wouldn't go for the pancakes though. They tend to *burn*."

He flipped the menu over again. "Thanks for the tip."

She stared down at her pen and paper. "Can I get you folks anything to drink?"

Greg looked up. "You have coffee?"

"Yep."

"What kind of roast?"

She looked at him, then at Molly. "Roast coffee," she said, un-ironically, but like she was being quizzed.

"I'll take a cup," Molly said.

Greg stared at her quizzically. "Me too."

Sarah turned for the front counter. "I'll give you folks some time."

Burn.

It wasn't that she said it, but the way she said it. Was she trying to imply something, to remind Molly of the fire? There seemed to be an air of resentment in her voice. Would she spit in her food? Molly looked down the menu. Which items would be least effective at veiling Sarah's possible desecration? Fries? Salad?

No dice.

It was just as plausible that the menu had been created to keep prices down as it was that it had been created to satisfy the passive-aggressive whims of disgruntled employees.

"What kind of roast?" Molly chided, turning then to a higher pitch and faster cadence to mock the waitress. "Well, sir, we have whole bean, light roast from the freshwater plains of New Guinea, and..." She stopped, watching his face for a reaction.

He laughed. "What?! I prefer breakfast blends. The darker roasts are usually used to veil or burn mold off bad crops."

"Pretty sure that's what they do with a well-done burger as well."

"Guess I'll scratch that off the list then." Greg continued poring over the menu. "What do you recommend?"

Molly watched Sarah chatting behind the counter, eyeing their table from time to time. "Somewhere else."

Greg shrugged, eyes still on the menu. "You suggested it."

"It's hard to give up on this place." Molly sighed. "It's like going to Christmas dinner with your dysfunctional extended family. You know it'll be unpleasant, at least a little, but there's part of you that wants to see how everyone's doing. There's something that keeps bringing you back, at least once in a while, despite the difficulties."

"I get that. Love the place, hate the people. That's what my mother used to say about Philadelphia."

"Except in cities it's easier to ignore the people. Around here, everyone sticks out like a sore thumb."

Greg followed Molly's eyes to the waitresses at the front counter, turned back. "I'm going to order the pancakes, just to piss her off."

"Here she comes," Molly whispered.

Greg turned, eyebrows raised.

Molly laughed. "Your eyes were almost as big as your talk for a minute there."

He leaned in and whispered, "I don't want her to spit in my food."

"She's coming for real this time." Molly set down her menu. "I don't think you have anything to worry about."

Sarah set two mugs on the table and poured to the edge. "So what'll it be?" she asked.

"I'll go for a burger. *Medium*," she said.

Greg handed his menu to Sarah. "Same."

"I thought you wanted pancakes?" Molly chided.

Greg rolled his eyes. "Only because you dared me."

Molly handed her menu to Sarah, smiling through her words. "I did no such thing."

Sarah walked away from the table, refusing to engage.

Molly reached for the creamer, noticed the cup was near overflowing, set the creamer down and drank the coffee down to a more manageable level.

Greg did the same.

"So what roast we dealing with there, connoisseur of coffee?"

"Dark. It's always dark when folks run a place on the cheap."

Molly filled her cup with creamer until it brimmed over.

Greg took the creamer out of her hands and did the same.

"Mirroring me already," she observed.

"What?"

"Eating the same thing. Copying my gestures...it's a sign of attraction."

"Asking you out on a date wasn't a clear enough indication?" Greg brought the cup to his mouth. "Analyzing my every move...seems like you might be obsessed."

"Mildly interested." Molly took a drink and set her cup down. "At best."

"Ouch." Greg set the cup down. Coffee cascaded over the edge and onto the table on its slow descent. He scrambled for a napkin.

"They only give you the one your silverware is wrapped in unless you ask for more."

"Really?!" He unraveled the silverware and dabbed at the coffee. Once the expanding pool was contained, her wadded up the napkin. "So what drew you to the class?"

"Tired of working at..." She caught herself, remembering her system of check and proceed to ensure she wasn't dating a creep. *Don't give away too many details yet. Or ever, maybe.* "Retail."

"I hear that."

Acknowledgement without invasive follow up. That was a check in his favor. "What about you?" Molly asked.

"Ah, career change. Just like you."

"Mr. Spearance says you used to work EMT."

"I still get called in sometimes. You were asking about me?" Greg smiled. "Mildly interested."

"Actually, he brought you up. Said you were the 'resident expert,' self-proclaimed of course."

"He's probably just jealous that I get to sit next to you."

"Pretty sure he's married."

"The man's still human. It's what, a set of vows and a ring, not an off switch."

Molly shook her head. "Pretty sure it was an off switch for him. I've known him since middle school. Known of him anyway."

"Family friend?"

"He gave a speech to my junior class about firearms. I've seen him around since then. Baseball games, ice shows, school concerts, things like that. He's about as asexual as they come."

"He seems all right."

"He can get a bit long-winded at times, but I suppose that's just the way with some people." She looked up at him. "They never get tired of hearing themselves talk."

"That a hint?"

"No, but this is." Molly rubbed at her nose, then picked at the outer edge of her nostril.

Greg cleared his nostrils with his right knuckle, face reddening. "I get it?"

She shook her head.

Greg continued rubbing his nose as Sarah set their food on the table.

He waited for her to leave and gave his nose one more run with his sleeve. "How about now?"

She pulled her plate to her side of the table. "There was nothing there."

"But you would have told me, if something was there, right?" He picked up his burger, looked it over.

"Sure. I'll let you know if you shit your pants too." Molly took a bite of her burger and covered her mouth as she chewed.

"Ugh. Trying to eat here, woman."

"All right. Change of subject." She set the burger down. "How long did you do the EMT gig?"

"About a decade."

Her eyes widened. "How old are you?"

"Thirty-one. I started a few years after high school. Spent a year or two just puttering around, doing odd jobs."

"You must have some interesting stories."

He shrugged. "They're not really dinner conversation."

"Try me." She took a small handful of chips into her one hand, plucking them one at a time with the other and putting them into her mouth, immediately wondering why she had just voluntarily coated her hand with chip grease and prevented herself from picking up her burger until the small pile of chips in her hand was gone. *Christ, I'm just as awkward as he is,* she thought, taking just a little solace in the fact that maybe they were right on par with one another in terms of their interest.

"All right." He wiped his hands on his coffee-soaked napkin and started. "Around here you're mostly just cleaning up after drunk drivers. Occasional cardiac arrests. But by the time we get there, it's too late most of the time. In a bigger area we'd have helicopters to medivac people, but out here, taxpayer dollars only go so far."

"You had me right up until you said 'taxpayer dollars,'" Molly joked.

"It had its intended effect then." He took another bite of his burger. "If I couldn't persuade you away from the topic, I figured I could bore you away from it."

"Almost worked," she said. "You must have at least a few good stories though."

He set his burger down. "I'd characterize them more as bad stories, low points in an overall dark period of my life."

She knew she was prying, but she couldn't help herself. She felt comfort in the suffering and subsequent survival of others. It wasn't schadenfreude. It was just camaraderie. Comfort in numbers. "Such as?"

"The usual, I suppose. Unspoken milestones in every EMT's career. You see someone dead. You see someone dying. Then you see various causes of death. Car crashes, burn victims, suicide. If you're really unlucky you see people dying in different ways. And if you're the most unlucky, you have to deal with situations that involve kids or infants." He paused. "One time, my second year on the job I think, we got called out to a car crash. The driver and passenger had been launched through the windshield. Both dead on scene.

"We packed them up, just glossed over the car seat in the back I guess. Then one of the officers noticed the car seat was buckled, like there had been a child in there..." He still hadn't looked up. "There had been, but because he was so light he'd been projected through the hole in the windshield his parents' bodies made and, god, it was terrible." He stared into his coffee, white knuckles gripping the handle tight. "I didn't sleep for a week." Finally he lifted the cup to his lips and made eye contact with her again.

"Sorry."

"You didn't do it."

"I pushed you to talk about it. You didn't want to."

"I know plenty of folks who will volunteer those kinds of stories, even if you don't want them to, at the most inopportune times even. Some folks live for it. I couldn't. I can't."

Molly folded her two-ply napkin and set it on her lap, another thing she never did when eating by herself or with her daughter. "I shouldn't have pried."

"It's all right. It was kind of nice to talk about it again. Gotta get it out, even if by degrees, you know?"

"You ever tell anyone else?"

"My brother." He took another drink.

"A brother, eh? He taller, maybe just a tad more handsome?"

He nodded. "He was. He's gone now."

She gritted her teeth and sucked in a deep breath. "I'm not going to be able to dig us out of this dark path our conversation took, am I?"

"Let's talk about you," he suggested.

Me.

She took in another deep breath. "Okay."

"What about you? Any family?"

"My mom."

"Any brothers or sisters?"

Molly took the final chip out of her hand, bit into it, and shook her head. She figured if she kept her mouth full, the conversation would be relegated to yes or no questions.

"Kids?"

She always resented men who went there on the first date. There are only two reasons men ask that question, and she had almost said as much, but stopped short. She decided, this time, to trust him. Not only because he seemed like a halfway decent guy, but because he was registered for an evening class, and their professor was a local officer. If he were hiding anything, he wouldn't be combing the classroom for dates. "One." She immediately regretted saying it, even before she could read his reaction. Sure, maybe he wasn't crazy. But maybe he was a creature of habit. The more she read about high-stakes crime, the more it seemed like many murders and kidnappings without apparent motivation were bred by opportunity rather than methodical thinking. So to avoid talking about Jolie, she anted up with her greatest shame. "My mother has helped out since my husband died."

"I'm sorry."

She chuckled from behind her coffee mug. "No you're not."

"Well, it would have been a bit of a shocker if you had still been married."

"Doesn't stop most guys."

"I think it depends on what they're looking for."

She cradled her cup in her hands, hiding the upward arc of her lips. "What are you looking for?"

He rubbed his stomach, which she now noticed protruded more than she initially thought. "Dessert."

"I would." Molly looked up at the clock. "But I should go." She pulled her coat and purse off the back of the booth.

Greg leaned in to stand, then stopped. "Can we do this again?"

"Sure." She put her hand on his shoulder, the warmest gesture she could muster in haste, and then headed for the door. She turned as she left. "Thanks."

"No problem." He waved, but didn't stand and didn't follow. For Molly, this was a small consolation, another one of those first-date checkbox items that put a potential partner in her favor. He had pried a bit, but so had she, admittedly. But he didn't try to follow her to her car, which meant she didn't have to worry about him making a mental note of her make and model, or her license plate, which in turn meant she wouldn't have to peer through the blinds for the next two hours waiting for cars to circle her street suspiciously slow.

And all of that was reassuring, but she couldn't help but worry that perhaps he hadn't followed because he didn't care. She watched the front door of the diner as she unlocked her car. She popped the door open, and waited a moment.

Still no sign of him.

Fucker was probably in there flirting with the waitress.

She turned on her car and looked in the rearview mirror. "Last chance," she whispered.

She checked the clock, promised herself she'd wait only one minute.

Just one minute.

After three and a half, he stepped out the door, staring first up at the sky, then around. He was looking for her.

She pulled out of the parking lot and watched as he headed for his vehicle. She drove slow enough to see him fumble with his keys beside a small pickup truck.

It occurred to her then that every red flag she checked against her dates—every damned one—she exhibited. She pried. She waited. She followed.

She didn't care.

When he left the diner, he had looked for her.

For tonight, that was enough.

Molly drove down Prospect Street and turned into her house just outside village limits, marked by a 45mph sign and an abrupt end to the orange glow emanating from the street lights above. As always, the front yard was dotted with garbage from passersby who tossed their trash as soon as the speed limit changed. Too tired to pick it up, she resolved to leave the trash to the whims of the wind. It was strong tonight, which meant by morning the trash would be strewn along the roadside.

She looked toward a heaven blanketed by a black coverlet so dark the clouds were indiscernible from sky.

She felt that specter. The impending. It cascaded out of the past, carrying with it all of her anxieties. She let it wash over and past her.

Whatever was coming, let it come. Tonight served as a reminder that good could puncture the veil of darkness inside her mind.

Hell, maybe karma didn't exist at all.

She loved nights like this. Quiet nights.

Since Jolie had been born, quiet nights were few and far between. She hoped against a steady routine that entailed Jolie staying up until 10pm. *Please be asleep*, she thought. But the small head poking through the curtains told her that her prayer was in vain.

Shit.

It wasn't that Molly didn't want to spend time with her daughter. Rather, it was that only two dichotomous variables existed when it came to their late-night interactions. At one end of extremes, she came home to Jolie fast asleep, allowing Molly to regard her sleeping daughter while sipping a cup of chamomile tea. At the other end, Jolie was reinvigorated by Molly's arrival, no matter how tired they both were, and refused to fall asleep for hours. As Molly approached the door, she braced herself for said hours. She walked up the concrete steps to the storm door, turned the handle and, as always, let the wind tear the door from her grip. It slammed into the siding, another reminder of her husband and his unfinished projects around the house. He'd never had a chance to install the pneumatic closer, but in all honesty probably still wouldn't have, had he survived. It used to infuriate her. Now it made her smile.

Then came the pitter-patter of tiny feet storming through the dining room and to the front door. Then the awkward semi-silence as Jolie fumbled with the lock before opening the door.

Finally, the door opened. "Mommy!" Jolie ran up to her, standing in her space but avoiding physical contact, as was her modus operandi. She pushed a softcover book into Molly's thigh. "Let's read this."

Molly took the book out of her hand and set it on the table. "Hang on, sweetie. Let me catch up with Grandma real quick."

Molly's mom stepped out of the kitchen, glass of red wine in hand.

"Planning on staying tonight?"

"I'll be good to drive." Her mother held up the glass. "This is my first, and only."

Molly took off her coat and hung it on the overtaxed, slumped coat rack. She hated that her mother still drank in front of her, refused to stop, even after she struggled to keep herself on track. "How was she?"

Her mother downed half the glass.

"That bad, eh?"

She exhaled and set the glass down on the dining room table. "She was fine. No worse than you were."

"Thanks."

"Thanks for stocking the wine rack."

Molly rolled her eyes playfully. "You know I don't keep alcohol in the house." *Can't*, she corrected in thought.

"So how did things go on your end?"

Molly walked into the kitchen and took a glass out of the cabinet. "It was all right."

Her mother followed. "He a keeper?"

Molly eyed the bottle of wine, filled a glass of water and brought it back to the dining room table. "He's not a creeper. That's a start."

Her mother brought the bottle of wine to the sink and poured it down the drain. "What's he do again?"

"He was an EMT." Molly sat down. "Not sure what he does now. He's taking night classes, so he must have a day job."

"You didn't find out?"

"I'm usually one for higher-order concerns."

"Employment status isn't a higher-order concern?"

Molly brought the glass to her lips, expecting wine. Vicodin. Anything bitter to take the edge off awkward conversation.

Just water.

"You tell me, Mrs. 'I've-never-worked-a-day-in-my-life.'"

"You think being a housewife isn't a job?"

"Not in this day and age."

"Your father felt the same way." Molly's mother shook her head. "If I had a dollar for every shit stain I had to clean off of his underwear—"

"Mom!"

"What?" She took another drink. "Sometimes I wish you appreciated the work I did to keep our house together."

"I do. I have to do the same thing *plus* work a full-time job."

"Times they are a-changing." She mock-strummed an invisible acoustic at her waist.

"Yeah, well, it sucks."

She dropped her hands to her sides. "I know it does. But were you honestly any happier being holed up in the house all day while Tom was being shipped all over the state?"

"It was all right."

"You were just as miserable then as you are now." Her mother picked up her glass and stepped away from the table. "Only now you're responsible for your own misery. That's a perk, right?"

"I wish he was still alive."

"Even if he was, the way things are going in this country, you would have had to get a job anyway. Jolie's off to school. Bills are through the damned roof. Take if from a single mother living on a fixed income. Things keep going the way they are, I'll have to get a job."

"Gasp," Molly chided.

Her mother walked to the window and looked outside. "I'm serious. There are a lot of women out there in the same situation. We bought into a lifestyle that had been pitched to us since childhood. Nobody told us we'd become obsolete. We're a dying breed. June Cleaver sure as hell didn't show us how to navigate the Reagan era. The son of a bitch."

"Mom!"

"Sorry." Molly's mother turned from the window. "So is this guy a good fit for you?"

"Seems like it."

Her mother reached across the table and put her hand on Molly's. Her hands were hot to the touch. She was buzzing already. "You're still young. You have plenty of time."

The acrid smell on her breath took Molly back to childhood, to sitting on her mother's lap while reading picture books, to family reunions, graduation parties, Jolie's birthday parties...her mother had become synonymous with the smell of fermented fruit such that she smelled her every time she had opened a bottle of wine. She wondered what this would mean for her when her mother passed. Another addiction that had been so hard to break, another thread of memories carrying with them a sangria of sweet innocence and a whole range of emotional baggage.

Forget when her mother died. She wanted a drink *now*.

She followed her mother's hand up her arm and to her face, her features, softened by a life of few stressors and a husband who had passed before retirement. She still looked so young, but Molly couldn't help but remember in these tender moments that someday her mother would be gone.

"Thanks." Molly pulled her hand out from under her mother's, patted her mother's hand gently.

Jolie stood at the edge of the living room, practically reverberating with anticipation. "When are we going to read, Mommy?" she asked.

Molly set her cup down. "I guess we'd better settle in."

"I'll let myself out." Her mother finished her glass of wine and carried it into the kitchen. "Call later if you get bored."

"Mommy's going to bed with me," Jolie announced.

Molly's mother stepped into the dining room. "Sometimes mommies get back up after their kids fall asleep."

Jolie's eyes widened.

Molly's mother squinted. "Maybe we'll even have a little party."

Jolie pushed the book into Molly's hands. "You won't."

Molly's mother took her coat from the rack and tucked it under her arm. "See you tomorrow."

Molly waved. "Say goodbye to Grandma."

Jolie was already on her way to the couch. "Bye!"

Molly watched her mother from the window as she pulled out. "How much of her juice did grandma drink tonight?"

"Just one. She said."

Molly nodded, closed the curtain, and turned to see Jolie pulling a tome-sized photo album off the shelf near the sofa. "I want to look at this instead."

"Instead of reading?"

Jolie nodded, barely able to remain upright as she tossed the album onto the arm of the couch.

"You should be reading," Molly said, tossing the book onto the other arm of the sofa. She'd already resigned to the easier alternative.

Jolie slapped the couch. "Come on."

Molly sat as Jolie opened the album across their laps. It was Jolie's birth album, from the nine months prior up to the big day and onward to two years old.

Jolie pointed at a picture of Molly on the second page. "Look how round you are."

"That's you in there."

"I know." Jolie smiled. "I wrecked you."

"It wasn't so bad." Molly turned the page. It was a picture of her husband, diaper bag slung over his shoulder. Her water had broken, and he still convinced her to take a picture of him heading to the car. Jolie had his smile, always smug and self-satisfied.

Every page thereafter, he was center shot or dangling in the periphery. Even on the day Jolie was born, he had to be the center of attention. It was one of his personality traits that had driven her away. But she could never go far enough.

Even now, as she looked at the photos, her memory locked her into the moments surrounding the photos, superficial details long-forgotten to most. Like his face in the photos, her time with him always hung center stage or in the periphery, poking in from the edges of her new life. There was no getting away from him. But tonight she humored his return, for Jolie's sake. She never asked about her father, about who he was or what he did. Molly chocked it up to Jolie's naïve confidence in her limited knowledge of the world around her. To Jolie, these photos told her all she needed to know about her daddy.

As they were flipping into Jolie's second year, lights cascaded across the living room ceiling and came to a stop. Someone had pulled in.

Molly slid out from under the album and checked the window.

Jolie set the album down on the couch and got up to look. "Who is it?"

Molly furrowed her brows, perplexed, as she watched Mr. Spearance step out of the car and run up the stairs. She took solace in the fact that he had left his car running. Whatever he wanted, it wouldn't take long. "My professor."

The trademark sound of the storm door latch turning, and the wind catching the door and sending it into the siding reverberated outside. Spearance knocked gently at the door.

Molly pointed to the couch. "I'll be right back."

Jolie ran to the couch and pulled the album back onto her lap.

Molly answered the door. "Hello?"

Spearance stood in the doorway, hands in pockets. "Sorry about the door."

"Happens to everyone."

He peered around the dining room. "I didn't wake you, did I?"

She pointed over her shoulder. "We're just getting ready to go to bed."

"Can I talk to you, just for a moment? Police business."

Reluctantly she stepped out of the doorway to let him in. "Sure."

He stepped in and took off his coat. "I won't keep you long."

Molly reached into the rain for the storm door and closed it behind him. "What's going on?"

"The night of the fire, you had mentioned a camera." He pulled an old photo out of his pocket. "Did the photos it took look like this?"

"Camera?"

"You asked me where your camera was, if it was all right."

Molly shook her head. "I—I don't remember."

He sighed. "Okay."

He didn't believe her.

Her eyes darted around the room, resting on Jolie, who was staring from the couch. "Honey, sit down."

Spearance waved to her, trying to break the tension.

Jolie waved back and plopped down on the couch.

He handed her the picture. "Have you ever seen older photos, like this?"

Molly reluctantly took the photo. "What is it?"

Spearance took the photo back and tucked it in his pocket. "It's an old photo Lola found in her storage unit. She's trying to track down the camera that took it, but says she'd lost it. Maybe recently, maybe years ago." He took the photo out again, looked at it quizzically. "I thought it looked like that portrait you had the night of the fire."

Why does he have this? The police told her it had been lost. Molly shook her head. Her chest tightened. "I don't know what you're talking about."

"The night of the fire? You had a picture with you. It's still in evidence down at the Johnstown station."

She could feel her heart racing now, all of the memories flooding back from that night. The sound of her jacket scraping her shirt as she ran from the house. The cold air turning hot in her lungs. Samantha, burning the photos. The flames emerging from her body as she tore off her clothes, trying to find the source of the fire. "I need to get my daughter to bed." She gasped for breaths between every few words.

"Are you okay?"

She shook her head.

Spearance guided her to the table. "Sit down."

The barrage of memories continued—Sam flailing on the porch, the house catching fire, "Your camera's fine," the smoke clearing—her body responding, building to a crescendo of panic. Was she having a heart attack? What the fuck was this?

Jolie peeked above the couch.

Oh god, Jolie. She didn't want her daughter to see like this. "Sit down, Jolie!"

Jolie—unfamiliar with any semblance of disciplinary tone—dove for the cushions. "Sorry, Mommy!" she said as quickly as the words could be carried from her mouth.

The memories continued—the smell of creosote on her jacket, in her nostrils. The smell of her dog. Bone, oh god, Bone. The sweat broke on her forehead. She became light-headed. She could feel Spearance's arms on her shoulders as she began to slip.

And suddenly, everything felt right. The memories lost their grip on her as she entered this new state, this physiological panic that rocked her to her very core. This was new. This was the impending she had conjured up, a form of torture commensurate with that she'd imagined.

And she was glad to have found it.

She rocked back and forth in her chair, cradling herself. Tears welled in her eyes as her heart raced. This felt so right. If she had known that this lay at the center of her mounting panic, she would have never resisted all these years.

Jolie jumped up again. "Is she okay?"

Spearance nodded. "She'll be all right. She's just hyperventilating." He spoke into her ear. "Do you have any paper bags?"

Molly shook her head.

"Breathe into your shirt," he said. "Long, slow breaths. Concentrate on slowing your breathing. You're going to be all right."

The panic had already begun to break. She knew before she even put the collar of her shirt over her nose the reaction would subside. Still, the memories—the worst memories—remained at bay. But she did remember feeling like this before. During recovery, when the DTs grew so strong that she could only focus on her clenched teeth, the convulsions in her legs, like minor tremors in the earth. She felt the fault lines of her being beginning to come apart. She was being reborn then, and now.

Her breathing slowed, and she let the collar of her shirt fall back into place.

Spearance took his hands off her shoulders. "There you go."

Jolie watched intently from behind the couch. "You okay?"

Molly took in one more deep breath of air. "Mommy's fine."

Spearance put his coat on. "I'm sorry, Molly. I didn't mean to upset you."

"I just wish it could be over, you know?"

He nodded, in part to acknowledge her, in part to himself. He'd asked about the camera without context to gauge her reaction. He wasn't anticipating the degree of resistance he'd witnessed. What was she hiding? He'd have a chance to parse that out later. For now, he needed to come back into the questioning from a less ominous angle. See what she'd tell him if he absolved her of whatever guilt she was feeling.

He leaned onto the storm door handle and turned to her. "I know you have plenty of reasons not to talk. Not to remember. This camera I'm looking for, it's not about you." *Don't say anything else,* he thought. But he didn't have much of a choice. *Tell her only what she needs to know,* he told himself. He sighed. "Someone broke into Lola's storage unit a few nights ago. She's been freaking out about this camera ever since. When she showed me that photo, it reminded me of the one you had. I thought maybe you had a similar camera that might help us more easily identify her missing one."

Molly reached for the door and began gently closing it. "I'm sorry. I can't help you."

"Okay." He nodded. "Okay." Spearance turned the latch and stepped into the rain. "Look, I'll keep the police business and teaching separate. I don't want this to dissuade you from coming back to class. But if you do think of anything, feel free to reach out."

Molly closed the door to a veritable sliver. "I'm sorry," she added, then closed the door.

Spearance gently pushed the storm door back into place and headed for his car.

Jolie popped up from behind the couch. "That was your teacher?"

Molly nodded.

Jolie ran to the window. "He looks old."

"He is old." She closed the album and set it back on the shelf. "Older."

Jolie ran to her mother's side. "Aren't we going to finish?"

"Not tonight, honey."

"What's wrong?"

"Nothing."

"Did the pictures make you sad?"

"Yeah."

Jolie grabbed Molly by the hand and pulled her toward the bathroom. "We have to brush our teeth, then I'll put you to bed."

Molly allowed herself to be dragged along. "*You'll* put *me* to bed, eh?"

"M-hm." Jolie smiled, and for the second time that night, Molly's husband smiled back at her from stage left. Molly imagined him physically occupying the space in her mind. *I hope they find your camera*, he whispered to her. *I hope they find that, and your photo, and they tear you limb from limb for what you did.*

She tried to clear her mind of him, of the camera. But as she stared, eyes glazed, into the mirror to brush her teeth, as she checked Jolie's teeth for "sugar bugs," as she stared at the ceiling trying desperately to fall asleep, she could see him there with that derisive smile. And she refused to look away, because to some small degree, that smile was her penance for infidelity. *Just one drink*, she thought.

One pill.

Anything to take the edge off.

But she knew deep down it wasn't the drink or the pill she wanted. That wasn't a strong enough distraction. What she wanted was the consequence, the requisite pain that blossomed in her mind the following morning. The pain centered her, because in memory, physical pain begat only the memory of physical pain, which was a one-track journey back and forward. There were no detours. There were no segues.

Only pain.

That was the closest thing to controlling her hyperthymesia she'd ever had.

LOLA

Later that evening, after Lola had closed her blinds and settled into her armchair with a cup of frozen, non-fat whipped cream, the phone rang. She picked it up.

"You were toying with your locket again, weren't you? Everything okay?"

David.

She sighed. "Yes." She shook herself out of the childlike butterfly-inducing effect his voice always had on her. "No. I need to see you."

"I'm halfway across the country, Lola. You're still planning on flying out in the fall, aren't you?" He paused, taking in the possibilities. "Oh god. You're ill?"

"I'm fine, David...I'm not fine, but I'm not ill. It's the camera. Someone took it, and the pictures. They think it's one of the local kids. He broke into my storage unit."

"Do they know what it's capable of?"

"He must know something. Police found a few prints, looks like he'd cut into them."

"I'll fly you out first thing in the morning."

"No. Distance isn't going to save us. You felt me tonight, didn't you?" The question was rhetorical. She knew he had. That's why he had called.

"I'll be there tomorrow."

"Thank you."

"Goodbye, Lola."

"Goodbye." She dropped the phone back onto its housing.

MILES

G.H. Maier had emigrated from Germany to California in '34, just as his films were beginning to reach the peak of their popularity in his home country. Unfortunately, his success decided not to emigrate with him, and the cost of living proved too high for him to sustain his garish lifestyle on diminishing royalties, so he packed up and headed as close to the east coast as his budget would allow, which put him in Hamburg, NY, about twenty minutes south of Buffalo. Since taking up residence there, he had become somewhat of a public figure, volunteering for the school and village board, ending his tenure in local government with a failed campaign for mayor. But he never left his small house on Stone Street, and though he had taken to withdrawing into his home on most occasions, he still welcomed fans to visit him at his house.

As such, finding him was easy.

Getting there undetected with Pennsylvania plates proved a little more difficult, however. Miles settled on public parking in Buffalo and took a bus south to Hamburg. From there he waited until after dark to visit the historic district.

He arrived at Maier's house at 8:00pm, knocking lightly on the side door neighboring the driveway.

No answer. Just as well.

He tried the knob.

Locked.

He peered over his shoulder quickly to take in the sidewalk. It was empty as the evening was silent. He reached into his pocket, pulled out his library card, and ran it down the seam between the door and its casing. No bolt lock. No chain lock. Just the lock at the door. He pressed the card gently into the lock and slid the door open. He wanted desperately to look back one more time before going inside, but it was too late. The gesture would arouse suspicion if anyone was there, so he stepped inside, closing the door quietly behind him.

Once the porch light had been extinguished by the doorway, Miles found himself in an ill-lit living room, with curtains thinly veiling the street. The photos on the walls—stills from Maier's work, photos with the last celebrities of the silent era—suggested Maier still lingered in the past. The world outside he wove into and through perfunctorily, only to sustain himself and the time capsule he insulated himself in at home. Maier reveled in a time forgotten, and his reluctance to reach out to his contemporaries suggested that when it came to his past, Maier had a very narrow memory of what had happened. Maier had a carefully curated past that, like a Faberge egg, could easily be shattered if held. It was to be observed from a distance, preferably away from the company of anyone who might devalue or challenge its value.

It was likely Maier had taken so much care to preserve his past because he feared what had already happened outside of his living room walls. Save this modest shrine, he and his contemporaries had been forgotten.

He walked room to room, searching for signs of life until he found light pooling out of a room at the opposite end of the house. Miles listened at the door. It was quiet, save the gentle sound of currents working against body in the bathtub.

Miles turned the knob and walked in to see Maier's emaciated body, draped only in the loose skin that sagged along his skeleton, in the bathtub. "There he is," Miles said. "The prime innovator."

Maier leaned over the tub and pulled a towel into the water to cover himself. "Who are you?!"

Miles walked in, closing the door behind him. "A fan. A historian." He took another step. "People called you the prime innovator. Ironically, the innovation of silent film was a step backward, but it had to be done. You were more of a gap closer than anything. It had always been the intention to create a film accompanied by sound and voice. A lack of technology led to the illusion of causality: that films with sound sprouted forth from silent film. In reality, quite the opposite is true. Silent film was just a necessary intermediary, pre-determined to die at its conception. One of the first of many art forms destined to die at the hands of innovation."

"Leave! Now!"

"Don't be rude. I'm here to help you. Have been helping you. Keeping you alive." Miles noted the flowered wallpaper, ran his hand down the fraying edges near the wall dividing tub and sink. "Many are still drawn to silent film. It has experienced much resurgence over the years. It is a medium never meant to be: the improvisation of an ideal, turned into an ideal in itself. Currently it approaches another rebirth. But the audience diminishes each time. People are losing interest and thus the immortality of silent film slowly dissipates. I watch the films to keep the dying alive."

Maier pulled himself up, one hand on the edge of the tub, the other covering himself with the now-soaked towel he'd pulled from the floor rack. "You just broke into my house! You expect my gratitude?! You're completely lacking in social grace at best, a common thief at worst!"

Miles reached into his coat pocket and pulled out the photo of Lola, Maier, Rothman, and Tigerstedt. "Do you recognize this?"

Maier's eyes widened.

"I'll take that as a yes." Miles held the photo in one hand, fished a lighter out of his coat pocket with his other. He lit it and drew the flame toward the photo. "It was inevitable that silent film die, of course, as its greater counterpart had been conceived before it. Not only was silent film predestined to expire, it was created with the explicit knowledge of its function as a temporary compromise. Other inadvertent factors, such as the short life span of chemicals like cellulose nitrate used in production of film, caused the history of silent films to literally fade away."

"Stop!"

Miles drew the flame closer to the photo. "But it wasn't cellulose nitrate that destroyed the industry as a whole, per se. It had something to do with that camera. What happened?"

"Wait."

Miles held the flame just short of the photograph.

"Can't a man get decent?!" Maier took one foot out of the tub and planted it on the floor. "It wasn't intentional. Lola had taken a picture of the studio. When they didn't renew her contract, she destroyed everything from that period in her life." He swallowed, then carefully stepped completely out of the tub. "That was the night the studio burned down." He stared at the pile of clothes on the floor.

"So the camera has power over inanimate objects as well?" Miles followed Maier's eyes. "You can get dressed when we're done." He took his thumb off the fork, letting the flame die. "There's more to it than that. The only record of that studio is in printed documents and what's been passed down orally. You know what happened?"

Maier shuddered. "You have the camera, don't you?"

Miles smiled. *Apparently you don't.*

"Oh god." He leaned against the wall and closed his eyes. "Just kill me."

Miles flicked the spark wheel, bringing the lighter to life once more. He brought the flame to the edge of the photo, where Maier stood. The flesh on Maier's arm began to bubble. He cried out in pain.

Miles stifled the flame and brushed away the ash. "What happened to the studio? Talk."

"That's all we knew, and even that we couldn't confirm." Maier shook his head. "Correlation isn't causation...we relied on that adage for years to absolve ourselves of the guilt." He reached for the burned flesh on his arm and recoiled at his own touch. "Decades later...*decades!*" he shouted, "when historians started trying to piece together our era, they couldn't find any pictures of the studio. Most were gone entirely, but the ones that were attached to other things—photos in newspapers or books—were jet black."

"The rumors about you, that you could bring any woman to her knees with as much as a glance in their direction...it was the camera, wasn't it? The photographs?" Miles shook his head. "What else is it capable of?"

Maier caved, falling to a lump on the floor, still covering his genitals, which were buried under him anyway. "For the life of me, I can't understand why that bastard made the camera."

"Tigerstedt?"

Maier looked up. "Do you really have it?"

Miles flicked the strike wheel again. "How'd you do it? How did you make women climax with their photo?"

"It reacts differently to different people. Like it's alive."

"Where is it now?" Miles brought the flame to the photo once more. Steam began to waft off Maier's back.

"I don't know! I swear!" He screamed again, a deeper scream, coming from empty and exhausted lungs that still needed to release the pain, or share it with the world surrounding.

Miles pulled the flame away. "I'm somewhat of an innovator myself. You should see my work in photography."

"You have to stop! That film is highly combustible!"

"I'm switching to a new canvas now, however, ushering in the era of the next dying art, as it were. It'll only be a matter of time before we reach utopia. Until then, we have the intermediary arts, all the subgenres of criminality and justice. You have to admire their symbiotic relationship, for lack of a better term. Crime pushes justice to new heights. Justice pushes back, causing criminals to expand the depth and breadth of their art. But they won't last forever. Eventually they'll extinguish one another. But I'm happy to serve as an intermediary, and my canvas is prone to rapid degradation, just as your celluloid was." Miles ran the lighter quickly over Maier's body in the photo, igniting it. "I wonder whose genre will last longer, yours or mine." On the floor, Maier bucked, kicking his legs out from under his body, overturning as the flames grew on him. "What do you think the life expectancy is for serial murder as an art form?"

Miles watched as Maier writhed on the floor and flames lapped at the wall. He dropped the lighter, went to his knees, and waved Maier's image over the bath water, finally immersing it completely to extinguish the flame.

Maier's convulsions stopped. So, too, did the flames. He gasped for air.

Miles continued staring, unblinking. Their eyes locked. As Maier's breathing slowed, so too did his heart rate.

He was going to live. He would tell, but he was going to live. Miles didn't care. He just wanted this to be over.

Maier took in another breath. It cut short midway, replaced instead by an efforted gasp and a faint gurgling.

Maier exhaled. Bathwater poured onto the floor from his mouth.

He tried to breathe in again. The gurgling grew more pronounced.

He clawed at his throat, coughing more bathwater onto the floor.

Maier reached for the photo, which Miles realized was still partially submerged in the water.

Maier's eyes reddened. His lips turned from a soft red to a softer shade of blue, then purple.

The convulsing began again.

Miles pulled the photo from the water and dried it as fast as he could. He checked the others. Only Maier had been damaged by the water.

His hand, still reaching for the photo, dropped to the floor. His head followed. Another surge of water shot from his throat onto the floor.

G.H. Maier, the prime innovator, was dead.

CHAPTER NINE

LOLA

SHE WAS GOING to be okay.

That's what she'd told herself, what she'd told Mike on the phone when she gave him the day off. It wasn't really in her power, neither mentally or physically, to excuse him, but he respected her enough to violate protocol.

The fact that he was salaried probably helped.

She heard his voice growing distant. No pleading. Nothing. "You call if you need anything."

She matched his brevity, in part because she was in a hurry, in part because his apathy hurt. His tone reminded her he was kind because he was paid to be kind. "Yes, yes. Fine." She hung up the phone and fumbled with the modest collection of VHS tapes she had sent Mike to collect for her before excusing him. She suddenly regretted labeling the tapes herself. She needed *Everyman*, the only film she and Rothman had leading roles together in.

She'd been priming herself on the opening scenes since, waiting for Rothman to knock on the door. But watching the film alone didn't feel the same as she had imagined it would in her mid-30s. There was a time when she thought reminiscing would be welcome, when acting had been an investment. She spent most of her youth cultivating a future for her aged self to passively view. She would become her own audience, watching her films, reading her books. But the time traversed from then to now rendered the experience too painful to savor. Reminiscing no longer evoked nostalgia. It just hurt. That's why she had packed up most of her pictures to begin with.

Solitude made temporary by an impending visit made it hurt just a little less today, however.

Where was he?

David arrived in the second scene, knocking so gently it was barely audible.

Lola turned down the television. "Hello?"

She heard his voice from the other side of the door. "Lola?"

Lola walked as fast as she could, a slight spring in her step that burned in her joints. She didn't care. She unbolted the front door and pulled it open to reveal the leading actor in her life, David Rothman.

He opened his arms. "Look at you."

She took one step forward and all but fell into him.

He embraced her and set his cheek on the top of her head. He hadn't changed a bit. Not to her. He towered over her still. His dark eyes were still set deep in his face, not sunken but cradled by his still-strong forehead and cheekbones.

Lola, on the other hand, had changed considerably. Her features had coalesced into an oatmeal-like palette of pale white and grey, green eyes losing their vibrancy day by day. At least that's how she saw herself, and that was with the kindness day-to-day changes allowed the senses to adapt to. She imagined the abrupt shift in her appearance was more pronounced for David.

He pulled back from her to take her in again. "Look at *us*."

She looked up in disappointment, donning the disarming smile she'd used to beguile men for years. "It's terrible, I know."

"Oh stop." He embraced her again. "We both knew this was going to happen."

"I didn't think it'd take this long."

"To get old?"

"To see you again."

David stepped back and began taking off his coat. "How long has it been?"

Lola turned for the living room, leaving the door open. "Too long to denote in years."

"Events, then?" He waited at the door. "May I come in?"

Lola waved him in. "Not too long to feign courtesy, though, apparently."

He folded his coat over his arm. "After I got back from the Korean War. That was the last time I saw you."

"I was still in town for a decade after you returned. Longer even. You could have reached out to me any time." Lola sat down on the couch and offered him a seat next to her.

He dipped into the room and sat down next to her. "*Everyman*." He waved dismissively. "I probably haven't seen this since the Korean War either."

"It's been about that long for me as well. I had my aide dig it out of storage when you said you were coming."

"It feels like a different life." He set his coat down on the neighboring chair and watched the television for a moment. "Who is that man?" He watched himself on the screen, his gestures and expressions overemphasized. "And why can't he act?"

"That's Maier's failing." Lola smiled. "Looking good was our job. Making us look believable, that was his."

"Somehow I feel we should have met him halfway."

"He never complained about our performances."

She paused, appeared to recognize him again for the first time. "David? When did you get here?"

He placed his hand over hers. "I never left."

They turned to the screen, letting the black and white light flood their features, drowning out all of the lines time had carved into their faces. Their screen-bound counterparts then disappeared, replaced by the supporting actress. Lola rolled her eyes. "Jamie," she muttered.

David smiled. "But you *loved* working with her."

"I didn't mind her, but she hated me after I took lead in *Kronos*."

"There's a stinker."

She turned to him, mouth agape. "I loved that film."

"I'm not surprised. Maier had you pickled on set from sun up to sun down."

She turned back to the screen. "You were stone sober, I suppose."

He laughed. "I didn't even know I was a villain until the premiere."

"Look at us, longing for lost time we can't remember."

David watched Jamie on screen. She shouldered her way into the forefront of the tight shot, glanced back at Lola, and then continued. "You can still go back."

Lola stiffened.

"Can't you?"

"I haven't tried. I'm not sure I want to."

"On that note..." David turned to her. "What's going on, with the camera?"

"The police think one of the local boys stole it out of my storage unit, or my house." She crossed her arms.

"You said you think he knows how to use it?"

Lola eased herself off the couch and headed for her bedroom. She returned with the one photo she had left from the camera, handing it to him.

David remembered the day. It was in the early '30s. Tigerstedt had set him, Lola, and Maier down for a group photo, set a brief timer, and ran to their side. Tigerstedt was always a little blurry in the image as a result of his running to beat the timer. "Is this from the camera?"

Lola nodded.

"Thank god." David held the photo against his chest. "I remember he made copies for all of us. Maier set one of the copies on fire in a drunken rage, trying to burn me when he found out about...well. Thank god the copies weren't dangerous." He set the photo on the table. "So we're safe then. You have the original. The others are duds."

"Tigerstedt took two photos. Remember?" She picked the photo up and flipped it over. "I think that kid might have the other."

"What does he want?" David placed the remaining photos in the tin. "Has he contacted you?"

"We don't know. He might just be a fan, an odd one at that."

David shrugged. "Wouldn't be the first time."

"The police say they found a lot of photos in his house, all sliced and defaced. If he has that original, it's only a matter of time..."

He placed his hand over hers. "If he knew everything he wants to know about the camera, I think we'd be dead by now. If he's oblivious and he just likes dicing up photos...we've had a good run, Lola. We can take solace in the fact that this will probably end with us."

She turned to him. "*Maybe* it'll end with us. We're lucky to have made it this long. It's not being dead that bothers me. It's dying." She turned the photo and held it before herself. "Like that. Look at us." She put her hand over her mouth.

David took the photo and placed it back in the tin. "For how important that damned camera was to us, I can't remember much about it."

"What do you remember?"

"That it was safest with you." He paused. "Or that you were safest with it after the accident at the studio."

"We should have just destroyed it. Who cares what would have happened to us?"

"That's easy to say now. We had a lot more to live for back then."

"Two broken people trying to piece together our pasts. Between the two of us, we might just have a bit of luck." She laughed. "Things haven't changed much, have they? Only difference is back then we couldn't piece together a future between the two of us."

"I know you're scared." He held the photo out between them. "But can you try? Take us back, Lola. You know I could never get these photos to work without you."

"They weren't meant to work for you." She stared at the photo, then at David.

He wrapped his fingers around her hand. "I'll be with you."

Lola reached for the photo, closing her eyes as she touched it.

***

"You need to keep your eyes open." Laughter echoed across a vast landscape. "And hold still!"

Lola turned her head to the hand squeezing hers and opened her eyes. She followed the hand up the arm of a navy-blue sport jacket to David's face. He stared ahead, talking through the corner of his mouth. "You did it," he whispered. "We're back!"

"Over here!"

Lola turned toward the voice. It was Tigerstedt. "It takes a minute to process. If you keep moving, the picture will blur."

"Sorry," Lola said, trying to keep her lips pursed.

Tigerstedt ran into frame next to them and smiled.

The camera flashed.

"Stay put for a second," Tigerstedt muttered through his teeth. He counted down. "Five...four...three...two...okay. We should be all set." Tigerstedt lowered the camera and turned for his house, a baronial hotel on the north edge of Dierhagen. The waves lapped at the shoreline below.

David turned to Lola. "I knew you still had it in you."

She half-sobbed through short breaths, breaths that no longer carried the weight of age. She squeezed David's hand with fingers that no longer carried with them the frailty she'd come to know so well.

David's face confirmed what her body implied. They were young again. She wasn't prepared for this. It had been so long since she had tried to go back—thirty years at least—that she only suspected the process changed not only her surroundings, but her as well. The last time she'd ran her fingers across this photo, found herself in the lens of Tigerstedt's camera once more, she attributed the receding pain to the warm air carried in from the Baltic Sea. But she was wrong. It was youth. Would this camera ever cease to surprise her? Would Tigerstedt ever cease to surprise her?

David let go of her hand and tucked his arm in hers. "So this is, what, 1931?"

She nodded.

David sighed. "We're in the death throes of our career, then. Didn't know it at the time."

In the distance, Tigerstedt and several others stood at the edge of the hotel. Someone, a young woman, it appeared, recognized them and waved.

Lola waved back. "Who is that?"

"I'll give you one hint." David laughed. "She's not waving at you."

The woman ran toward them.

Lola rolled her eyes. "Jamie."

"Play nice." David pulled her closer.

Jamie stopped before them, barely winded. "So nice to see you, David." She appropriated his other arm and looked over at Lola. "Bridgette."

Lola ignored her.

Suddenly she remembered why she and David had stopped talking all those years ago. Or maybe she didn't remember, but saw it through eyes no longer veiled by the naiveté of her youth, no longer clouded by her failing mind.

David was fucking her.

Or had been.

Or will be.

They'd never discussed the details of his indiscretion. Not when, or how many times, only that it had happened. And that he was sorry.

Not sorry enough to avoid repeating it a second time, it seemed.

She glared up at him.

He smiled, making light conversation with Jamie until they reached the hotel lobby. Inside, Tigerstedt had gathered at the center of a throng of visitors, all cast and crew from *Everyman*. Jamie ran to the circle, leaving David and Lola at the doorway.

"Was this when it started?" She nodded at Jamie. "Did you sleep with her when we were here?"

"Please." He looked away. "She's dead." He walked toward the circle. "Let's just savor this while it lasts."

Lola resisted his pull. He stopped, allowing her to take the lead. She dragged him away from Jamie, to the opposite end of the circle.

As she looked forward she could feel his eyes averted, reaching out to meet Jamie's.

"Quiet, everyone." Tigerstedt held out a stack of photos he had taken during the day. "I want to show you something that will change your thoughts on photography anymore."

Almost everything was as she remembered it, except David's demeanor. It was such a stark contrast to the relationship she'd thought they had. She'd been blind to everything back then, presumed herself untouchable. She'd found a new venue for her celebrity. Tigerstedt, obsessed with earning the favor of his native country's industry, had invited them to northern Germany, roped them into contracts to incentivize the use of his equipment. She had been his biggest bargaining chip. As such, she was treated like royalty. Jamie was just along for the ride, a starlet who had exhausted her chances in Hollywood before she even headlined a bill. She had idolized Lola, and her submissive preening had proven so disarming that Lola lost everything to her without realizing it had happened. Pride was to blame as well, but that was something she could only admit after Jamie's passing. Now that she was alive again, in this moment, all of those realizations were out the window. With Lola's youthful appearance came the same petulance she had long since abandoned. All that had been forgiven in Jamie's death was back on the table.

And she hated Jamie even more for bringing it back.

She reminded herself that this wasn't real. Nothing she did here could change what had been or would be. This was just some small piece of the past partitioned off for her perusal.

She tried to distract herself by reminiscing about superficial items, taking inventory of the people around her, akin to counting tiles on the ceiling. She saw Renoir, a Frenchman in charge of lighting. His wife, Elizabeth, an American who had started in dance and shifted over to makeup. She saw another young man and his girlfriend, but couldn't recall their names, only that he had been a failed protégé of Fritz Lang who had taken up with one of his lesser competitors...who was oddly not present.

"Do you see Maier?"

David looked around the room. "No."

"He was here, I remember."

"He's probably entertaining someone upstairs with a few parlor tricks of his own." David winked at her.

She hated him.

She loved him.

Tigerstedt took out a photo of Lang's protégé and held it up to him. "This is you, no?"

The protégé nodded.

"Tell me, what do you feel?" Tigerstedt ran his thumb across the photo.

The protégé held his chest.

"A pressure, right?"

The protégé nodded.

Jamie laughed. "And we're supposed to just take your word for it?"

Tigerstedt shuffled through the photos. "I can show you." He held up a photo of her.

He held the photo out before her and squeezed her arm between thumb and forefinger.

She reached for her upper arm in shock.

Tigerstedt cocked his head and raised his eyebrows.

Jamie pulled her dress down over her shoulder, revealing a red welt. "You've bruised me!"

The smile on Tigerstedt's face dropped. "I am sorry."

Jamie pulled up the shoulder on her dress and stormed up the stairs to her room.

David started for her.

Lola tugged at his arm.

As he turned, she shook her head.

"Shouldn't we follow the course of events from the night?"

"We're not in the past. Nothing you do tonight will change what happens in the future." She pulled him in her direction. The truth was, she couldn't remember exactly what had happened on this day so many years ago anyway. But she knew she wanted David with her. Or rather, she wanted him *not* with Jamie. She nodded to herself. She was here for two reasons. First, to remember. Second, to keep David off that slut Jamie. "Stay with me."

He turned to watch Jamie running up the stairs, then settled back into Tigerstedt's presentation.

"I'm sorry, everyone. I didn't know that would happen." He turned to Lola. "Perhaps a gentler display, for a lady of gentler disposition?"

She smiled.

He took out a picture of her from the stack, ran his finger down her leg. "Do you feel that?"

Pins and needles coursed up and down her thigh in sync with Tigerstedt's finger on the photo. It didn't feel like a gentle touch. Whatever it was, it reverberated beneath the surface of her skin, at the core of her, a dull ache of sinew and bone. She clasped David's jacket to prevent her legs from giving out. "That's enough," she said calmly.

Tigerstedt looked perplexed. "Are you okay?"

"Yes. It's just, it's strange."

He spun around the crowd slowly.

"Do me next!" someone in the small crowd exclaimed.

Another stepped forward. "Did you take a picture of me?!"

Lola looked up at David. "Can you help me to my room?"

David put his arm around her waist and they started for the stairs.

"That's all for now, folks. We will try again." Tigerstedt tucked the photos in his pocket and ran to catch Lola and David. He placed his arm around Lola's waist, under David's. "Let me help."

David tugged at her gently. "I've got it."

Tigerstedt stopped them on the stairs. He looked at Lola for confirmation. "Actually, I was hoping you'd excuse us."

She nodded.

David kept his arm tight around her waist.

"It's fine." She reached for his arm and pushed it off gently. "I need to talk to him anyway."

David stood on the bottom step, watching Tigerstedt lead her upward. "You're sure?"

"I'm fine." She nodded. "Will you come and see me later?"

"Maier." Tigerstedt held the stack of photos out as Maier entered the room. "Take your pick."

Maier shuffled through the pictures. "All of them!"

"Pick three."

Maier separated the photos one by one, settling on three images containing as many partygoers as possible. He handed the remaining photos back to Tigerstedt.

"Come, Bridgette."

David watched Lola grow more distant, shrinking toward Tigerstedt's bedroom.

Lola disappeared inside.

Tigerstedt closed the door. Lola remembered the way she felt the night this had initially happened. Tigerstedt's small stature did little to offset the unease she felt about being closed into a room alone with a man who had, in his mind, done a small favor for a woman. First, it was rare to find a man who thought of any gesture he made as small. In their mind, taking out the trash was moving a goddamned mountain, and reciprocation had to parallel the delusion rather than the reality of whatever small gesture had been made.

The higher up she went in Hollywood, the larger the expected reciprocation became.

But Tigerstedt wasn't only small in stature, he was small in self-image, and too in expectation.

He sat on the bed, but did not gesture for her to sit beside him. "Sit, stand, wherever you feel comfortable." He turned to his nightstand, set the camera and photos down, and reached into the top drawer for a bottle of brandy. "I won't keep you long."

Lola looked around the room.

Tigerstedt pointed to a seat opposite him. "If you move this chair to the edge of the bed, you'll have close access to the door, should you feel the need to flee."

She sat down in the chair. "I'm fine, thank you."

"You're very kind, and very trusting. That's rare for someone in our industry." He pulled two glasses out of his nightstand and set them on top. "Tell me, are you trusting because you've had no harm done to you, or because you have had so much harm done to you that you've become reckless?"

Lola crossed her arms. "I know to trust people to the degree that they've given me reason to trust them."

Tigerstedt unsealed the bottle and filled the glasses, set down the bottle, and offered one to her. "Why do you trust me?"

She took the glass. She hadn't trusted him this much when this first happened. But what little trust she afforded him, he never broke. Tigerstedt was one of those rare good men. Had he come packaged like David, she might have fallen in love with him. But, were he packaged like David, he likely wouldn't have been so trustworthy.

"I trust I can run faster than you, should you lunge at me."

Tigerstedt laughed. "That is true." He held up his glass. "To you."

Lola raised her glass. "I'm not sure I trust the seal on that bottle."

Tigerstedt drank. "I brought a new bottle up for just this occasion. And if you're worried about the glasses, we could trade."

She drank. "So tell me what you want."

He reached for the camera. "I am a man of modest proclivities, but I understand that my desires come at a price." He turned the camera over in his hands. "I created this for you." He handed it to her.

Reluctantly, Lola took the camera. She knew this wasn't the real Tigerstedt, but she still wanted him to enjoy the pursuit. "What do you want in return?"

He waved her off. "Have you ever been to the Middle East?"

She shook her head. "Too hot, I've heard."

"Yes. It is very hot." He smiled. "There is a small tribe there, when we visited, they turned from our cameras. Our guide said they feared it would take their soul." He leaned forward. "So I asked them what they thought of film. Do you know what they told me?"

Lola looked at the camera, trying to dedicate every facet of it to her memory. "What?"

"They told me all art captures the soul, from photographs to paintings to written and spoken word. It exudes soul and captures soul. But this is not a good thing. The muse loses herself in exchange for immortality, but only if the artist's soul is as strong and plentiful as her own." Tigerstedt poured another glass of brandy. "Do you believe this?"

Lola turned the camera over, running her fingers along the edges. It had a wooden base. Would it be warped and cracked, wherever it was outside of this photograph? "It's silly superstition," she said.

He frowned. "A romantic superstition, no?"

She looked up from the camera. "Perhaps."

"It is real." He opened the bottom drawer of his nightstand and took out a leather-bound book. He extended it. "Feel it."

Lola reached out, anticipating that jolt she'd felt several times before, like a nine-volt battery coursing through her. She placed her hand on the book, and there it was. That soft tingle that penetrated to the bone.

"This book cost me a small fortune. It's over one hundred years old—one of a kind—written by quill that channeled the author's soul directly onto the page." He pulled the book from her hands. "The book is a physical testament to the power of soul in art." He opened the book. "The words tell the story of soul in art. The soul transfers to everything we touch, a flame slowly disseminated through the darkness that is our existence, until we extinguish. But we can choose where it is invested." He pointed to the camera. "What you hold in your hands is a piece of my soul."

"I am not a strong man, not of body." He sipped from the cup. "But I do have soul. I have an untempered passion for life, one I've been generously rewarded for." He looked around the room at the ornate oak spires that jutted upward from his bed. "I want to give that to you. I want to help you live forever."

"And this camera's going to help us do this?"

"You felt it, downstairs. Our souls touched." He picked up the stack of photos. "And with these you can do so much more." He handed them to her. "You can caress, heal, harm."

"And you want me to have it?"

"It is just a prototype." Tigerstedt nodded. "I am making another one, for film. This one was just to see who had soul strong enough to withstand the duress of creation."

Lola tucked the photos into her pocket. "Thank you."

"Be careful with it. I am trusting you."

A knock at the door stirred them from the moment. Tigerstedt walked to the door and opened it.

David.

"Is Lo— Bridgette in there?"

Tigerstedt nodded. "She is."

"Can I speak to her?"

Lola called from her chair. "I'll be right out."

Tigerstedt closed the door.

Lola rose from her chair. "So what do you want from me?"

Tigerstedt shook his head. "I just want people to feel us, through the ages. With this I believe we can make that happen."

Lola nodded. "Thank you, Eric." She reached out to hug him.

He held his hand up and backed away. "No. no." Tigerstedt walked her to the door.

She followed, watching Tigerstedt bow to David and descend the stairs.

David glared at him, a flash of jealousy in his eyes. "So what happened between you two in there all those years ago?"

She held up the camera. "I told you everything, David. Don't try to use your paranoia to justify your infidelity."

"You expect me to believe you?"

She stared at him, eyebrows raised. "You want to inspect me? Now's your chance." She took his hand and placed it between her legs.

"All right." David pulled away. "I believe you." He looked downstairs to make sure nobody was watching. "I believe you, all right."

"What would it matter anyway? Just two years from this moment, Tigerstedt died. He's gone." She turned to him. "So where were you while I was with Tigerstedt?"

"I was waiting for you."

Lola rolled her eyes. "The first time, when we were actually here all those years ago?"

David followed her into her room. She closed and locked the doors behind them, set the photographs on the nightstand, and lay on the bed, camera in her hands.

David lay beside her, facing her. "It looks different than I remember."

She regarded it. "Looks the same to me."

He rolled onto his back. "So when does this end?"

Lola set the camera on her nightstand and shook her head. "One of two ways. When I will it, if my faculties are still intact."

"If not?"

"We exit through the next photograph taken by the camera." She could feel him shaking beside her, trembling with anticipation, but too afraid to ask her if he could be with her, just as he had all those years ago. She had initially fallen asleep like this all those years ago, content with knowing she was furiously desired. But tonight was different. Knowing what she knew about Jamie, coupled with the knowledge that they might never meet like this—in these bodies, at this point in time—again, drew her to his lips.

She rolled onto him and began kissing him. His hands steadied on her waist. She waited for him to begin unraveling the bow at the small of her back. He fumbled with it nervously. She sat up and took over as he unbuttoned his shirt. Lola stood and shimmied out of her dress, flesh exposed to the warm summer air inside Tigerstedt's hotel. The darkness rendered their bodies nearly invisible, but her milk-white skin radiated against the dim lighting. David unbuttoned himself and kicked his pants to his ankles. She tore them off, tossed them onto the ground, and crawled on top of him. His fingers found her womanhood almost instantly. She exuded that wet warmth that only a body in prime can deliver, a wetness that, when pulled away from his body, grew slightly cold, all but forcing their bodies together.

She pulled her panties to the side and slid onto him. She'd wanted to remember the night like this for so many years, but nothing, not even the onset of dementia, that soft tide of age that washed memory away, allowed her to forget that this had never happened before. That now was her chance to take this night back.

She grabbed onto the hair of his head and tugged until her entire body reverberated. As she climaxed, her mind went immediately to Tigerstedt's manuscript. This was soul.

This, their two bodies together in this moment, at this time, was art.

CHAPTER TEN

MOLLY

SHE CLIMBED THE stairs to Lowell 214 as slowly as possible, checking her watch every other step.

6:52.

Early.

She slowed down to a crawl. *Please be canceled*, she thought. The previous evening, she'd asked Spearance to leave in haste, not thinking about a sustainable outcome that would have allowed her to avoid the topic of the camera *and* continue to take his class. All she knew at the time was that she wanted him out. All she knew now was that she didn't want to be here, but she had to be here. This was for Jolie. This was for her future.

6:56.

She peered down the hallway and slid into the women's room, preening herself in the mirror for the last three and a half minutes, giving her thirty seconds to get down the hallway and into the class right as the clock struck 7:00. She rolled her eyes at herself. Christ, was she in high school again? It's like she'd never grown past that phase in her life, except then she would have risked late arrival, especially to avoid her teachers.

She took a deep breath and stared at herself in the mirror. What was she going to tell him when class was over? There's no way she could dart out after securing her seat in the back of class the first day.

She walked out of the bathroom, resolving to mull it over during the class.

And of course, there he was, standing outside the door. The closed door.

Shit.

He turned to her.

"Hi," she said, walking briskly toward the door.

"I was worried you wouldn't come." He smiled nervously.

"Can't afford to miss yet. Pretty strict attendance policy." She put her hand on the doorknob and began to turn.

He stopped her. "I'm sorry about last night. This case..." He shrugged. "I really should have thought more about how that line of questioning would make you feel."

She held her bag tight and looked at him.

"If you're willing, and if you have time, I can tell you more about why I want to know about the camera. Then you can decide whether or not you want to tell me, if there's anything to tell, of course."

A small wave of panic washed over her, like an electric shock. She wanted more. She nodded. "Okay."

He stepped out of her way. "After you."

She turned the doorknob and walked in.

Spearance followed, matching her pace to the front of the room. He spoke without making eye contact with the class. "How's everyone doing tonight?"

The response was a raucous shuffling of papers, zippers on duffel bags.

"Excellent," he said, completely deadpan. "Love the enthusiasm." He started writing on the chalk board, caught a few chuckles. He still had a few of them. That was all he needed. He'd passed the point in his career where he dwelled on the disengaged. As long as he had a few who were there to learn, a few who didn't greet his lecture with death stares, he was all right. He finished writing the central theme of tonight's lecture on the board: SURVEILLANCE.

He turned to the class. "You ever feel like you're being watched?"

A few people nodded.

"If so, when, where?" Spearance asked. "In what context?"

An older woman in the front row raised her hand. Spearance was terrible with names. He nodded at her.

She lowered her hand. "The grocery store. Those secret shoppers. I have a twelve-year-old son, so they follow us down the aisles, looking at items on the shelves, but they never check out."

Another hand went up.

Greg.

Spearance gave him the go-ahead.

"We used to have neighbors that would call CPS on my parents all the time. Just really stupid stuff. The tree house was built too high, leaving my brother and me in the car while running back inside to get something off the kitchen table, anything really."

"Good. Good," Spearance leaned against his desk. "Not good that they called on you. Just...good examples." He stood upright. "The first is a sort of manufactured surveillance. People are paid to watch you with the intent of preventing crime. The second is naturally occurring surveillance, and that particular example is more designed to detect and punish crime that has already transpired." He returned to the board. "So preventative surveillance and detective surveillance are two important variables." He wrote them on the board. "The problem today is that preventative surveillance is invasive, and detective surveillance is often too little too late, in all honesty. I shouldn't admit that because it's my bread and butter, but..." He paced across the classroom. "We like to tell ourselves detective surveillance is preventative to some degree."

"Isn't it?" the woman in the front row asked.

Spearance shrugged. "In some cases, yes. A couple teens get drunk and get into a car crash out on route 36, we put it in the paper, spin it as a cautionary tale, then it might help prevent future accidents." He paced to the other end of the room. "But let me offer up another scenario. John Wayne Gacy murders over thirty young men, gets caught, and becomes the center of a media frenzy. He's cast in a negative light, but he's reached celebrity status. People are fascinated with his mind. His name comes up in psychology courses, criminology courses. His face is everywhere. Detection suddenly switches from deterrent to a potential incentive." He stepped behind his desk and opened his textbook. "You guys see that chart on page 49?" He flipped to the page and held it up. "Correlation isn't causation, yada yada, but look at the influx of serial murder and how it has grown exponentially since it's been given exposure at the headline level."

"Why don't they just stop media coverage?" another student asked.

"Freedom of the press. They're driven by ratings, and killings make a killing, pun intended," Greg countered.

Nobody laughed.

Spearance let the silence work its way into Greg, hoping it'd serve as a deterrent for the rest of class. "So how do we deal with this?" Spearance set the book on his desk. "That's up to you folks. Take some time now to brainstorm. One preventative measure and one detective measure to help reduce the instances of serial killing in our society. Then we'll discuss."

Molly put her pen to paper, and her mind immediately went to the camera. What was she going to say if he did ask again? If they found a link to her, some kind of tangible evidence...what if she just confessed to having the camera on the night of the fire? Would it be so bad? She could join the ranks of the John Wayne Gacys and Ted Bundys of the world. Paid interviews. A book deal. She might even drum up enough to help out with Jolie's college someday.

She laughed the thought off. She didn't want any of that. She just wanted to live her life, small and inconspicuous. Why weren't people happy with that anymore?

She came back to mid-conversation, watched Spearance listening to her classmate's ideas with a calm demeanor, nodding with feigned engagement, even when one student suggested microchipping every citizen at birth. Spearance was either a pro at poker face, or he'd suffered a severe stroke that just happened to benefit him in an occupational capacity.

He pointed to the board. "What do all of these ideas have in common?"

The room was silent.

"They're innovations." He pointed to the items one by one: "video surveillance, increased patrols, more manpower, even microchipping, they're all innovations." He started to erase the items on the board. "For me, that's what makes this field so compelling." He turned back to the class after erasing the list. "Any of you heard about the most recent innovation?"

Silence.

"Across the pond they're starting to use DNA evidence to convict rapists. It's like a fingerprint that exists in every part of our bodies. Hair, skin, even saliva. Someday all it will take is one hair, or a few flakes of dead skin, to catch a perp. Finally, we'll have a deterrent that outweighs the potential incentive of media attention." Spearance eyed the clock. "All right," he said, disappointed. "That's it tonight."

She decided, as the discussion came to a close, that she'd hear him out.

The large hand on the clock finally struck ten to. On cue, the textbooks closed, and the class emptied out. Greg watched Molly as she packed up slowly. "You in lot 2?" he asked.

Molly nodded. "I have to talk to him first, though."

He smiled. "I can wait."

She didn't look up. "It'll be a while."

He slid his textbook under his arm and headed for the door. "You okay?"

"Yeah." She looked up to watch him leave, vaguely aware that she might have hurt him, but too distracted by the uncertainty of the conversation she was about to have to worry about it. She'd catch him later.

She watched Spearance gather up his things at the front desk while working through the modest line of students there to suck up. She tried to look busy while, one by one, they left the room. Finally, they were alone. She immediately felt uncomfortable.

He sat down in the seat next to her. "You stick around to talk, or are you just waiting for a ride, or...?"

"I'm here to *listen*," she corrected.

"Okay." He took in a deep breath, his belly expanding against the desktop. "I already told you about Lola's storage shed being broken into, right?"

"Yeah."

"She thinks the Singleton kid took her camera. He definitely broke into her storage unit and took some photos, but the camera, I'm not so sure. What she describes, it's like the one we found near you that night. An old accordion camera, folds out. I thought maybe she'd pawned it off, or gave it away as a gift. But you say you didn't have a camera. Maybe I'm misremembering."

She looked at him, that signature poker face. "What's so important about this camera anyway?"

"I'm not sure," he lied. He had ideas, but he couldn't afford to give her an out yet. "Lola thinks it's important." He stood. "Can I walk you out?"

Molly slung her bag over her shoulder and headed for the door. "Sure." She didn't notice Greg outside the door. He scrambled for the nearest stairwell that wouldn't force him past Molly's line of sight.

He watched them leave the room, then the hallway, before following.

Spearance waited until they left the building and took a few steps away from Molly, hoping the distance would put her at ease. "I might be misremembering, but I was certain you had a camera that night. If you did, and you're not telling me—"

"Are you going to tell me I'm obstructing justice or something, because if you are—"

"No." He looked at her, confused. "I was just going to say I'm sure you have your reasons." He sustained the look of confusion, almost hurt. "Man, law enforcement really played hardball with you back then, didn't they?"

"They never stopped treating me like a suspect."

"I'm sorry."

"It's not your fault."

"It's not your fault either, not how you feel now, and not what happened then. Survivors of tragedy always carry some sense of guilt or accountability with them. My father's a vet. He never forgave himself for living." He looked at her. "Just for living."

Molly looked up at the sky, again unrepentant in its darkness. There was no light to dry the tears beginning to press against her lids. She tipped her head back further to subdue them, but they ultimately won out, finding the path of least resistance down her temples and around her cheekbones. "If just one other person would have made it out that night, I could believe that." She lowered her head to look at him. "When I ran out, there were people feet—inches, maybe—from the door. I could hear them." She ran her thumbs under her eyes.

"They panicked. It's a more common phenomenon that you might think...if you ever want to see the coroner's report..." He cringed at his own words. Why would she want to see that?

"I'll be all right."

"Do you need a ride home? I could come back with you in the morning to get your car, or send Bo over to pick it up."

Molly shook her head. "I'm...I'm not going to do anything rash. I've got a kid at home."

"I was more worried about the...you know." Spearance turned for his car. "If you have anything—need anything," he corrected. "If you need anything, you know where to find me."

Molly took a few steps toward her car. "Thanks."

"One more thing."

Molly opened her door and stepped behind it. "Yeah?"

"You have a copy of the North Cambria yearbook from '79?"

"My mom might have a copy."

"Can you bring it next time?"

"I'll see if I can find it."

"Thanks."

SPEARANCE

Spearance sank into his front seat, started his car, and waited for Molly to turn left out of the lot. He watched her tail lights cascade across the pools of water down Main Street until her car disappeared. Spearance eased out of his space, rolled to the roadway, and signaled right, toward Johnstown Police Department, wishing Molly had taken him up on his offer to drive her home. The thought of visiting JPD's evidence room filled him with a vague sense of dread, but the cocktail of potential reasons why was too much for him to discern what exactly left him feeling off. It might have been guilt. He was being invasive when Molly had given him little reason to pry. Part of him simply didn't feel like re-visiting the case. He paused. If he stopped digging right now—if he just turned left for home—he could follow Molly to ensure she made it home safely. He could forget about the idiosyncrasies of the case, ignore the loose ends, and just go back to his weekly routine of traffic tickets, processing civilian complaints, and discouraging Bo's obsession with Publisher's Clearing House. He could finally get that gym membership in Johnstown and hit the treadmill before classes on Tuesdays and Thursdays.

It all sounded wonderfully mundane, which made his decision to turn right all the more peculiar. For that brief moment as he merged with traffic, he felt like he was watching himself, a vessel floating in the aether. Connected by some immaterial thread, the vehicle dragged him onward, toward JPD.

MOLLY

Molly pulled into her mother's driveway, already dreading the inevitable interaction. It coursed through her head, calculated via a cornucopia of memories that essentially boiled down to, "Mom, could you please not smoke in the house when Jolie is over?" *Or ever?* And, "Mom, could you please not feed Jolie two boxes of chocolate-covered cherries every time she comes to visit?"

Molly stepped out of the car and walked up the front porch steps into the house. Through the window she could see her mother butting one of her signature Misty 120s in the ashtray, trying to disperse the smoke with her other hand.

Molly had all but given up on changing her mother. When Jolie had first been born she'd made some headway, getting her mother to quit smoking in the house until Jolie was three, at which point her mother decided Jolie was old enough to cough herself back to health after each visit. And she did just that. Every. Time.

Molly knocked on the door and opened it. Through the clouds of cigarette smoke, Molly could see Jolie sitting at the dining room table, purple crayon in one hand and cordial cherry in the other. Her face and hands were caked with the sweet sap inside the cherries. "Mommy!" she shouted emphatically without looking up from her picture on the table or changing her expression in the least.

"Hi, honey." She dipped in behind Jolie to pull her hair back into a pony tail, hoping the shoulder length curls weren't already coated in cordial. "How'd she do?"

Her mother pulled a cigarette out of her pack, paused to gauge Molly's reaction, then put it in her mouth. "Her stomach's a little upset."

"I see she's still nursing a box of cherries."

Her mother lit the cigarette. "She's a kid. Let her indulge."

Jolie turned to her. "It burns when I swallow."

"I gave her a Tums and some crackers. She'll be all right."

"Thanks for the professional opinion."

Her mother rolled her eyes. "So how was class?"

Molly walked into the kitchen and opened the fridge. "You got any juice?"

"Grape, of the fermented variety." Her mother followed her into the kitchen. "Was your boy toy there, Gary?"

Molly took a cup out of the cupboard and filled it with water. "Greg."

"Whatever." She set her cigarette down in the overflowing ashtray on the counter, where the last cigarette she smoked in the kitchen was still smoldering. "Was he there?"

"That's where I met him, so yes."

She followed Molly to the bathroom. "He still look as good as he did through the lens of desperation on your first date?"

She closed the bathroom door in her mom's face gently. "He's all right."

"When do I get to meet him?"

Molly sat down on the toilet. "When you quit smoking in the house."

"So, never?" her mother chided.

Molly washed her hands and opened the bathroom door. "Can you help her get her shoes on? She's still having trouble tying them."

"You have two free hands."

"I want to check the bookshelf in the living room. We still have the yearbooks from when I was in high school?"

"Maybe."

"Where else would they be?"

Her mother picked up the cigarette in the kitchen and headed for the dining room. "What you didn't take I tossed. What I didn't toss, Jolie trashed."

"The yearbooks?"

"Well, maybe not those. She does have a penchant for books, though."

Molly let her mother's words slip out of focus as she headed for the bookshelf. Her father's old *Guns & Ammo* magazines still lined the shelves, nearly all of them. He was an avid gun collector, and most of that collection remained upstairs, tucked away in his hunting room. Her mother couldn't bring herself to get rid of them, but at the least she'd agreed to place them under padlock after Jolie grew old enough to take the stairs. Even that—getting her mother to padlock the door— had been an uphill battle.

On the bottom shelf a few of Jolie's books rested. Molly regarded them solemnly. Beautiful white books with minimalist drawings, coated with a thin layer of brown tar from her parents' excessive smoking. Tar so thick Jolie's little fingerprints remained etched into the front covers of each.

And next to those, Molly's yearbooks, the last of which she had purchased a plastic jacket for. Already at seventeen she could see the yellowing of the wallpaper and knew to protect anything she cherished. She sorted through them until she came upon '79. She tucked it under her arm and headed for the dining room. "You got your shoes on?"

Jolie nodded.

"All right. Let's get you home and in the tub."

"Awww."

"Don't start. You need a bath. You haven't had one in days."

Jolie held her hand up to her nose and inhaled. "I smell like cherries."

Molly pushed her out the front door. "You smell like grandpa's tobacco pipe at best."

"You're welcome." Her mother lit another cigarette.

"Thanks." She nodded toward the kitchen. "You've got another one lit out there."

"Gives me something to look forward to on my way to the bedroom."

"Bye, Mom. Love you." Molly closed the door behind her.

"Love you too. See you guys tomorrow."

Jolie stomped through every little water-filled divot in the driveway, splashing water all over Molly's pants. "Do I have to take a bath?"

"Yes. But we'll make it quick."

"Good."

Molly strapped Jolie into her car seat, rounded the back of the car, and started up the car.

"Grandma says you found us a new daddy."

"Jesus," Molly whispered. "I just met a guy in my class. We're not going to use the 'd' word around him."

"Grandma uses the 'f' word sometimes."

Molly backed out of the driveway. "I bet she does."

"Can I?"

"N—"

"Fart!" Jolie interrupted. "Farty fart fart!"

Molly turned to her daughter. "Say it one more time. See what happens, missy."

Jolie smiled. "Ffffffffffffffff."

Molly turned to stare at her again.

"What? I'm not saying it."

She watched her daughter in the rearview mirror, her infectious smile spreading from the car seat to the driver's seat. "Brat," Molly chided as she pulled into their driveway.

Jolie grinned.

Molly unstrapped Jolie and helped her hop out of her car seat. Jolie reached up for her, both arms outstretched. Molly carried her into the house. She was nearly asleep after only a few minutes in the car, and Molly hoped she'd stay that way. She lay Jolie on the bed, took her out of her dress, and tucked her in.

"What about my bath?" Jolie asked.

"We'll give you one first thing in the morning."

Jolie rolled onto her side. "Okay."

"Goodnight."

Jolie snuggled against her pillow and fell back asleep.

Molly watched her as she rested, wishing her waking moments were this tranquil. She almost lay down beside her and fell asleep, but longed for a few minutes of down time before bed.

She went to the living room, picking up the '79 yearbook off the kitchen table on her way. The minute she sat, she remembered a six pack of Coke in the fridge, then sunk into the cushions and decided the call of the comforter draped over the edge of the couch was too inviting to leave its warmth again. She opened the yearbook and was immediately greeted by the scent of her childhood, which consisted mostly of stale smoke and a vanilla perfume her mother had worn religiously.

She started at the blank signature pages. She remembered deciding to leave the pages pristine, thus the plastic dust jacket she'd paid five dollars extra for. When she looked back at this book, she wanted to remember the moments captured in photographs within, not the events surrounding the acquirement and passing of the yearbook. By seventeen, when she had gotten this book, she already understood the importance of isolating memories as much as possible, otherwise memories became obscured by discussions of said memories, and subsequent discussions and experiences that cued those memories. After a while, it all became too difficult to manage. But while everything else became sandwiched atop an endless procession of experiences and memories, this yearbook remained isolated on that bookshelf. Everything therein was just a few layers of the past rather than memories infinitely stacked atop one another.

She opened to club photos, took in all of her friends from Spanish club, and remembered the senior trip they were supposed to take to Europe. Their small town made it nearly impossible to raise the funds, and so only four members whose parents could afford the $500 ended up going. As a consolation, Molly and a few of her friends went to Pittsburgh to see a football game. She had never liked football, but she was grateful they got to do something while their better-off friends traipsed across France and Germany.

She flipped through the pages of her class, stopping on her old boyfriend, James. He left for a state college in New York and never came back, though she did see his parents from time to time. They said he was doing well, working for Niagara Mohawk or some electrical outfit.

She turned the page.

There she was in all her permed glory. She was one of the first to get one, earning her the moniker "poodle pelt" for her entire senior year, a moniker she was glad hadn't stuck. It was all in light jest, however. Some kids didn't have it so easy.

She turned the page.

She pored over the pictures, trying to find someone she knew. She remembered them all vaguely, caricatures, archetypes from television made real in her memory. Every school had a Moose, the thick-necked footballer who towered above the rest of the kids. He dated Sam. Sam the cheerleader.

Sorority Sam.

Seared Sam.

On-the-next-page Sam.

She swallowed.

She turned the page.

And there she was, staring back at her like some cruel joke.

Sam. Hair-singed-into-cheeks. Flesh-mottled-in-blackened-scars Sam. Marred in nearly the same way, the same way they had found her six years prior, when they picked Molly up in front of the Theta Phi house. The same way she looked when a gentle breeze caught the sheet covering her face for a brief moment, revealing Molly's inadvertent handiwork to her.

She never forgot that face.

Now the memory of it stacked with the yearbook photo.

She flipped to the cheerleader team photo.

Samantha, one of the flyers, arms outstretched, charred, held in the arms of her squad mates, leg turned outward, revealing a matrix of scarification up her thigh.

White teeth through an ash-black face.

Molly slammed the book closed and threw it on the floor.

SPEARANCE

Spearance walked into Johnstown headquarters to find it unchanged, even after six years. Younger faces dotted the hallways, sure, but those hallways were still built up with large, glossy bricks the color of bluebird's eggs. The ceiling tiles were still stained at best, missing at worst. It had always been an unnerving place to visit, but today he felt oddly at home.

One of the younger faces sat at the front desk, but Spearance knew him from night classes. He'd been a student only a few years earlier.

He had an in.

"Good to see you..." He drew a blank. "Jeremy, right?"

He nodded.

"Can you buzz me into evidence?"

"Sure." Jeremy stepped out from behind the desk and led him down a narrower hallway. He unlocked the door on the right and opened it.

Spearance stepped inside.

Jeremy started to close the door behind him.

Spearance turned, anxious.

"Protocol. Gotta lock you in. You call out from the phone on the wall and I'll let you out."

"Can I still sign out cold case materials?"

"Depends on what you want." Jeremy pointed to the far wall. "All of that is low priority. Won't be missed. Center rack is cooling down, but there might be some extenuating circumstance or it could be a case of interest for one of the guys in the office." He pointed to the last rack. "That shit's like the reserves in the library. Dig all you want to while you're here, but it isn't supposed to go anywhere."

Spearance started browsing the low-priority shelf. "You organize this?"

Jeremy nodded. "Yeah. It's chronological too. Oldest on the top, newest on the bottom."

"You've cleaned the place up nicely." Spearance stepped back to glance at the top shelf, starting on the left with 1974. "Going to make it hard to get what I need out of here under your nose."

Jeremy laughed.

Spearance did not.

"Well, guess I'll lock up. Let me know when you need me."

"Will do."

Spearance followed the dates down the first shelf.

Nothing.

He turned to the middle shelving unit, finding materials from 1981 on the second shelf. Three boxes. He popped open the first. Missing persons case from early in the year. They found the kid, but never found the person who dumped him. Spearance dropped the lid back into place.

He reached for the next box and peered inside. The smell of creosote wafted up into his nose.

Bingo.

He pulled the box off the shelf and set it down on the evidence table. He set the top down on the floor and began rummaging through the contents.

Inside, there was no evidence of anything gleaned directly from the fire that night. Just a litany of paperwork bound by paperclip and, when the size rendered paperclips no longer useful, rubber band. He pulled out the manila envelopes one by one, setting them on the table. He opened each, smelling the contents. All smelled of ash, but the largest bundle smelled the strongest.

Spearance pulled the stack of papers out of the envelope and spread the pile of paperwork. He was looking for...what was he looking for?

There was a lingering hope that he would find the camera stashed away inside the evidence box. Now that that was no longer a possibility, what was left?

He brushed the moment of doubt aside and took the first stack of staple-bound papers into his hand. He'd look at scene inventory conducted by EMT, police, and the hospital. If a camera was mentioned anywhere between them, he might have something to go off. Something to prove that memory of Molly asking for her camera wasn't just a fabrication his mind conjured up to draw non-sequitur connections and provide a personal sense of resolution.

The Johnstown Police Department joint incident report. They'd shared the responsibility with state boys. Spearance wondered if one of the other envelopes might contain his initial report, or if the contents might be appended.

He flipped quickly through.

His notes were not present, but that was only a minor disappointment, the weight of which could be carried easily by his ego. The fact that it was missing wasn't cause for any concern beyond a personal one.

He flipped through to the incident report on Molly, to the "items taken" section at the bottom of the page.

Two photos, one partially burned. The other smoke damaged.

No mention of a camera.

He opened the next envelope. A shorter report compiled by Indiana University, an internal investigation, citing the sorority for hazing with the consequence of indefinite suspension.

The next was his report. Modest, but exact. He had always prided himself on his "just the facts" approach to reporting, until today. Today he wanted the superfluous details. He wanted the minor details, digressions, anything and everything.

But aside from a few spelling errors, Spearance found nothing his young, agile mind wouldn't have found back at the start of his career. He'd been as thorough as protocol required. Nothing less. Nothing more.

The next envelope contained patient treatment reports from the EMTs. In some cases, three separate reports for the same patient. Spearance sorted through the respondents. Sheila Marshall, Indiana Emergency...Gregory Peck, Johnstown Em...Greg. Resident expert in the class Greg. Hang-around-in-the-hallway-for-Molly Greg.

He sorted through the pile for the reports Greg filed. Molly was in the stack. Had either of them made the connection?

He scanned the assessment for mention of belongings. Two photos and non-restrictive clothing.

Spearance sorted through Sheila's reports until he found Molly.

Belongings: Two photos...non-restrictive clothing...a camera.

He checked the times on the reports. They were synonymous, both stamped for patient observation at 7:12pm.

Spearance set the reports aside. He didn't need to sign them out. He could make copies.

But the police report included two photos. Those items carried from first responder through to the police.

They had to be in the box.

Spearance tore through each envelope.

The thickest was a stack of interview transcripts. Page after page of cross-examinations, depositions, court room transcripts. Parents v IUP. IUP v PXO. Molly Richards v. IUP.

The cases had stretched well beyond his brief time with the case, and yet, all were marked in their brevity. Simultaneous out of court settlements that brought everyone's initiatives to a close.

No matter. He needed the pictures.

He continued tearing open the folders.

Fire Marshall report...

Copies of the insurance forms...

Coroner's reports...

He slowed his search when he reached the photographic inventory of the incident. He knew both from the smell of the envelope and protocol that the pictures he wanted wouldn't be inside, but he still had to look.

Documentation had been incredibly thorough. The photos were arranged in linear fashion.

First Picture: the outside and inside of the house, bodies collectively captured where they had found them.

Second Picture: the site after cleanup.

Third through Eighth Pictures: The few bodies that were able to be separated from the aftermath, individually catalogued, after being extracted from the charred detritus.

Spearance thumbed through them quickly, settling on Sam, her charred face rendering her revealed teeth in an upturned grin, too exaggerated to be pleasant. He knew this image from the North Cambria yearbook.

Ninth through Fourteenth Pictures: corresponding images of the victims from when they were alive, demarcated with red ink where identifying features were comparable to the victims'. Except Sam's photo, which was indiscernible from the post-incident photo of her.

Same blackened face. Same sunken eyes. Same charcoal smile, as if every picture of her was altered the day she died.

He set the photos down.

Last envelope: Non-perishable items recovered.

Spearance opened it and immediately met the acrid stench of creosote.

This was what he had been looking for.

He reached in and pulled the thin strip out, already sensing the glossy surface with his fingers.

He extracted it and flipped it over.

Molly.

The edges were blackened and frayed, curling off the image.

She stood, arms akimbo, in a windbreaker and jeans. Comfort clothes.

This was one of the photos, straight from the mouth of the camera. Spearance slipped the photo inside his jacket and headed for the phone. He dialed out. "Jeremy?"

"You all set?"

"Yeah. Need some copies."

Spearance waited by the door as Jeremy opened it. "You got a copier?"

Jeremy extended his other hand. "I can get it for you. How many copies you need?"

"Might as well get two of each to be safe."

Jeremy locked the door behind him.

"I'll need to clean up after I get my papers."

Jeremy shook his head. "I'll clean up after you."

"Thanks." Spearance followed Jeremy to the neighboring room. "I think?"

"I'm supposed to do it anyway, to double-check inventory."

"They keep trying to retrofit distrust into our profession, don't they?"

"It isn't very hard, given all the corruption." Jeremy propped the top of the copier open, set the first sheet down, and closed the top. "I trust you, of course. But you have to admit there are problem people out there." He pushed the button. "Two copies?"

"Yeah." Spearance suddenly felt guilty for the photo lining the inside of his jacket.

Jeremy watched the copies roll out and placed the other sheet in the machine. "So what's bringing you back to this case?"

"I better not let the cat out of the bag yet."

Jeremy laughed. "Understood." He handed the four copies to Spearance. "There you go."

"Thanks again. You're doing me a solid here."

"I am." Jeremy eyed his jacket. "You bring that back when you're done, all right?"

Spearance looked at him quizzically.

"Surveillance camera." Jeremy gave him a subtle salute and smiled. "Later, Professor."

"Later." Spearance tucked the EMT incident reports under his arm. "Thanks."

Once in the car, Spearance had no reservations about his next stop. He set the EMT incident reports on the passenger seat, placed the picture of Molly into his glove box, and closed the door gently. He opened and closed it again to make sure it wasn't warping inside, then headed for Monopole.

For a main street bar in a college town, Monopole was unusually spare most nights. It was your quintessential small-town bar, reserved for those who lived in town year-round and most likely had a family tree that coursed through the county for three or more generations. There were no formal requirements for entry, but informally, most people knew you weren't welcome unless you worked for the country or state, and being a registered Republican didn't hurt. As such, it never felt like home to Spearance. But it did to Greg.

Spearance walked through the front door and scanned the room, finding Greg at a two-person booth near the bathroom, facing away from the door.

Spearance approached the booth, giving Greg a hearty pat on the back. "Mind if I have a seat?"

Greg looked up. Shrugged.

Spearance sat down across from him.

Greg stared at his drink. "So what'd you keep Molly after class for?"

"Just a few questions."

Greg finally mustered the courage to meet Spearance. "You ask her out?"

"What?" Even as he answered, it took Spearance a moment to get his bearings straight. "No."

"I saw you guys in the parking lot. You had your hand on the small of her back." Greg took a drink. "She didn't look interested."

"I'm at least a decade older than her. Not to mention the fact that she's one of my students."

"Like that stops your type."

"My type?" Spearance shook it off. "Look, I came here to talk to you. I'm not going to humor this line of questioning."

Greg looked over his shoulder, at the floor, anywhere but Spearance.

Spearance held up the EMT incident reports. "You were there. The night that sorority burned down."

"So were you."

"And I discussed it with Molly the first night of class." Spearance set the papers down on the table. "Have you told her yet?"

Greg took another drink, wiped the excess moisture from the table, and set his beer back down. "I didn't want her to get upset."

"You sure it wasn't about something else?"

Greg rolled his eyes. "Like what?"

"There's no way you and Sheila Marshall arrived there at the same time. She was minutes away. You had a bit of a drive, coming in from the neighboring town."

"We were already on call in Indiana." Greg slid the papers to his side of the table and double-checked the times. "We got there at the same time."

"And the two of you worked on Molly together?"

"Yes."

Spearance pointed to the items inventoried. "Know anything about this camera?"

Greg leaned back. "I don't remember any camera."

"Yeah." Spearance folded the reports and slid them into his coat. "I figured." He stood up. "I better be going. Long drive." He tapped the table, hoping to secure Greg's attention one last time before leaving. "I'm telling you as a friend, as someone who wants you to find happiness as much as you do. You need to tell Molly you were there. It'll come up eventually. And if you do know anything about that camera, I hope you'll let me know. Off the record. As a friend."

Greg finished the beer and stared forward blankly. "Will do, Prof."

MILES

Maier's body, steam still exuding from the pocks and blistered on the right half of his body, lay against the tiled floor. Miles stared in shock. He'd seen plenty of mutilated bodies in his time. Felt them even, but only within images. Never had the act of defacing another been accompanied by the absolution of death. He felt vomit crawl up the back of his throat, but forced it down.

He needed to clear his head. But first, he needed to dry off the photo. The towel hanging on the rack near the sink was too abrasive so he used his shirt, dabbing at the wet end of the photograph until only subtle water damage remained.

The next item of importance was the body. He'd never had to deal with cleanup. He always left them where they were, as they were.

He ran to the kitchen, combed through each drawer looking for rubber gloves, and settled on two large Ziploc bags to cover his hands. It was haphazard, but he wanted to get the job done as quickly as possible.

After putting the bags on his hands, he grabbed Maier by the wrists and pulled him toward the tub as gently as possible. He slung one arm over the tub, into the water. He reached under Maier's naked body and pulled him up and into the tub, Maier's appendages sprawling down and out as he did so.

Miles resolved to make it look like a suicide. To explain the burn marks, he'd try to access the water heater and turn the temperature up. Then he'd leave the hot water running when he left, hoping the water would scald the rest of Maier's body, making the current burn marks indistinguishable from the others.

But first he had to cut Maier's wrists.

He took the straight razor from the sink and took the photo into his hand.

He raised the straight razor to Maier's image and drew it across his wrist. Blood coalesced at the wound, both on paper and in the bathtub.

Miles drew the blade across Maier's other hand. He sliced upward this time, hoping gravity would aid in bleeding him out. He let the arm rest again at Maier's side, wiped the blade off on the inside of Maier's shirt, then folded it and cradled it in his hand.

The tub water was now a bright red. One of Maier's arms had been left slung over the edge of the tub. It now bled out onto the floor.

He set the photo in his hand on the toilet lid and looked carefully into it. A thin trail of blood ran down Maier's hands from under the cuff of his jacket.

Miles slid his hands into the Ziploc bags on the edge of the sink, dunked the straight razor in the water, then wrapped Maier's right hand around the blade. He let the blade fall into the tub.

He dropped the bags in the sink and washed his hands. Then grabbed another pair of bags to cover his hands with. He moved quickly through the house, checking the doors for Maier's basement. Once he found it, he descended and searched for the water heater. It was in a small room near the boiler unit. He pried the unit control panel off the heater and turned the thermostat as high as it would go. He heard the natural gas spill onto the pilot light. The unit fired up, and Miles stuffed the panel back into place and ran upstairs.

Once he closed the door behind him, he looked down at his Ziploc hands, hoping they were secure enough. He'd never feel confident in getting away with this, but he always had the option to hide in images. He took solace in this thought as he began rummaging through Maier's room for something, anything, that would lead him to the camera. But after an hour, he found nothing.

After years of research, after killing a man during inquiry, he had still found no trace of the camera.

But he knew it existed.

And he had a better sense of what it was capable of.

If he couldn't find the camera, he'd draw the remaining survivors in the photo out, or he'd kill them one at a time until those remaining told him where it was. The rumors suggested they knew what it was capable of as well. As such, it was too valuable an item to forget or misplace.

Miles turned the hot water on, setting it at a slow trickle, and then closed the door behind him. Against his better judgment, he decided to go back to Hastings to see who, or more specifically what, he could draw out of hiding.

CHAPTER ELEVEN

MOLLY

Molly clocked in at the Hastings IGA Monday through Friday around 9am with an occasional 9:30am delay due to extenuating circumstances, those extenuating circumstances being Jolie or Jolie-related. Today she managed to get there a few minutes early after dropping Jolie off at school. She signed in at the front register, relieving the new store owner.

Even though the store had been taken over by new ownership, they kept the original namesake, Toulman's IGA, because it was so prominently featured in the town's history. From newspapers to fundraisers to pre-existing place holders at the local diner, you could find traces of Toulman's IGA just about everywhere. Legacy overrode ego in this one small way, but in all others, the new owner was hellbent on making the store his own, even if it was to the detriment of business.

The first mistake he made, in her opinion, was cutting her hours down to part-time so he could hire his friends and relatives. The second was cutting any and all inventory that didn't contribute to profit margins on a weekly basis. Light bulbs, thumb tacks, and other minor hardware were removed because they didn't move fast enough. Molly knew from her tenure there that those items were not on the front wall for profits. They were there for customer convenience. And every visitor who came in looking for said hardware after its removal was one less return visitor.

The customer pool was shrinking faster every day, which led to the next mistake: marking every item up in the store 20% to compensate for reduced traffic.

The way things were going, Molly knew she wouldn't have this job much longer, which made her all the more grateful that she'd been able to purchase her grandfather's house at a pittance from her aunt. Small mercies, and sometimes, rather large ones.

Molly had been dropping applications off around town, and had even picked up a few in Johnstown after class to supplement her income in case the store closed before she got her degree. In the meantime, she burned the hours away by reading for school between the steady yet spare stream of traffic at the checkout counter, which, generally speaking, did not include Greg. Yet there he was, almost immediately after the opening hour, staring down at her.

"Greg?" She looked up from her book. "Bit of a drive from Johnstown for the same produce, isn't it?"

"I came to talk to you."

Molly looked at the clock. "I'm here four more hours."

"That's fine." His eyes darted around the room. "Can we meet somewhere afterward?"

Molly hesitated. "How'd you find me?"

"You told me you worked here."

"Did I?"

"You said store. You mentioned living in Hastings. It wasn't an admirable feat in deductive reasoning." He smiled. "But I did stop at the other two stores in town before this, if it makes you feel any better."

"A bit better, yes." Molly closed her book. "But still not sure if I should be flattered or creeped out."

"If I had any say, I'd choose the former."

"You don't." She smiled. "Have any say."

"Yeah, I figured that's what you meant." He took a deep breath, let his shoulders fall. "So can we talk, after work?"

"Sure. Diner?"

"I was hoping somewhere a little quieter."

She shuffled through her mental inventory of neutral zones in town, added the variable "quieter." "How about the library? We can find a study booth or go upstairs there."

Greg cocked his head and raised his eyebrows in resignation. "All right."

An elderly woman approached the counter with a small cart.

"I better get back to work." Molly turned to the register. "See you around 2:00."

Greg headed for the exit. "All right."

"I won't have long though. I have to pick up my daughter," she shouted.

He turned, continuing to walk backward. "Just keeps getting better."

"Take it or leave it," Molly said.

"You know I'll take it." He waved at her as he turned to the door.

LOLA

Lola woke to a familiar ache in her joints, reminding her that the prime that allowed her excessive bouts of sleep had long passed.

She was in the present once more, but with an added clarity: a residual effect of entering the photo, perhaps? She wished she had tried going back again sooner, and suddenly realized the slow degradation of her memory had escalated when she resolved to go back no longer. Once again, her stubborn predisposition had gotten the better of her.

David lay beside her, one arm draped over her waist. She rolled onto her back and stared at the ceiling, stirring David awake. He pulled closer. "That was wonderful."

Lola nodded.

"You know, if you asked me to go back and stay there, I wouldn't refuse."

Lola rolled out of bed and immediately felt herself to make sure she was partially clothed. She was relieved to feel her soft bathrobe still cradling her as it had when they first entered the picture. She wanted the memory of her body to remain in the past. "We can't stay forever."

David sat up. "Why not?"

"Stay long enough and you just get ejected through the next photo." Lola re-tied her bathrobe and headed for the kitchen.

David followed. "What if you keep going in, right through to the last photo?"

Lola turned. "You really want to find out?"

"I might." David embraced her from behind.

Lola edged away from him, smiling. "Get off me." She laughed. "Coffee?"

David beat Lola to the cupboard she reached for. "I'll get it. You relax."

Lola leaned against the countertop.

"Does it make you tired?" David pulled the coffee from the cupboard, opened the can, and poured two scoops into Lola's press. "Going into the pictures?"

"Twenty years ago I might have said yes." She turned to the window. "But the level of exhaustion I felt back then after coming out, it's pretty much perpetual now."

"I'd say that's the hardest part of getting old. Knowing that the threshold on exhaustion doesn't end, and it doesn't get better." David shook the kettle on the stove. "Still full." He kicked on the heat. "It's perpetual degradation."

"By the time I realized it, it was too late to enjoy what I had left."

David laughed. "It's not so bad" He stood behind her. "And last night was such a gift." He reached into her robe.

She slapped him away playfully. "Not here."

"In that case..." He walked into the living room and picked up the picture on the table. "Shall we return for a little afternoon delight?"

The kettle rang out in the kitchen.

"Let me have my coffee, old man."

David set the photo down and headed for the kettle. He poured the water into Lola's press. "Who're you calling old?"

Lola took two cups from the cupboard and set them on the counter. "Good to see your vanity hasn't escaped you." She poured some powdered creamer into her cup. "You know you have to leave that behind when you die too."

"I was hoping the Lord might make an exception in my case." David took the creamer and poured some into the bottom of his cup, then filled both with the coffee. He picked up his cup and tapped it against hers. "Down the hatch."

"Don't rush me." Lola picked up her cup and took her first sip. She headed for the living room. "All right, let's go."

David followed. "So soon?"

They sat on the couch together. David took a large drink from his cup, burning himself. "Christ!" He set the cup down. "I forgot room temperature powdered creamer doesn't necessarily heat down a hot cup."

Lola sipped again. "You get used to it." She set her cup down and picked up the picture. "You ready?"

He wrapped his hand around hers and closed his eyes.

She closed hers and sat back on the couch. Before she hit the cushions behind her, she could feel the warm air of the Baltic Sea once more.

"We're back," she heard.

She opened her eyes and there was David standing beside her.

"Was there any doubt?"

He let go of her hand. "We could do this one thousand times. I'd still be in disbelief every time."

"You need to keep your eyes open." Laughter echoed across a vast landscape. "And hold still!"

Tigerstedt stood behind his camera waving his hands maniacally. "It takes a minute to process. If you keep moving, the picture will blur."

Lola straightened her dress. "Of course."

Tigerstedt ran to their side and waited for the camera to work its magic. "Okay. We should be all set." Tigerstedt took the camera and turned for his house, a baronial hotel on the north edge of Dierhagen. The waves lapped at the shoreline below.

"It's exactly as I remember." David turned to her. "Is it the same every time?"

"We're re-living the moment. We change, but the others rarely do, only to the capacity that we interact with them."

"I'm starting to understand why you were reluctant to come back for so many years."

The camera flashed, and Tigerstedt headed toward his house. "Going to take a while to develop. You're free to wander."

"It depends on what you come back for." She waved him toward Tigerstedt's hotel. "If you're here for them, it can get old. If you're here for yourself, your autonomy is intact. We can go anywhere. Do anything."

David ran to her side. "So what do you have in mind?"

In the distance, Tigerstedt and several others stood at the edge of the hotel. Someone, a young woman, it appeared, recognized them and waved.

Lola rolled her eyes. "Do you know how many years it took me to forget her?"

The woman ran toward them.

David held his hand up to stop her. "Jamie. You'll have to excuse us."

Jamie stopped. "Oh, sorry."

David pulled Lola past her.

Lola cocked her head back, eyes to the sky, as they passed.

David laughed under his breath. "You bitch."

Lola kept her nose in the air. "She deserves it."

Inside the circle of viewers, Tigerstedt held out a small pile of photos. "I want to show you something that will..."

His voice drifted into the background as Lola pulled David past them. "We've heard this before."

She led David upstairs and down the hallway toward her quarters.

"Getting right to business, eh?" David caught up to her and kept her brisk pace.

She looked at him from the corner of her eyes. "No use wasting time."

He pushed her gently against the wall and kissed her neck. "Might as well start now."

She put her arms around his neck and pulled him closer, tilted her head back to give him unrestricted access to her exposed flesh. He followed her neckline to her breasts, then tugged her dress down. In the heat of passion, Lola heard his heavy breathing—almost gurgling— as he pulled her dress down below her nipples and took one into his mouth. He had always been predictable in foreplay, but she savored the routine now.

Then the gurgling started again. But it didn't match the pace of David's breathing at her chest.

And again...the gurgling. From beside her now.

She turned.

Inches from her face was Maier, face pallid, water dripping from the edge of his mouth.

As she screamed and pushed David off her, Maier projectile vomited bathwater down her dress. The gurgling continued.

"What in god's name?" David shouted.

Maier walked past them and headed down the stairs. Tigerstedt turned and greeted him as if nothing at all was amiss. "Maier! Come down here!"

Tigerstedt welcomed Maier into the circle as he approached the bottom step.

Lola looked over the balcony.

David joined her. "They don't see it?"

"Something's wrong."

Lola closed her eyes. She inhaled deeply. Never in her life had she recalled the smell of her small apartment in Hastings being such a comfort. They were back.

David regarded her, asked with a nearly accusatory tone, "What was that?!"

"I don't—I've never seen anything like that." She slid down the couch to the phone on her end table. She reached for the small moleskin notebook beside it and shuffled through the pages. "Something's wrong." She settled on a page, picked up the phone, and dialed. "With Maier."

She let the phone ring until his answering machine picked up, then hung up and tried again. "Come on."

The answering machine picked up again.

She reset the line and dialed Spearance's office. On the second ring, Bo picked up.

"Hastings Police Department, will that be delivery or pickup?"

"Is Mr. Spearance there?"

"He's out at the moment. Can I take a message?"

"Is there any way I can reach him? This is an emergency."

"To be frank, I'm not sure exactly where he is at the moment, but can I help?"

"I'm trying to reach a friend in Buffalo. I think he's ill. Something's wrong."

"This Lola?"

"Yes."

"Who you want us to check in on?"

"It's Maier, G.H. Maier."

"He local?"

"He's in Hamburg, New York. Can I give you his number?"

"Go ahead."

"It's 716-365-1712."

"All right. I should be able to call the department up there and send someone out to check on him. You got an address?"

"34 Main Street."

"I'll see what I can do."

"Thank you."

David called to her from the neighboring room. "Lola!" He walked in, photograph in hand. "Look." He handed her the photograph.

In it, Maier's wrists were now slashed. His face swollen.

"It's too late." Lola dropped the photograph onto the table. "We're next."

MOLLY

Molly walked into Hastings Library and looked for Greg. The front desk was empty, as usual, and the quiet was almost unnerving. Today it carried a different connotation, however, one of imminent safety. The silence would mean any noise at all would be picked up by staff. She wasn't sure what she was afraid of. Perhaps commitment, perhaps the fear of disappointing Greg if they grew any more serious. In either case, some lingering sense of dread washed over her every time she thought about him, and it was starting to bother her.

She walked past the card catalog up the stairs into the stacks. Around the first corner, Greg sat on one of the couches. She donned her best disarming smile and approached him. "Hey."

He reciprocated.

He had a cute smile, one that sort of squelched that growing sense of dread as she approached. As such, she sat down beside him against her better—scratch that—worse, she'd refer to it as her worse judgment. Or paranoid judgment. Both were equally accurate, she presumed. "So, what's so important that you drove all the way out here to track me down?"

"Spearance stopped by to talk to me last night. After class."

"And?"

He turned to her. Here, again, was this stern, solemn look he'd carried with him at the grocery store earlier. "I have something—some things—to tell you. After I say what I say, I don't expect your forgiveness or friendship. However you react, I understand."

That overarching sense of dread returned. She watched his face carefully. The smile that washed away her anxieties was nowhere to be found. "What's going on?"

He reached out and took her hand in his. "All I ask is that once I start talking, you let me finish."

"Okay?"

"I don't know if you remember...I was one of the EMTs at the IUP sorority fire."

She thought back to the night, as painful as it was. She had no recollection of his face, which was unnerving since she had involuntary recollections of virtually everything.

"Are you mad?"

"Why didn't you tell me?"

"I just thought...if something like that had happened to me, I wouldn't want anything even remotely associated with that night near me."

"Great intuition there." She pulled her hand away.

"Yeah, well, I didn't want that to happen." He tapped his fingers, looked down. "I like you."

"Thank you for being honest." Molly leaned in to catch his downcast eyes. "Is that all, though? Why all the dramatic buildup?"

Greg continued to watch his feet. "There's more. When I talked to Spearance last night, he asked me about your camera. He knew I was there that night. He had my old incident reports. Started interrogating me."

Molly leaned back, rubbed her thighs in frustration. "There was no camera."

Greg looked at her. "There was, though." He opened his duffel bag and put it on the table. "I took this, the night of the fire."

Molly froze. This was it. The source of the dread. Not just the dread when she looked at Greg, but the dread that she had carried with her from her marriage, from childhood even. Everything boiled down to this moment and those that followed. She looked down each side of the stacks. They were alone. "So what now?" Molly swallowed back the tears, but they came anyway, and she refused to fan them. She let those that escaped her eyes fall down her face. "What do you want?"

"I—I thought you'd want it."

She dried her eyes on her shirt. "Could you put that away, please?"

He put it back in the bag and zipped it up. "I'm sorry."

"Did you really find it that night, or did Spearance dredge up a similar one and put you up to this?"

"I took it that night." He put his hand over hers again, tried to console her with whatever gesture of compassion their tenuous relationship would allow. "Why are you crying? You should be *really* mad at me right now." He finally looked up at her. "Like really *really* mad."

"Why'd you take it?"

"So, remember how I asked you to let me finish once I started?"

Molly nodded.

"I'm starting now."

GREG'S STORY

I'm not proud of what I did, but I was never really ashamed of it either. I suppose the only thing I felt when I robbed the personal effects of bed-bound hospital patients was apathy or indifference. Most of them were going to die anyway, and I never took anything that looked like an heirloom. No St. Peter necklaces, no engagement rings or photographs, except the one I picked up one evening six years ago. It was a sliver of a thing, the picture, a partially scorched image of the girl lying in bed beside it.

You.

What struck me about the image was how old it looked. I could tell the camera beside you was a dinosaur, some generic Polaroid camera so ancient it appeared to predate even the earliest models.

My first impulse was to sell it to Tim's Antiques. But Johnstown isn't large enough to obscure the sale of something so unique, and you, despite how frail and emaciated you looked, were only in shock. You weren't going to die, and I knew eventually word would get back to you. So I kept it.

I'm sorry.

I left the picture. The edges were blackened and frayed, curling off the image. I ran my finger down a coarse edge to smooth it over. Ash scattered and slowly fell to the ground like the feathers of a small bird taken mid-flight by shotgun. You squirmed like a felled deer, and for a moment I was back in Dad's truck as a kid, watching my brother drag his first doe out of the woods.

I could never bring myself to fire on a living creature, but my brother had a strong taste for it. And every time he did, every year he tagged a deer, he'd come into my room that night and ask if we could "celebrate." I didn't understand what we were doing at the time. Sometimes I wonder if he even did, but I still blame him for it. I blame him for what he took, whether life or innocence.

I think that's why I became an EMT, so I could restore the things he took. I'd like to think I started with honorable intentions, anyway.

Over the years I've watched every type of person in rural America die by every lethal force imaginable. I've been called to bodies five days dead on bathroom floors, bodies not found until the mailman notices that the deceased haven't collected their flyers in weeks. I don't know. Maybe I did start the job with good intentions, but after my first year on the job something happened. I didn't grow callous. Nothing simply "turned off" like some of my co-workers described. My pity transitioned to hate. It was such a strong hate that there was no room for anything else inside. After a while, hate was the only thing that made me feel human. Then even that feeling started to die. So I kept it alive, feeding it with what little kindling I had, like tossing dry leaves and brambles to a flame on the verge of extinguishing. I started taking pictures of the accidents and going through them when I felt empty. In doing so, I started to understand why my brother liked his trophy room. The only thing I couldn't understand was why he wanted to preserve his kills as they were before he put a bullet in them. It was the memory of self-destruction I wanted to preserve.

But I'm too weak to kill. I had wanted to take my brother's life for years...maybe not really, but in some capacity I had imagined it. I know it's wrong, but have you ever been touched...like that? Too young to know it's wrong and then one day this overwhelming shame and disgust blossoms into something you can't do away with. I hated him.

I hated myself.

And every time I saw an unidentifiable body, imagining it was him made cleanup so much easier. Every time I had to roll some morgue-bound body onto the stretcher, I thought of my brother. I thought of him squaring away three-hundred acres of family-owned farm land, leaving me with nothing. I thought of him flirting with the girls I brought home from college, marrying my high school crush, becoming a doctor after I told my mother I wanted to be a nurse.

I thought of him as I watched you settle into your pillow, but I couldn't hate you. You were a victim. Innocent. A survivor.

You tucked one arm under your head, revealing a small stretch of raw skin that coursed over your elbow to your wrist. I looked at her picture again, at the modest smile and downward glance you cast onto the ground before you, and I ran my hand down the edge of the photo again, to brush away the last of the black flakes obscuring your image in the picture. You flinched, and I knew I had to leave before you woke up. As I scratched at the charred edge of the picture, you cupped your arm, the same arm I was whittling away at in the picture. I stopped, and watched you ease back into a deep sleep. Then I dug at the uneven edge of the photo. You began sweating and covered your elbow.

Coincidence, I thought.

***

Two nights later I was called to a car accident on route 11. On a Saturday night the odds that the driver was drinking were two to one, which meant we had to get there fast to prevent him from bleeding out. I was so caught up in the urgency of the situation that I almost forgot the camera. Almost.

The scene was excruciatingly anti-climactic. At thirty miles per hour, the driver veered off the road into a shallow ditch that slowed him to a grinding halt. He was non-responsive, probably more from copious amounts of alcohol than any physical trauma caused. And though he probably deserved what he got, we packaged him up nice and tight and prepared to transport him to the ER like he was an infant we found cradled by a mesh of steel and glass on the verge of death.

I was to accompany him on the drive in. The liquor on his breath as his chest expanded and deflated at a snail's pace told me he was still alive. But I had to check his vitals. Protocol, you know how it is. After that I pulled out the old camera, and realized there was no flash.

I turned the lights on and waited for the driver to check on me. She was too busy wolfing down a bag of corn chips to notice. So I stood up, stepped back as far as possible, and took a full-body shot of the drunk. A grainy photo came out of the camera. I turned it over to review my work. I checked on the driver again to gauge her progress on the bag of corn chips. She was fingering the bag casually, shoveling handful after handful into her mouth.

I thought about how many people he could have killed during his drunken joyride, the irresponsible nature of his actions. I wanted to tear the picture right then and there, just to see if he'd respond. But I couldn't bring myself to do anything. So I tucked the photo away in my pocket and waited until he was hospitalized.

After we'd shipped him to the ER, the other EMTs stood in a circle, chatting about the usual: his blood alcohol level, how he was somebody's brother, cousin, or uncle, and the "he said, she said" secondhand account of how and why he ended up the way he did. It all boils down to justifications and excuses...I guess that's what I'm trying to do now, make excuses.

Anyway...

I just listened calmly, waiting for them to probe each other for feedback, to really get into the conversation like it's a bag of fucking corn chips so I could wander off the grounds and have a cigarette.

When I finally did get that opportunity, I walked to the school parking lot across the road and lit up. The cherry burned like a flare on the shoulder of a highway. It smoldered like a freshly fired muzzleloader in the cool autumn air.

I wondered then how I got to a point in my life where everything signified death and the only thing that made me stop thinking about it was seeing or hearing about death, accidents on the highway, emergency calls, and conversations about accidents on the highway and emergency calls. I wondered how the rest of the people I worked with lived with themselves as I fished my pocket for the drunk's photo. For a moment, his face made me forget. Then my mind wandered back to convulsing animals, rock bass suffocating under the weight of my father's strong hands, people whispering their final words as blood invaded their crushed lungs. And as I came to the conclusion that I'm too human, I watched my cigarette draw closer and closer to the picture of the man. I aimed for his head. But when I finally reached the photo, I lit it from the bottom edge, watching the flame build in a slow crescendo as it worked its way up his legs. Then the electric wing doors of the hospital burst open, and all of the EMTs rushed in. I extinguished the flame, stuffed the photo back into my pocket, and ran to join the others.

When I got inside, the man had awoken. His hands trembled over his legs as he screamed for the nurses to put out the fire. Only there was no fire. But when they pulled back the blankets to investigate, his legs were covered with third-degree burns.

It worked.

It actually worked.

And I couldn't have been more terrified.

***

Every Sunday my brother used to invite me over to our old house to reminisce about childhood, eat dinner, and then remind me how different we had become, i.e., how he had a job, a wife, and two kids, while I volunteered as an EMT. As much as I had grown to hate it, every week I came back. Sometimes I went to remind myself how much I hate him. Sometimes I went because I was hungry, or to soak in the beauty of my old heartthrob. Mostly I went because I had nobody else.

The Sunday after I found out what the camera did, I was there again, sitting in the driveway working up the courage to step out of the vehicle, walk up the front steps and knock on the door that was always open after school when we were children.

When I finally did, my brother jumped out at me with a beaver fur on his hand, complete with plastic eyes and teeth still intact.

"It's got me, Greg!" he shouted.

I smiled and nodded to his wife.

He took the beaver pelt off his hand and set it on the table next to a large bowl of tossed salad. "Remember that time we had to dynamite the beaver dam by Dad's turnip field?"

"Yeah," I said reluctantly.

"How long did you cry after I shot old papa beaver?" He looked at his son, Ryan, and asked, "Was it a week, two weeks?"

"Just that night," I said. "Can I sit down?"

"Of course you can." He pulled out a chair. "Door's always open. Can I get you a beer?"

"He'll probably need five to deal with you." His wife looked at me. "He's in one of those moods again."

"Better give me two then."

My brother laughed, way too hard, always harder than he needed to when I said something, even when I was dead serious. Then the camera slung over my shoulder caught his attention. "What's that?"

"Camera I picked up." I held it in my hands, looked at it intently to avoid eye contact. "It's an antique."

My brother reached for it. "I'll say."

I pulled away. "I can't find film for it anywhere. There's a few slides inside, but don't try to take any pictures with it."

He held his hands in the air. "I won't touch it. How's it work?"

"Barely," I joked.

My brother didn't laugh. He was transfixed by the camera. His inquisitive nature was one of the few things I grudgingly respected him for.

"Just like a Polaroid." I showed him the slot where the photos eject. "But I think it's older. I've never seen one like this."

"It's probably worth a pretty penny. You going to sell it?"

"I think I'm going to keep it."

"You should ask around the antique shops."

I shook my head.

His wife pulled a small ham out of the oven and placed it between us. "Let's eat first."

So we ate, and after five days of midnight drive-thru, it was undeniably the first good meal I'd had all week. We talked about

Ryan's progress at school, the beaver pelt, his daughter Jamie's dance recital, the beaver pelt, my job...the fucking beaver pelt. Finally I finished my second helping and asked him what he thought about the camera, more as a way to get him to shut the fuck up about the beaver than out of interest.

But there were no distinguishing marks. There was no date, no brand name, nothing on the camera. It was just a solid box with a lens, an activation button, and a slot for the pictures to come out. We looked back at the most primitive cameras through history. I learned more about Polaroid than I'd ever cared to, and they didn't have a single model like this.

"I'm starting to think that's a one of a kind you have there, Greg."

"You ought to see the pictures it takes."

My brother stood up. "Let's see it in action."

"It'll only take pictures in heavy light. There's no flash."

"We'll take it outside. Kids are probably getting restless anyway."

So my brother took the family to our old back yard, and stood with them at the opposite end of the porch. "What're you waiting for?"

I held the camera at my waist. "I was hoping to get just a picture of you."

"Come on, Greg, the kids want to see how it works."

His wife stepped out of range. "Let him take a picture of you if that's what he wants."

I angled the camera upward and snapped a shot as soon as she moved, hoping the lens would catch him from the waist up. Success. For once, something worked in my favor.

My brother pulled the photo out of my hand. "Can I see it?"

"Be careful!"

He looked at it, shook it, and looked at it again. "Delicate, eh?" He held the picture close to his face. "Looks like the wild west or something. Mind if I keep it?"

I gently tugged it away from him. "I want to make an album."

He shrugged. "All right. You want another beer?"

"I should probably head back home. Might get called in again tonight."

Before I could justify leaving, he was already racing inside to get me another. So I set the camera down and decided to stay for another, and another. Before long, the conversation led to Dad and how merciless he could be when we used to hunt. In truth, Dad held a strange mixture of respect and hatred for nature. He had personal limitations. He wouldn't shoot fawns or their mothers, but he'd laugh about his friend hitting a pregnant doe and then cutting it open to see if the fawn could live. For some reason this was the shit my brother would always bring up, as if we were trying to quantify desensitization. Like cruelty somehow made us men. That's sure as hell not what I meant when I thought I was too human.

About the time he finished the story about Dad using the leftover dynamite from our beaver dam to blow one hundred bass to the surface of a nearby pond, we heard Jamie scream. Then Ryan rounded the corner of the house with my camera. "I don't know what happened!" he shouted.

We followed him to the far edge of the house, where Jamie lay in a heap. She was still breathing. Thank god she was still breathing. I knelt down beside her. "Honey, you've got to tell me what hurts."

She didn't answer, but I knew when she turned to look at me that she was conscious.

"Is your neck okay?" I asked. "Does your back hurt?"

She shook her head, so I picked her up.

"What hurts?" I asked.

She reached down and clutched her leg tightly. When she let go I saw the protrusion through her tights. I handed her to my brother. "Her leg is broken. She needs to go to the ER."

He and his wife rushed to their car, leaving me with Ryan.

"Where's the camera?" I asked. "Where did you put it?!"

He pointed to the back porch. "It's on the swing."

"Did you use it?!"

He started to cry.

"Did you?!" I shouted, shaking him.

He pulled away. "I just took one picture, of Jamie."

"Where is it! Give it to me!"

He led me back to the edge of the house, pointed to the photograph, one corner bent, lying on the ground.

I picked it up to confirm what I already knew. The upturned corner had caught the image of Jamie's leg. "You could have killed her!" I shouted.

"What?"

I paused. "Just don't touch my camera, okay?"

"Is she going to be all right?" he asked.

I tucked the picture in my wallet as carefully as possible. "It's just a broken leg. She'll be fine."

***

After that day, I carried three pictures in my wallet. One, partially scorched, of a drunk whose legs were scarred by third degree burns; one of my brother, the only man I've ever truly hated and from which all of my hatred stems; and one of my niece, an innocent girl who I never want to see hurt again. I flattened that corner of her picture out and tucked it in plastic casing. I hid it in an opening in my wall until I feared the mice might take from it to build their nests. I have wedged it between the pages of books on my shelf I know nobody reads. Even in my wallet, I feared it would be marred by the effects of time. No matter where I have put it, I never felt safe. But I carried it with me because that's the closest thing to security I can find.

I carried it as she crossed the stage and graduated from high school. I carried it when the Saturday night drunk with third degree burns on his legs crashed his car again three years later and I was the first to arrive on the scene. It remained tucked away in my wallet as I said goodbye to my first photograph, and watched as the drunk's car was engulfed in flames and his image burned to my fingertips.

It stayed with me when I was called to a hunting accident on my father's property, when I stopped worrying about the man in my second photograph, not out of hatred, but out of mercy. My brother lay on the ground, upturned to the sky, suffering a shot to the lower intestines. Someone on the bordering state land had mistaken him for a deer. I realized then that although I had wanted him to die for so long, I couldn't watch him suffer.

I thumbed the photo as I stood before my brother's casket, watching the polish on his teeth catch the funeral home lights. I tucked the photo of his daughter and the remains of his picture into the lining of the coffin and returned to my seat, waiting for the funeral director to finally close the lid.

Even after the lid was closed and we loaded my brother into the hearse, it didn't feel like it was over. So I stayed until one of the other pallbearers handed me a shovel, and I scattered a few grains of sand into the ground. They fell in slow motion, like ashes from the edge of a charred photograph.

I waited until they covered my brother and packed him in tightly, and returned when the ground settled and grass began to grow before my brother's stone.

I come back every year, and every year I'm reminded that whether six feet under or ten years older, that photo of Jamie will stay with me. Even though it's tucked away in the lining of a casket, I hold the life of another in my hands.

And I couldn't be more terrified.

CHAPTER TWELVE

SPEARANCE

THE WEDDING PHOTO had gradually made its way around the imaginary clock in Spearance's head, initially facing at 9:00, now facing him directly at 3:00.

He wasn't ready for this, but had promised himself once that photo faced him, it would remain fixed there forever. Refusing to look at the image was the last bastion of his denial.

He closed his eyes, then imagined the image on a wall-sized collage, etched with every blemish their relationship had suffered.

Every inch they'd taken from her. Every stitch they'd put in her.

This. This liminal space between being too afraid to open your eyes and too tortured by keeping them closed. This, he decided, was his personal hell.

Look, damn you. Look!

He forced his eyes open.

They were fine. Tammy was fine.

He reached out for the photo and rolled onto his back, photo in hand.

He studied the contours of his wife's body, the odd way her delicate frame so perfectly cradled his expanding waistline. They looked like two puzzle pieces fit together, a mesh of night and day. Black and white. "I feel like shit, Tammy."

He took in the photo like a glass of water. Silence was as good a response as any, so long as he was awake.

"At this point, I'm not sure if it's because I think the Singleton kid could have been saved, or if it's because I always knew he was beyond saving. I was always the naively optimistic one out of the two of us."

He laughed to himself. "Maybe you should have been the officer in the family. Lord knows you wore the pants."

He gently set the framed picture face down on the nightstand and rolled onto his back to take in the ceiling. He knew right away it was going to be a restless night. The exhaustion needed to caress him into dream state evaded him. His mind raced. He tried to distract himself with his next lesson plan, superficial innovations to the assignments he'd already created. He closed his eyes and let the gentle hum of the baseboards creaking to life serenade him.

Silence.

Silence begat dreaming.

Dreaming begat Danielle Ohst's ashen body, twisting on a funeral pyre of celluloid and memories.

Then screaming.

Then ringing.

The phone.

Spearance rolled to his side and pushed himself up shakily. He was getting old, and he felt it more every day. Consequently, he felt Tammy's death more every day. They were going to do this together, and now...

He stood and walked to the phone, took a deep breath, and picked it up.

"Hello?"

"This the head of Hasting Police Department?"

"Yeah." Spearance pushed the exhaustion out of his voice. "Who is this?"

"Dick Lowe. I'm with Hamburg PD."

"New York?"

"Yah. Your friendly neighbors to the north." Papers shuffled on the other end of the phone. "One of your boys called in a request to check on G.H. Maier."

"Who?"

"G.H. Maier. Directed silent films?"

"Ah. Okay. And?"

"We checked on him this afternoon. He's dead. Any idea why or how your man, Bo, I think, might have been tipped off? We're checking the phone records, but—"

"We're working with one of Maier's friends, an actress he used to work with."

"You think they spoke before Maier passed?"

"I can ask her."

"Don't do that. I mean, tell her he passed if she's the one who inquired, but leave the questioning to the folks on my end. We might have to send someone down."

"How'd he die?"

"I can't discuss that right now."

"Must be homicide if you want me to keep quiet."

Dick's tone became unnervingly formal then. "I can't divulge any further information regarding the case."

"Understood." Spearance opened the drawer below his tabletop rotary phone and reached in the dark for his phone book and a pen. "You got a number I can reach you by?"

"Yah. You got a pen?"

"Go ahead."

LOLA

By early evening, Lola and David had recovered from the initial trauma of seeing their friend Maier. Still, Lola waited by the phone in silence to hear from Bo, Spearance, or whoever might call. David sat beside her, doing his best to console her, but he grew restless. "We should go back in, see if he's still there."

"I'm not going back."

"We should check on him."

Lola shook her head.

They continued to wait in silence until the sound of upturned gravel in the driveway pulled David away from the couch. "Police."

Lola met him in the kitchen. "Thank god."

She watched Spearance step out of the car and ran to the front door to let him in. She twisted the bolt lock free, opened the door, and peered out. "Is he okay?"

Spearance didn't respond as he made his slow descent up the stairs.

"Did you hear anything?"

Spearance stood before her. "Can I come in?"

Lola stepped out of the way, her hand already covering her mouth. "He's dead, isn't he?"

Spearance nodded. "I'm sorry."

David embraced her, not with the intent to console, but in mutual fear. His arms trembled around her back. "What happened?"

"They wouldn't say." He struggled only for a second against his professional inclinations. He wasn't supposed to talk, but he didn't care. "They're treating the investigation like it was homicide, at least that's the impression I got from my conversation with them." He looked at David, then back to Lola. "Can I speak to you alone for a moment?"

David held her closer, almost with the demeanor of a child. It made Lola pity him and despise him simultaneously. "He's fine. He knows everything."

"Do you have any pictures of him, of Maier?"

Lola slid out from under David's arms and walked into the living room. "I have a few."

Spearance followed her.

Lola picked up a picture from the modest pile on her coffee table and handed it to him.

He flipped it over, then back to its front. "Turn on the light, please."

Lola waved David into the room. "Get the light."

He walked to the edge of the room and flipped the switch.

Spearance pored over the image. There was nothing in the picture, no indication that anything had happened to those photographed. "Any others?"

Lola reached down and grabbed two more photos. She handed them to Spearance.

He flipped through them. Then again.

Nothing.

"I don't understand."

David took another step into the room. "What's wrong?"

"Just a hunch. Looks like I was off, though." He set the photos on the table. "Do you mind if I sit down?"

Lola stepped back and sat on the far end of her couch. Spearance dropped onto the opposite end. He stared at the photos on the table. "Do you think there's a possibility of another camera like the one you owned?"

David sat in the arm chair beside the couch. "That was one of a kind."

Lola agreed. "Why?"

"I don't think Miles took your camera. I'm not sure how or when it came into her possession, but I think a young woman had it as far back as 1981. She may still have it."

"Miles still broke into my storage unit. He still has my pictures."

"I know. And we're still looking for him. In the meantime, if you see him, steer clear."

David leaned into the chair. "I don't even know what this man looks like."

Spearance took several photos out of his jacket, shuffled through them, and handed one to David. "That's the guy we're looking for."

David took the picture. "He looks...off."

"He is off." Spearance took the photo back and presented another. "You recognize her?"

"This woman." Lola leaned in to look at the photo. "Is she 'off' as well?"

Spearance shook his head. "She's a good kid."

"I don't recognize her, no." Lola reached for Spearance's arm. "You have to get it from her."

"I'm working on it." Spearance reached into his jacket. "But you need to be honest with me."

Spearance watched her as her eyes scanned the room and fell upon David.

"I need you to be completely honest." Spearance pulled out the photo of Molly from evidence. "Do you think this photo was taken with your camera?"

Lola took the photo. "Is she still alive?"

"She is. She lives in town."

"That poor girl." She handed the photo back to Spearance. "Have you spoken to her?"

Spearance nodded. "She claims she doesn't have the camera." Pause. "Do you remember that yearbook photo we spoke about? The picture of the girl who died in that sorority fire in Indiana?"

Lola nodded.

"The girl in that picture I just showed you was the only survivor, and I'm starting to suspect the camera may have somehow contributed to or caused the fire. There's just one thing I don't understand, and I need you to explain it to me if you do."

"Okay."

"Is that camera capable of what I told you about in the yearbook?" He rephrased. "If that girl died somehow as a result of that camera, could it spread the image of her post-mortem body to images that pre-date the incident?"

Lola stared at him blankly.

Spearance leaned in. "What can you tell me about the camera?"

"It reacted differently to every person who had it in their possession." David turned to Lola. "We have to tell him. We're in danger."

"So if this young woman had the camera, and the camera or its photos somehow led to that sorority fire, that might explain how those yearbook photos were retroactively altered?"

"It might," David said.

Spearance turned to David. "Why do you believe you're in danger?"

Lola finally spoke. "Because there's one variable that never changes with that camera." She looked down at the images on the table. "Its pictures capture a part of you. Like those dolls we saw down in New Orleans. You remember those, David?" She paused in thought. "Voodoo dolls," she recalled. "And whatever happens to the picture, happens to the person in it."

Spearance tucked the photo of Molly into his pocket carefully, just in case what they said was true. "I wish you had told me this before."

"You would have thought me crazy."

Spearance conceded to her point. "Anything else?"

"No." Lola whispered, still staring at the remaining photos on the table. "But you can understand now why we're still concerned about that boy who broke into my storage unit. If he has my pictures, and Maier's passing suggests he does, he can still harm David and me, possibly others."

Spearance sat up, preparing to leave. "Do you remember anyone else from the photos, people we could check on?"

Lola cycled through her memories, but found only photos of herself and her three companions in her mental inventory. "I don't."

"Of those who knew about the camera after its creation, Lola and I are the only two left." David rose and headed for the door. "I'll see you out."

"Wait." Lola stood and walked to the bedroom, returning with another photo. "There is another photo, from the camera." She handed it to him.

He pored over it, noting the cuts across Maier's wrists and his bloated countenance. "This just happen?"

Lola nodded. "He's gone."

"So this camera harbors the wounds of people, but it doesn't save them from those injuries. It just reflects them?"

"So it seems," David observed.

Spearance handed her the photo, shook his head. "Every answer dredges up a larger wealth of questions." He pushed himself off the couch. "Thank you both."

David opened the door. "Drive safely."

Spearance looked back at Lola, who was still transfixed by the images before her. "Thank you. Both of you."

David nodded, closed the door, and waited for Spearance to pull out of the driveway.

"What if he comes for us? That boy with our photos? What if he's like me?"

"Nobody's like you, Lola."

"He could be. He could find us, force us to tell him where we think the camera is."

"We'll cross that bridge when we come to it, *if* we come to it." He leaned into her, slid his arm around her shoulder. His reassuring demeanor had returned.

"I think it's best we take precaution now." Lola gathered her photos together and took them into her bedroom. "We'll keep the group photo in the living room fire safe and lock the bedroom door. Just in case." She waved David into the bedroom. "If he has any of the photos, he could find his way here, whether intentionally or inadvertently."

He pushed himself off the couch. "I suppose you're right."

"Of course I am." She smiled at him as he stepped through the door. She closed the door behind him, locked it, and fell onto the bed. "Poor G.H."

David sat down beside her. "He's still alive." He nodded toward the living room. "In that photo. Perhaps we could save him still."

"He's gone, David."

"Take us back, to see."

Lola shook her head. "I'm not going back."

"Then send me in alone," David suggested.

"No." She took his hand and pulled him down beside her. "I need you here."

David let his body obey her gentle tug. "I'm here."

MOLLY

Molly held the camera up. "I can't believe it."

"I'm sorry." Greg folded the box up and put it back in his bag. "So, on a scale of one through ten, how mad are you?"

She shook her head. "I don't even know how to process this." She shook off the urge to prioritize her feelings for Greg, particularly the urge to snuff them out as soon as possible by maintaining distance given what he'd told her. There were higher-order concerns she needed to deal with first and, unfortunately, she might need Greg's help. She held up the camera. "What am I going to do with this?"

"It's yours. You can do whatever you want with it."

She wanted to smash it right there on the floor, but given her history—and Greg's alleged history—with the camera, she worried what might result from an impulsive move like that. She set it down between them.

Greg grabbed his bag and set it on his lap. "Look, I'm really sorry."

"Stop apologizing." She grabbed the camera and rose to leave.

"Where are you going?"

"I'm going to show it to Mr. Spearance." She turned to him. "And we're going to tell him everything."

"We?"

"You're telling him your story too. We all have a piece of the puzzle. I think if we bounce ideas off one another, we might be able to understand just how dangerous this thing is, or if its effects can be reversed."

"Maybe I should hang on to it." Greg followed her as she walked toward the exit. "Until we meet with Spearance."

His pursuit made her anxious. Not the general sense of dread that accompanied her time with him. Not the impending. A genuine, acute discomfort. "You've had it long enough."

"It isn't safe."

"Then why did you offer it up in the first place?"

"I just wanted you to believe me."

She entered the main area of the library, making sure not to be too obvious as she took the room in. Empty. Where was everyone? "I'll take my chances."

"Let me come with you."

"I'm not sure I want you to know where I live." She stopped, frightened by her honesty, or perhaps by his potential reaction to it.

Greg stopped pleading with her.

"Can you blame me?!" She saw the hurt in his eyes, but shook off any residual guilt she felt. "How do I know what you told me is even true? All I know is that somehow, you got your hands on this camera."

"Why would I paint myself as a thief and a coward?" He looked down. "You deserve my honesty. You deserve to know who I am, good and bad." His eyes remained fixed on the pea green carpeting. "Can you forgive me?"

"I don't know." She shook her head. "I told you, I've got a lot to process right now, and frankly you and me is the last thing on my list of what needs to be sorted through." She paused to gauge his reaction, but he just kept staring at the ground, brow beaten. "And I can't believe it's so high on yours." She leaned in to whisper. "People's lives could be at stake."

"You're right. I'm sorry." His chest heaved. "What else can I say?"

Molly cradled the camera under her arm. "You don't have to say anything else. I think I've heard, and *seen*, enough." She opened the front door and stepped into the evening air. "Don't follow me."

She walked to the edge of the street, unlocked her vehicle, watching the front door of the library to see if Greg would trail her.

He did not.

She lay the camera gently into the passenger seat and headed for home. She checked her watch. She had a bit of time before she needed to pick Jolie up from her mother's, time she desperately needed to think her next steps through. She was going to show the camera to Spearance. That was certain. But after that, what? What if he wanted to use the camera as evidence against her? Start a civil suit or something and sue for damages to Sam's family. Molly shrugged it off. This fucking camera needed to be dispensed with, and if it took her down in the process, so be it. As long as Jolie made it out alive, that's all that mattered. She'd put the camera in the attic, where Jolie had been too scared to venture since she was a toddler, and she'd keep her mother out of the house until she could get the camera to Spearance.

As she pulled onto her road, she suddenly felt like everything she'd resolved to do was a terrible mistake. What if Greg decided he wanted the camera back? He could easily track her down, and—

She checked the rearview mirror. Only darkness greeted her there.

She was safe.

She turned into her driveway, stopping halfway when she noticed a black sedan parked near the house.

Greg?

Molly put the car in reverse as someone stepped out of the vehicle. He turned to see her.

Spearance.

A sense of relief washed over her. She put the car in drive and eased into the driveway.

He walked briskly to the edge of her car. He reached into his jacket, pulled her picture out, and held it against her window.

She reached into the passenger seat and held the camera up to the window.

Spearance's eyes widened.

Molly opened her door and stepped out beside him. "It's a long story."

Spearance put the picture back into his jacket. "I've got time if you do."

"I want immunity."

Spearance laughed. "From what?"

Another pair of headlights entered the driveway.

Spearance reached for his gun. "Do you recognize that vehicle?"

Molly shook her head.

The car parked. A tall figure stepped out.

Greg.

"What the fuck?" Molly whispered. "I told you not to follow me!"

"You forgot your coat." Greg handed it off to her. "Sorry."

Molly pulled it out of his hands. "You need to start listening." She turned to Spearance. "Come on."

Greg stood at the edge of the driveway, hands in his jacket pockets. "I thought you wanted us to tell him together...about the camera."

Jerk. He'd added that last detail to pique Spearance's interest. Molly liked Greg less and less as each minute passed.

"You told him about it too?" Spearance asked.

"He's got his own story." Molly waved Greg toward the house.

Molly unlocked the door and let them in. "Before I say anything, I want to know what you know," she demanded.

"If I talk first, you'll disclose only what you have to, to corroborate with my story." Spearance kicked the mud off his shoes and stepped inside. "Shoes on or off?"

"Off." Molly held the door open for Greg. "Come on."

Greg stepped inside, wiping his shoes on the welcome mat. He kicked his shoes off and stepped onto the hardwood floor.

Molly pointed to the dining room. "You can sit down in there."

She waited for Spearance to untie his shoes and followed him to the dining room.

She set the camera on the table between them.

Spearance stared at the camera, then at Molly. "I'm not trying to play hardball here. I know you have the camera now, and that opens up plenty of doors for me to fill in the gaps in what I've pieced together. But I'd rather hear it from you."

"It was a gift from my grandfather," Molly began.

"I stole it from her." Greg interrupted. "After the fire."

"Let her go first." Spearance nodded in Molly's direction. "What was your grandfather's name?"

"Barry."

"Last name?"

"Richards."

Spearance took out a small notepad and jotted the name down.

"Why are you writing it down?"

"I'll ask Lola if she knew him."

"You won't tell her he had the camera, will you?"

"Shouldn't have to. Either she'll recognize the name or she won't. If she does, I'll have something to follow. If she doesn't, it's a dead end from her angle."

Molly nodded. "He had it when I was young, maybe fifteen years ago."

"A handful of years after Lola moved into town," Spearance observed. "What did your grandfather do for a living?"

"Worked at a chemical plant in Johnstown, I think."

Spearance wrote down the detail. "Go on."

"He willed it to me when he passed away. I brought it to college..."

"Any experiences that suggest it was capable of bringing harm to anyone...aside from the obvious one?"

Molly shook her head.

"I suppose there's something I need to divulge here." Spearance clasped his hands together on the table. "Over the past month I have found several copies of the '79 North Cambria Yearbook. So far, every copy I have found shows your classmate, Samantha Ohst, post mortem in the photos that were taken before the fire."

Molly said nothing.

"I believe it has something to do with that camera." He waited for her to shift, to react even in the smallest way. She remained frozen.

"Look, whatever happened, it's off the record. I just want to understand."

Greg reached for her hand. "You know I'm not going to judge."

"I'm not like you." Molly pulled her hand away. She ran her palm across the table, kicking up a small layer of dust. "Sam killed herself. She stole the camera, stole my bag. They took my clothes. They treated us like garbage. I took the camera back, shot a picture of her hazing one of the rushes, and ran outside. Sam followed me, wrested the incriminating picture out of my hands, and set it on fire so I couldn't report her. The minute her lighter touched that picture...that's when it started."

"I was one of the first responders," Greg added. "But I didn't take the camera until she was at the hospital."

"And you've had it all this time?"

"The past six years, yes."

"And neither of you had any run-ins with the Singleton kid?"

"He worked at the store with me for a while." Molly shrugged, staring at her reflection in the table. "But we never interacted directly other than when our jobs required it."

Spearance and Greg looked at one another.

Molly shrugged. "What?!"

"Nothing." Greg pulled back. "Why so defensive?"

"I saw that look the two of you shared."

"Thank you. Both of you." Spearance closed his notepad and slid his chair back.

"What about you?" Molly asked. "You said you'd tell us what you know."

Spearance relaxed into his chair. "Did I?"

Molly cocked her head. "Cut the hard-boiled bullshit, *John*. This involves all of us."

"All right." Spearance leaned back in his chair. "Miles broke into Lola's storage unit. He took a tin filled with her photos, at least one of which came from that camera. Run-of-the-mill burglary case. Even Lola didn't seem all that concerned." He paused. "A few days later she contacted us, telling us another item was missing, the camera. Her aide had no recollection of the camera. He's been with her for quite a while, so we figured perhaps she was misremembering.

"We checked the Singleton kid's house. We found the tin, but some of the pictures were missing. Camera was also missing. The pictures he did have were sliced up. He had a...rather large collection of photos that were marred in a similar manner. Some kind of fetish, I figured.

"But when I showed Lola the images we found at Miles' house—the ones where her body and face were sliced up—she became more insistent we needed to find that camera. Just like you." He gauged her reaction. "For a long time that was all I had to go on. The matched insistence on the importance of a camera surrounded by tragedy was all I had to connect you to any of this."

He pulled the camera to his side of the table and turned it slowly. "So tangentially connected was the yearbook. Miles had a copy in his locker at the hospital. The picture of Samantha Ohst looked doctored or altered somehow, just like the photos he had of Lola. But then I found another copy of the yearbook, one it was unlikely he had gotten his hands on. That one was also altered. I still don't understand how or why that happened." He phrased it like a question.

Molly and Greg looked at one another. Neither had an answer.

Spearance sighed. "I think that's everything you *need* to know."

"Anything you don't want us to know?" Molly asked.

Spearance shook his head. "I've got nothing to hide."

"Do you think this Miles guy knows about the camera?" Greg leaned in. "What it does?"

"I think he might."

"Then let's just destroy the camera. If we destroy it, that takes care of the mess with Miles, right?" Greg looked at them both for affirmation, but got none.

"He's still got a picture of Lola and her friend. If what you and Lola have told me is true, we need to find that picture to ensure their safety."

"That's second priority. The first thing we need to do is get rid of the camera before it hurts anyone else."

Spearance set the camera on the table. "I know this has brought both of you a lot of grief, but I don't think destroying it is the answer."

"Then what?" Greg returned to the table.

"I think we might need this, to lure Miles out of hiding."

Molly shook her head. "I just want this to be over with."

"If he knows what this camera is capable of, anyone whose picture has been taken with this camera is in danger." Spearance set Molly's photo on the table. "That includes you." He slid it toward her. "Just because we destroy it doesn't guarantee its legacy ends."

Molly took the picture in her hand. She felt sorry for the girl in the picture, a shadow of who she was today. But still, through this picture, enough of what made Molly who she was today remained in that image to cut her down wholly if it fell into the wrong hands. "All right. But it can't stay here."

Spearance grabbed the camera. "I'll keep it at the station. 24-hour surveillance."

"This too." Molly slid the picture back across the table.

Spearance tucked the camera under his arm and slid the photo into his jacket with his other hand. "I'll take it in tonight." He stood to leave.

Greg looked at Molly. "I should probably go too."

Molly looked at him as he half rose. "Yes. You should."

Greg stood the rest of the way and headed for the mud room. He slipped his shoes on and waited at the door.

"I need to talk to John." Molly rose and pushed her chair in. "Alone."

Greg opened the door, nodding in submission. He waved before closing the door. "See you around."

Molly stood at the edge of the dining room, arms at her sides. "Bye." She waited for Greg to start his car and pull out of the driveway.

Spearance fumbled with his shoes at the front door. "You okay?"

"I'm fine." She leaned against the table. "I just didn't want him lingering around after you left."

"You don't trust him?" Spearance braced against the door and forced his left foot into his shoe.

"Not particularly."

"Probably one of the most important things I've learned over the years is that you can't trust anyone completely. I have friends I'd trust with my life, but those same friends, I might not trust them with my bank account number, or to take care of my pet if I went away on vacation. That doesn't make them bad people. It just means we need to think a bit more about the capacity to which we trust others."

"Do you trust him?"

"I can't make that judgment call for you, but I can say this." Spearance reached for the doorknob. "He seems honest to a fault. If he had wanted to, he could have just left this damned thing on your doorstep. No identifying information. You would have had the camera back and his relationship with you wouldn't have been tarnished in any way." Spearance cracked the door. "He chose to give it to you. I don't see any reason why, once he resolved to do that, he'd lie about anything else to you. He put a lot on the line to come clean."

"He followed me home after I told him not to."

"I didn't say he wasn't a creep." Spearance opened the door. "I just said he seems honest."

"Yeah." Molly walked to the door.

"Thanks." Spearance took the first step down. "I'll drop these off at work, then I'll spin back by on my way home to make sure he hasn't decided to drop in."

Molly slipped her shoes on. "I think I'm going to stay at my mother's tonight anyway. Be nice to get out of this house for a bit."

"Good idea." Spearance waved as he followed the walkway to his car. "Later."

Molly threw on her jacket and followed him. "Bye."

DAVID

Every night.

Every damned night so far in this frozen wasteland, Lola insisted on keeping the bedroom door closed. Incidentally, every heating vent on this side of the apartment was in her bedroom, leaving the thermostat in the hallway perpetually activating the furnace for heat. By morning it'd be 88 degrees in the bedroom, 64 in the hallway. Lola had the thermostat set at 75. Her heat bill must have been astronomical. In some small way, David had convinced himself this was part of the reason they had not married. They'd both been spared a lifetime together, so three more days wouldn't hurt.

Until then, every night around 2am the residual heat in the hallway would waft out of the house through various escape routes and the vents would kick on, blowing dust all around the room. And every night, David would wake up, eyes clouded and nose running profusely. He'd taken the precaution of bringing the tissues to bed tonight, and Lola had been kind enough to let him sleep on the side of the bed with a nightstand.

Small mercies.

It was when the vents kicked on for a second time that David thought he'd heard something in the neighboring room. He held a tissue to his nose and simply let it run to better hear—what was it?—a faint rattling. There was definitely something out there. Perhaps a mouse making its final rounds before abandoning its nest in the wall for the warming air outdoors.

Then the doorknob rattled.

That was no mouse.

David's eyes went to the shadow under the doorway.

Someone was inside.

After a few tries at the knob, the shadow disappeared. David gently rolled out of bed and crept toward the door, listening to the creaking floorboards in the living room. Was it Lola's aide? Mike? David almost called out his name. Instead, he unlocked the door as quietly as possible and peered through the crack in the door.

It was a man of small stature, standing over the coffee table. Emboldened, David shouted, "Who's there?!" in the deepest voice he could muster.

The man...disappeared?

David blinked.

The man was gone.

But something fell to the edge of the table.

He opened the door and switched on the hallway light. He followed it into the living room and flipped the switch there.

Nobody.

On the edge of the table was Lola's photo, the one she'd insisted on leaving in the living room.

Chills snaked out from a subtle knot in his stomach, coursing through his extremities.

What if Lola was right? What if the thief was like her?

David carried the picture back to Lola's room and tried to rouse her. "Lola!" he whispered. "Lola, you have to wake up!"

She rolled onto her back. "What?"

"The picture." He wrapped her fingers around it. "You have to let me in!"

Lola released her forced grip on the photo and rolled back over. "What, did you wake up with a stiff one that can only be soothed by Jamie?"

He rolled her back. "This is serious!"

"You're not whoring around at my expense. Let me sleep. We've got a shoot in the morning and I still need to practice my lines." Lola shrugged him off and fell back asleep.

"Shoot?" He shook her. "Lola, it's 1987. This is serious!"

She did not respond.

He wrapped her fingers around the photo again, weaving his fingers through hers. He closed his eyes. "Come on!"

Nothing.

He lay down beside her, closed his eyes again. Tried to feel that sinking feeling Lola had described to him so long ago.

Still nothing.

He remained in position, whispering in Lola's ear. "Do you remember our night together in your room, Tigerstedt's hotel?"

Lola smiled.

"Remember?" he beckoned.

She backed her body into his. He closed his eyes, and tried to match her recollection. When he opened his eyes, he was there again.

"You need to keep your eyes open." Laughter echoed across a vast landscape. "And hold still!"

David stared into the camera. "Thank you, Lola," he whispered.

She did not reply.

He looked down at her and squeezed her hand. She did not reciprocate.

"Over here!"

David turned to face the camera.

Tigerstedt waved at him from behind the camera. "It takes a minute to process. If you keep moving, the picture will blur." He ran from behind the camera toward the others. The timer on the camera activated, and snapped the picture. "Okay. We should be all set." Tigerstedt returned to the camera and turned for his hotel. David followed, with Lola in tow. He tried not to look at her again as he led them past Jamie, past the throng of visitors on the floor level of the hotel, and up the stairs to where they had seen Maier.

At the bottom step, Lola stopped. David tugged at her, but she had turned toward the guests. He pulled at her once more, then let her hand fall to her side.

He would go alone.

He retraced their steps to Lola's bedroom, waited in the shadows for Maier to emerge.

"Maier!" He saw a figure at the edge of the shadow. "Is that you?!"

David stepped into the relative darkness, his eyes adjusting quickly.

It was not Maier.

"David Rothman."

David backed into the light. "Who are you?"

"I've been looking for you." The man stepped into the light.

David recognized his stature from the living room. He recognized his face from the picture Spearance had shared with them. "How did you get in here?!"

"I could ask the same of you." Miles took another step. "Where is the camera?"

"With Tigerstedt."

Miles turned, a straight razor in hand. "The camera, out there. The *real* camera, not this facsimile."

David shook his head. "I don't know."

Miles opened the razor.

"You think you are strong enough to harm me." David laughed. "I'm in my prime here."

Miles reached into his pocket and pulled out his photo of Lola and her companions. He drew the straight razor across David's arm in the image. "I have to admit, I didn't plan on having to struggle with you, but I'm happy to cut you down here before I dispense of you via your actual body." He took another step toward David and sliced into his thigh.

David dropped to his knees, noted the blood pooling below his pants. "Oh god."

"There, now you're appropriately incapacitated." Miles raised the blade again. "It's amazing, this camera. We've become so accustomed to using photography to innovate the self, to immortalize our ideal self-image." Miles brought the straight razor down across David's face. "We use photography to mask our vulnerability."

"Please," David pleaded.

"But this camera undoes all of that. It takes the very thing we use to guise ourselves, and exposes vulnerabilities far deeper than those we intended to hide. It exposes us to our very mortality."

Miles drew the razor down across David's face again.

"Please stop," David begged.

Miles flinched. The pleading, that was something he hadn't accounted for. Not with Maier. Not with David. "You should endeavor to die with dignity."

David curled into himself on the floor and began crying. "Please."

Miles watched him collapse with a combination of pity and disappointment. He turned from the heap on the floor. "What a disappointment, meeting you." He took the picture out of his pocket and drew the blade across David's throat.

David sat up quickly, grasping his throat, then fell forward. He clawed at the heavy carpeting on the floor, thinking to himself—even adrift in the act of dying—that he'd never noticed just how red the carpet had been. Had he ever looked down? Had he ever beheld the minutiae that in large part made the world what it was? He clenched the carpeting, his fingers slick with blood, as if the stitching below was the very minutiae he never knew he longed for.

Miles watched from above as David's slow crawl toward the edge of the balcony slowed to a grinding halt, then stopped completely. Blood pooled at his neckline, quickly expanding toward the edge until it began to run down the balcony onto the guests below.

LOLA

Lola woke to an uncomfortable draft blowing in from the hallway. The open doorway reminded her of her brief interaction with David in the middle of the night. She turned to his side of the bed, which was unkempt and empty.

Someone knocked at the door.

She smiled to herself. The fool had locked himself out. "Hang on!" she shouted. She stepped out of bed, grabbed her bathrobe off the back of the open bedroom door and ran toward the door as fast as her feet would allow, through the hallway to the kitchen.

She unlatched the chain lock—couldn't be David out there, then—and opened the door.

Spearance.

He tipped his hat. "I—uh. I'm pretty sure we found your camera."

"Is everything okay?"

"We have it down at the station."

She re-folded the robe over herself to keep the cold air coming in through the front door at bay. "When can I pick it up?"

"I was hoping we could speak to you and your friend at the station. To formally identify the camera and ask a few questions."

"Sure." She turned for the living room. "David?"

Spearance stood on the porch, door still open. "May I come in?"

Lola waved him in. "Sure. Sure." She walked into the living room, now perplexed by David's absence. "David?"

She walked down the hallway, and into the bedroom to check the suite bathroom.

There was David, on the floor below the nightstand, picture still clasped between his stiff fingers dangling precariously above a thick pool of blood.

From somewhere Lola heard a deafening scream. Spearance ran to the bedroom, almost retching at the sight of David's body. He pulled Lola from the room as the scream persisted until Spearance sat her on the stool near her kitchen phone and asked her to take deep breaths, breaths that muted the scream. That's when she realized it was her own voice, drowning out everything around her from within her lungs, her throat, and her head. She began to breathe as Spearance picked up the phone. "Bo. We need state police." Pause. "Lola's." Pause. "No! Stay at the office. Call the state troopers."

CHAPTER THIRTEEN

SPEARANCE

SPEARANCE STARED ACROSS the table at Lola and set a mini-recorder between them. "If this interview were just between you and me, I'd have fewer questions to ask. I wish I could have kept the investigation local, but we desperately need more manpower on this. I'm hoping we can find a way to steer police toward the person responsible without...I'm getting ahead of myself." Spearance reached into a small cardboard box on the floor and pulled out Molly's camera. "Is this your camera?" He set it on the table before Lola. "Recorder's not on yet. This is between us."

Lola picked up the camera and turned it to view all sides. "It is." She set it back on the table. "Did you find the young man who took it?"

Spearance shook his head. "It's been in the possession of two people over the last six years. The first inherited it from her grandfather in 1981. She claims she remembers it from her childhood, so this model could have been in her family's possession since the early 70s. The name Barry Richards ring a bell?"

Lola shook her head. "No."

"You moved into town around that time, correct?"

"Yes."

"Any other possessions of yours come up missing when you made the transition to Hastings?"

She rolled her eyes. "Those goddamned pictures."

"The nudes?"

Her face reddened. "Yes. The *nudes*."

"Were they packaged with the camera?"

"I had help packing my things. I remember asking where it was before the moving truck left. They gave me box numbers with corresponding itemized lists and a shipment code, said I could call the moving agency or the airline during transit to check on the status of my items, but I never saw the camera or the photos." She nodded toward the camera. "Obviously they made it here."

"But you never checked your boxes when they arrived in Hastings?"

"I checked the boxes in storage, but there was no time to go through the contents of every box. I came here to start a new life, not revel in my old one."

"Do you still have the box number?"

"Are you kidding me?"

"What about the company's name?"

"I might be able to have Mike dig it up."

Spearance leaned back. "I was just a kid when I first saw your photos. When did you move here again, exactly?"

It took Lola a minute to conjure up the memory. "1965. Maybe '66."

"So whoever took the pictures must have taken them not long after you arrived. Did you have local help when moving?"

"It was all taken care of by the agency. I'm sure they had locals help instead of driving movers across the country."

"It'd be great if you could get me the name of that company."

Lola crossed her arms. "As much as I appreciate you delving into this mystery, there are more pressing matters at hand. That boy has at least one photo from that camera, possibly more. Two of my friends are dead, and I'm the last one alive."

"You're right." Spearance sighed. "I'm letting my curiosity get the better of me."

"If I survive and you capture that kid, *then* we can try to figure out who took the camera all those years ago. If I die, then it doesn't really matter, does it? I'm the last survivor in the photo he has. The threat ends there."

"Not necessarily." Spearance leaned in. "I've already established that several pictures were taken between '81 and '86. Those pictures we have in evidence. Those people are safe. But I have no idea where this camera had been prior to that. And if what you're telling me is true, then there are quite possibly fifteen years of photography unaccounted for." Spearance picked up the camera. "If Miles does his homework, there's a possibility he could find those photos. If he doesn't, there's still a possibility that a number of photos around Hastings could pose a threat to residents." He put the camera down. "And I'm still not convinced that the photos you remember taking or having are the only ones out there from your time with the camera. Tigerstedt had the camera. Maier had it. Others may have used it as well. But you're right. Priority one is helping you and finding Miles. We can worry about the rest after that. I hope when that time comes, you'll help me."

"*If* that time comes," Lola corrected.

"Don't talk like that." Spearance reached for the mini recorder. "We know that Maier and David's deaths are more than likely associated with the camera, but it's unlikely anyone is going to believe us. Even if they did, the learning curve of involving someone, even if they were to believe, would be difficult to manage. So, we're going to do our best to suggest Miles is responsible for David's death, and we'll do what we can to lead the state police to Miles. Follow my lead once I turn this thing on and we should be all right. State police think we're incompetent. They'll likely want to follow up with a more thorough line of questioning, at which point I suggest you lawyer up."

Lola nodded.

"Before we do this, is there anything else you want to tell me? Anything that might help me steer the interview in the right direction, or a different direction that will help the state police without wrapping this camera into it?"

"Just that you're right. There likely are more photos out there from Maier and Tigerstedt's time with the camera...and from when the camera was in my possession. My memory isn't what it used to be."

"We'll do our best to minimize risk as we move forward. Thanks for being honest." Spearance turned on the mini recorder.

Interview
Lieutenant John Spearance & Subject Bridgette Louise.
April 27th, 1987

LIEUTENANT JOHN SPEARANCE: Can you tell us what happened in the events leading up to David Rothman's passing, yesterday evening?

BRIDGETTE LOUISE: I'm not much for reminiscing, but David is, so we've been watching our old films together. That's how we ended the evening.

LIEUTENANT JOHN SPEARANCE: Let's step back a little further. When did Mr. Rothman arrive at your residence?

BRIDGETTE LOUISE: Two nights ago.

LIEUTENANT JOHN SPEARANCE: Was it a planned trip?

BRIDGETTE LOUISE: Yes. We had planned for me to visit him, but with my health, he thought it better to see me now that winter was over.

LIEUTENANT JOHN SPEARANCE: Okay. Back to the night of the incident. You woke in the bedroom?

BRIDGETTE LOUISE: Yes.

LIEUTENANT JOHN SPEARANCE: There's no television in the bedroom.

BRIDGETTE LOUISE: Well, obviously we turned off the television and went to bed. I locked the door to the bedroom because that boy who broke into my storage shed still hasn't been caught. I told David not to unlock it if he woke up, but the heat from the bedroom doesn't reach the hallway thermostat if you keep the door closed, which causes the heat to run all night. The dry heat is good for my arthritis, but David hates it. I suspect he opened the door once I fell asleep. He's a light sleeper, up off and on through the night, especially if it's warm.

LIEUTENANT JOHN SPEARANCE: Did you wake during the night?

BRIDGETTE LOUISE: No.

LIEUTENANT JOHN SPEARANCE: I want to go back to you two watching the movie. Give me every detail. What you ate. How you were dressed. Everything. Estimated time.

BRIDGETTE LOUISE: We sat down to watch the movie around 5:00pm. We had just eaten dinner. He insists on those boxed...abominations. I certainly hope he doesn't rely on those back in California, the food down there is wonderful, and...I'm rambling. We both ate turkey. The dinners come with peas. Who eats peas? I'm a corn girl, myself, coming from the Midwest...don't we have a shoot scheduled today?

LIEUTENANT JOHN SPEARANCE: No shoot, just the interview.

BRIDGETTE LOUISE: About the film?

LIEUTENANT JOHN SPEARANCE: About David, his passing.

BRIDGETTE LOUISE: He's passed?

LIEUTENANT JOHN SPEARANCE: Yesterday. You were with him. You ate frozen dinners. Turkey. Peas.

BRIDGETTE LOUISE: He liked the peas.

Subject uncontrollably sobs. Recorder turned off at 7:45am.

Recording resumes 8:06am.

LIEUTENANT JOHN SPEARANCE: What happened after dinner?

BRIDGETTE LOUISE: David took the dinners to the trash and carried the garbage down to our can out front. I remember telling him to wait another day because that was our last bag for the week, but it was starting to smell a bit. He took it down. Once he gets something in his head, he's going to do it.

LIEUTENANT JOHN SPEARANCE: What time did you finish dinner?

BRIDGETTE LOUISE: I don't know. We just picked at it for a while. Probably 5:30. Then we finished the movie...almost. We turned it off a few minutes before it was over, a bit before 7:00. I was already wearing my bathrobe, so I didn't have to change. I've been pretty modest with David around. We sleep in the same bed, but I'm usually in my bathrobe—I'll just untie it—and he wears boxer shorts and an undershirt.

LIEUTENANT JOHN SPEARANCE: Anything further you can add to characterize your relationship with Mr. Rothman?

BRIDGETTE LOUISE: We've got along all right since he's been here. It had been years since I'd seen him, though.

LIEUTENANT JOHN SPEARANCE: Were you ever romantically involved?

BRIDGETTE LOUISE: You think I'd let just an acquaintance into my bed? Yes, we were romantically involved, and we still were fond of one another, but we're getting old, and as such the way we express our feelings has changed. But that spark was still there.

LIEUTENANT JOHN SPEARANCE: You mentioned Mr. Rothman was a light sleeper. How do you know this?

BRIDGETTE LOUISE: He's constantly shifting through the night.

LIEUTENANT JOHN SPEARANCE: But you never woke yesterday evening, even among his shifting?

BRIDGETTE LOUISE: Oh, I probably did, just for brief interludes when he turned over, but not for any period of significance.

LIEUTENANT JOHN SPEARANCE: Okay. As far as our local investigation, my line of questioning is over. State troopers will likely have more details for you once they conclude their investigation. In the meantime, I'm not holding you in interrogative detention. You won't be able to return home until they have cleared the scene. I'll need to know where to reach you in case we have more questions.

BRIDGETTE LOUISE: I'll have Mike drive me to Hastings Inn. I'll call out from there so you have a number, but you can always contact the front desk. Once I'm in, I'm in for the night.

Spearance turned off the mini recorder. "Between my feigned incompetence and your banter, I think we're in good shape."

"My banter?"

Spearance smiled. "Sorry, just assumed it was acting."

Lola gathered her coat and headed for the door. "Banter," she whispered to herself. She reached for the camera.

"I'd like to keep that in evidence, if I could."

"That's fine." Her arm fell to her side. "I would like that picture, though."

"Picture?"

"The one you took out of David's hand."

"That's in evidence."

"Your personal repository, perhaps, but you're not turning that over to the troopers. Just like you're not turning that camera over."

"What do you want with that old picture?"

"I'd rather hold my life in my own hands, thank you."

"Fine." Spearance reached into his pocket and handed it to her. "You know they're going to chew me out for letting you go, right?"

"They'd be fools to suspect me. A woman of my size and stature, completely clean from head to toe upon finding him."

"No forced entry. Likely no fingerprints. Blaming you is the only way they'll be able to account for it, but you'll find someone to account for the inconsistencies. Right now they have nothing, and they don't seem to be in a rush to detain you. We'd better both hope they find evidence of foul play with Maier. Then you'll have an alibi here, and we'll be able to connect it to Miles."

"Thank you."

Spearance pocketed the mini recorder and led her out of the room. "No problem."

LOLA

Mike opened the rear passenger-side door for Lola. "Defective seat belt in the front passenger seat. Sorry."

"Are you serious?"

"Just until I get to a dealership. The seat belt mechanism could malfunction."

"We're in town. You don't even need a seat belt." Lola stepped into the back of the car. "This is ridiculous."

Mike closed the door behind her. "Sorry."

"You should have taken care of this when I was with David."

Mike popped the driver-side door open and stepped in. "Just got the notice in the mail. We're only going to the inn anyway. It's, what, a five-minute ride?"

"I need you to stop by the storage unit first."

"State police might be watching it."

"Let them. I have nothing to hide."

"What do you need? I could drop you off and get it for you."

"I'd like to visit myself, thank you."

"All right." Mike turned off Main Street toward Tiernan's Storage.

Lola, bored with the repetitive scenery, tried to make small talk. "So, what have you been up to in my absence?"

"You remember my girlfriend?"

"Denise?"

"Bev."

"What about her?"

"I finally got to meet her parents."

"How'd that go?"

"Better than expected." Mike pulled into Tiernan's Storage, waving as they passed the front office.

"I'm happy for you." She folded her hands on her lap. "I'm sorry I soak up so much of your time. I've grown rather needy in my old age, haven't I?"

Mike stared forward. "You're fine."

"I'm going to try to be a bit more independent." She could see the slight panic in his eyes as he looked at her through the rearview mirror. "Don't worry. Your salary won't be cut. It's just David's return keyed me in on how much I depend on others for things I could otherwise take care of myself."

Mike pulled over in front of her lot.

"Key," she muttered.

Mike took the keys out of the ignition and began sorting through them. "You want me to help you?"

"I'll take care of it, thanks."

After working the key around the ring holder, he handed it over.

"I won't be long." Lola took the key and opened the back door. Slowly, she put her feet on the ground and hoisted herself up onto her frail legs. She started for the unit door, finding that once she began, momentum made it hard to stop. She braced herself against the front door of the unit, unlocked it, then paused to catch her breath.

Her body was failing her. Perhaps choosing to add another set of criteria to her diminishing sources of pride was in poor taste. At least today.

"You okay?"

Mike's words prompted her back to action. "Fine." She tugged at the door. It gave more easily than she anticipated, sliding up with ease. She stepped inside. Where were the photos again? She kept them at the top of her stacks for easy access. As much as she purported to loathe reminiscing, she always liked to keep her history within reach.

She went box by box across the top of her stacks: Yarn—why did she have so much goddamned yarn? Antique silverware—there was something she could easily part with.

She promised herself, as soon as all of this was over, she was going to auction with all of this. She was going to enjoy the fringe benefits of her modest hoarding habit *before* she died, damn it. Who else was there to take on this responsibility?

In the second layer of boxes, Lola found her photographs. Everything sorted through remained in a heap on the right side of the unit, organization be damned.

There was one more thing. She had tucked it in the back of the unit in a small blue bag. In haste, she pushed through the stacks until she reached the box. She opened it and knew, at least for tonight, she'd be safe.

She strung the bag over her shoulder and carried it back to the car with her photos, tossing them on the seat next to her. She sat, trying to catch her breath, finally yielding the key to Mike. "Close up for me."

Mike took the key and locked up, returning to the car in time to see Lola loading a small pistol in the back seat.

"Lola!"

Lola nonchalantly continued loading the chamber. "What?"

Mike reached into the back seat. "Give me that!"

Lola pulled away from him. "I think not."

Mike remained turned in his seat. "Where did you get that?"

"I've had it for years."

"How old are those bullets?"

Lola casually rolled the window down, flipped the chamber back into place, and fired a shot into the ground. She returned the gun to the bag. "Still works."

Mike spoke through gritted teeth. "Damn it, Lola! Give me that gun!"

She raised the gun, pointing it at him. "Take me to my room."

"Not before you give me that gun."

"You'll take me to my room. You will leave me there. And I'll be keeping the gun."

"That's not going to happen!"

"Michael. Drive the damned car."

Mike turned to the steering wheel and started the car. "I can't believe you had a gun all these years."

"You're barely past adolescence. There's a lot you don't know about me. Even more, I suspect, you don't know about the world."

"There's no reason for insult." Mike pulled away from Lola's unit. "Great. Nathan's out front of the office. Probably heard the shot." He stopped at the front entrance and rolled down his window. "Sorry about that."

"Was that gunfire?"

Lola nodded. "I didn't realize it was loaded."

"I know it's against policy," Mike began.

"I'm sure we can make an exception for Ms. Louise." He tipped his mesh-backed baseball cap to greet her. "Ma'am."

She waved daintily. "Thank you, sir."

"Thanks." Mike rolled up his window and pulled away. "Laying it on a bit thick, don't you think?"

"On the contrary. It was one of my most modest performances to date. Have you ever seen a silent film?"

Mike rolled his eyes, leaving the question unanswered.

Lola smiled, opening the box of photographs. Judging from the pile, it'd take a while to find any that might have been generated by the camera. But if they were there, she wanted them, preferably with Spearance for safe keeping. As soon as she was done, she'd let him know what she found. In the meantime, she had her gun. She shuffled through them quickly, starting with a spot check.

Mike pulled into the inn parking lot. "You already reserve a room?"

Lola closed the lid on her photos. "I thought I asked you to?"

Mike stepped out of the car. "I'll do it now," he muttered to himself.

Lola pushed open her door and caught him at the door.

"Is there a safety on that thing at least?" Mike whispered as they stepped inside.

"No."

Mike glared at her.

The woman at the front desk smiled. "Can I help the two of you?"

"We need a double for—"

"Jamie—" She paused for a moment. She couldn't use the full name of another silent actress. "Craig," she finally settled on.

"Double bed," Mike added.

"Okay, Ms. Craig, and how many days will you be staying with us?"

"Two, I would imagine." She looked at Mike for reassurance.

He nodded.

"Ground floor okay?"

"That's fine." Lola grabbed her box of photos off the counter. "Get the key."

Mike took the key from the receptionist and followed her. "I only have clothes for one night."

"You're not staying."

"I think I should."

"I have my gun, and I have some things I need to take care of."

Mike stopped in the middle of the hallway. "You're going to..." He took a few steps closer, whispered, "You're *not* going to kill yourself, are you?!"

Lola rolled her eyes. "You really don't know much about me, do you?"

"Why are you so adamant that I leave, then?"

Lola stopped in front of her room. "Open the door." Once inside, she set the box of photos and her bag on a counter near the door. "I'm not going to kill myself, Michael."

Mike walked to the windows, peered out. "There's another set of parking spaces right outside your window. I could stay in the car. Just a shout away."

Lola stared at him, mulling over his suggestion. "Fine. But you don't come knocking unless I flag you from the window. Got it?"

Mike nodded. "Fine. Fine."

"You're really worried about that paycheck, aren't you?"

Mike braced her shoulders. "I worry about you, Lola."

She shrugged him off. "Go sit in your car."

"You sure you're okay?"

Lola took off her coat and slung it over a chair near the windows. "I'm fine."

Mike walked toward the door, head bowed in resignation.

"Mike?"

He turned.

"If anything happens, don't call Spearance. Go directly to him."

"You sure you're okay?"

Lola waved him off.

Once the door was closed, Lola took the gun and the photographs to the bed. She set the gun beside her and opened the box, resolving to start with two piles. Normal photos on the floor. Photos from the camera on the bed beside her.

***

By early evening, Lola had managed to find all of two photos she suspected might be from the camera, more than she had wanted to find. These were photos she had no recollection of. They pre-dated the photo she had from Tigerstedt's mansion and included several of his waitstaff, herself, and Maier. Again, she was likely the only one alive in the photos.

Once she had sorted through the entire box, she gathered the photos on the floor and returned them to the counter by the door. She turned on the bedside lamp, turned the overhead lights off, and went to the curtain. She parted it to look into the parking lot.

There was Mike, in one of the spaces opposite her room, waving maniacally. She closed the curtains again without waving.

Damned kid.

She lay on the bed, turned off the lamp, and took the two photos into her hand. She ran her hands across the first, closed her eyes, and heard something shuffle near the window.

She sat upright. *Mike?*

She peered into the shadow.

Not Mike, but somebody.

"Who are you?"

"*Where* am I?"

Lola slid across the bed away from the figure. "Somewhere you're not supposed to be."

"Bridgette Louise?"

"Who are you?!" she demanded as she stood opposite the wall.

"Just a fan." He took a step toward her. "What year is it?"

Lola crawled back onto the bed, scrambling for her gun. The figure did not move. She held it toward him, clutching the photos in her other hand. "Don't take another step."

He remained in place. "What year is it?"

"1987."

She could barely make out the smile that crept across his face. "It's good to be back."

"I'll shoot, I swear."

"I have no doubt you would." He raised his hands in submission, revealing a photo in his right hand. "I'm not here to hurt you. I'd just like to know more about the camera that produced this photograph." He waved the photograph in his hand, then looked behind him. "And how I got here." He smiled. "I noticed the camera in a documentary initially, a picture of you and Tigerstedt with it, but there's no mention of it in your autobiography, and there's no record of model or make anywhere. It's a one-of-a-kind piece."

Lola tried to focus on the photos in her hand. If he lunged at her, she could fire, but she'd need an escape route, and the photos in hand were closer than the door. But what if she was wrong, and they weren't from the camera? What then?

He lowered his hands slowly. "I'm a bit obsessed with photography. I'd like to add the camera to my collection."

"I don't know where it is."

He squeezed the photo in his hand, causing Lola to drop her gun. She dipped for it, but he squeezed again. "Ah ah. Stand up."

She rose against the wall.

"It's true, isn't it? The camera that destroyed the industry. Was it cursed?"

Lola rubbed the surface of the photo in her hand and closed her eyes. "I don't know what you're talking about."

"For the longest time I thought it was just a coverup, a myth you created to avoid blame for burning down the studio while on one of your petulant benders."

"No," Lola muttered.

"Maier talked." He reached into his pocket and pulled out a knife. "I don't need a confession if you're unwilling. But I need to know where the camera is."

"Nobody knows. I checked my storage unit after you broke in, but it was gone. We thought you had it!"

"We?"

"The police know. They're looking for you after what you did to David."

Miles took the knife and drew it across the image. Blood began to run from Lola's arm.

She rubbed the photo harder, keeping her eyes closed.

Nothing. It had to be from a different camera.

She dropped the first photo and clutched the second. *Please work.*
Miles raised the knife against the photo again.

Please, God. Lola closed her eyes, leaned against the wall, and felt that all too familiar sinking feeling.

Miles sliced the photo once more, bringing her back into the moment. "I always work through photography. Photographs are vision temporally delimited. Each photograph signifies an eternity—the eternity of a single state which can never be duplicated in reality, only re-presented. Like the silent film cuts implying death, photographs too provide a key to memories of actions. But the direct way the photograph prompts rekindling of a memory allows for all the distinct sensual and cognitive flavors to return in accompaniment. The guilt, the simultaneous paroxysm shared between victim and aggressor, the rush of the kill, etc. All aspects remain.

"Your body has been my canvas numerous times over the years. I'd like to show you my work." He reached into his pocket and pulled out a small stack of photos. He tossed them on the bed.

Lola looked down at the pictures, all of them featuring her body, mangled, torn limb from limb, mutilated in a multitude of ways. All so real.

He smiled. "Every new person we meet is like film we impress fragments of our identity upon. The photograph is the extension of their identification with you. So many selves in the world watching so many recreations of other selves. It's hard to say whether or not garnering a true, singular identity is even possible, as we begin to obscure our own the very moment we try to concretize it in society. We rethink our representations, change them and experiment on others. Meanwhile we're leaving the byproduct of previous social experimentation to fester in people's minds, as it is impossible to un-create the flawed aspects of self we have already revealed to the world.

"Ultimately, while we may immortalize the self we believe we are, the other selves are immortalized as well. Our development, our humanity, and thus our weakness, is immortalized as is our strength. Either we can anticipate exploitation and embrace our weaknesses or erase the immortalized past. Or we can re-create ourselves by remaining invisible, preparing to project ourselves outward into society once and becoming invisible again—build up one big statement and explode like a dying star."

Lola continued rubbing the photo, now afraid to take her eyes off Miles as he approached. "What are you talking about?"

"Once I find that camera, and figure out how to erase you like you erased that studio, I'll show the world my work. The ideal you." He spread the pictures out, revealing the plethora of gore in its full splendor. "But I want you to pick. Which one is your favorite?"

Lola leaned in to look at the photos, dropped to the floor, and grabbed the gun.

By the time Miles reacted, Lola had already raised the gun. A shot rang out, catching Miles in the shoulder. He dropped everything. Almost as quickly, Lola dropped the gun and took the photo he had used to cut her and ran for the bathroom, locking the door behind her. She fell against the wall, finally able to catch her breath, and begin processing the situation. How much time did she have? Mike had to have heard the gunshot. He'd come for her. In the meantime...the gun! She'd forgotten the gun. But she had the photos, both the photo she had found and the photo Miles had likely used to butcher Maier and David.

A gunshot burst through the bathroom door.

She had to get out. She just needed to disappear until Mike showed up. She looked at the photo Miles had dropped. The lacerations confirmed what she had suspected. This was his instrument of torture. She couldn't go back there.

She reached for the other photo and closed her eyes, ignoring another gunshot. That was it. She'd only put four bullets in the chamber; one she'd expelled at the storage area. She let her body go limp, except this time the sinking sensation didn't end. She was falling. She ignored the impulse to spring forward. The sound of Miles banging against the bathroom grew more and more distant, then she was there. In the past. In the photograph surrounded by Tigerstedt and his waitstaff.

MILES

With one final burst of his good shoulder, Miles finally rammed himself through the bathroom door.

The room was empty.

He sliced through the shower curtain, tearing it from the rod above.

Lola was gone.

His eyes scanned the room, finally resting on the two photos Lola had carried with her. She was like him. She must be. She must have escaped into one of the images.

He tried to catch his breath. He could do this. He'd have to try to follow her.

Someone knocked at the door. "Lola?!"

Miles stared at the two photos, uncertain of which to choose when one of the waitstaff in Lola's picture caught his eye. If Lola hadn't escaped there, he'd bide his time with the women in the photo until he could emerge and find her.

He dropped the other photo on the floor, closed his eyes, and fell inside.

CHAPTER FOURTEEN

LOLA

EVEN AS SHE adjusted to the moment, Lola was still trying to cycle through her next steps. If this photo pre-dated the one still in the motel, she might end up right back where she was. She hoped Michael had heard the struggle and come to check on her, but she had no way of confirming. However, one thing she was certain of was that Miles wasn't going to kill her, not yet. Despite her plea of ignorance, Miles didn't believe her, and rightfully so. She knew at least some information valuable to him, and would forfeit that information to stall him if she had to.

But all of these concerns were lower-order at the moment. The most immediate reality was that Miles might enter the image she did, which threatened her outside of the scope of any protection that existed in the outside world. As such, she did what anyone would do in such a circumstance. She ran.

Tigerstedt followed after her. "When I declared my intention to pursue you, this is not what I meant!" he panted.

"Why not make a sport of it?" she chided, continuing toward the hotel.

"I'll be out of breath by the time we make it inside," he called after her.

"Do you think you'll need your breath for something other than running once we are indoors?" Even in the heat of the moment, when escape was priority, she relished the feeling of her legs burning with the modest burden of carrying her light frame. "I'm not that easy." She feigned laughter then, allowing elation to struggle to the surface. Almost there.

She turned back to watch the scenery where the picture had

originally been taken. The waitstaff had cleared. The field was empty. Miles was nowhere in sight.

She climbed the steps to the dining hall and stepped inside to catch her breath. She scanned the building floor by floor, trying to conjure up a memory—or lack thereof—of a room she hadn't previously seen, some place within that she knew she'd never had her picture taken in. But she'd been everywhere. Likely photographed everywhere...except the basement.

As Tigerstedt's pace slowed to a crawl, he topped the stairs. "You never told me you ran."

"I don't." She put her arm under his and mock propped him up. "I just control my appetite." She slapped him on the belly.

"So," Tigerstedt panted. "Where to?"

"Show me the basement."

He looked at her quizzically. "Why? A sudden interest in soiled bedding, or the inner workings of our furnace perhaps?"

"Just show me."

"Very well." Tigerstedt guided her through the dining hall to the rear hallway. The corridor led to a small kitchen, inside of which one door to the basement could be found. "Come on then." He guided her down the stairs, flipping a switch at the bottom to reveal the four by four columns holding the hotel in place. "Here we are."

The first thing that struck Lola was the smell, like the outer layer of brie. She found it oddly favorable, especially when weighed against what she anticipated she'd smell. "It's quaint."

"Be honest with me, Lola." Tigerstedt turned her to himself. "Are you here to reminisce about the past, or escape the present?"

His question caught her off guard. "What?"

"You were running, possibly toward, but more than likely away from, something."

"I just wanted to see the basement."

"What year is it, out there?" Tigerstedt smiled. "How long have I been...gone?"

"I don't understand."

Tigerstedt unraveled the scarf around his neck, revealing a thick gash across his throat. "It's me. The *real* me, not some facsimile you've conjured up through your photographic projection."

Lola turned her face away from the wound.

Tigerstedt, sensing her discomfort, covered his neck. "Sorry."

"How?" She clarified, "How are you here?"

"I always suspected these images would harbor a soul. I tried for years throughout my forties to come here for good, but once I saw that I never changed, that my youth was preserved inside the images, my sense of urgency diminished, until I felt myself dying."

Lola ran her open palm down his cheek, felt the contours of his face. Tigerstedt. Her wise man. The only man she could truly call a friend. "It's really you?"

He nodded. "I was wondering if you'd ever come back."

"Do you know who"—she adjusted the scarf on his neck to fully cover the wound—"cut you?"

"No." He sighed heavily. "It may not even have been intentional. Intent doesn't figure into the photos, I've found." He placed a hand on the small of her back and guided her forward. "Had I known back then, I would have never taken the pictures. I put us all in danger, and for that I'm truly sorry."

"You didn't know."

He eyed her cynically. "I invented the camera. At best I had a vague notion." He opened the door to the laundry room and stepped inside.

"Why did you create it?"

He ran his hand through her hair. His touch was tender, accepting of unrequited love. For years she had resolved to settle with Tigerstedt if things didn't work out with David. But it felt so unfair to him, settling. Instead, all three of them spent their lives alone. "Because I could. Because I wanted to impress you."

"How did you create it?"

"That's a secret I'll take to my grave, should I ever die, that is. I can't have anyone attempting to reproduce what happened here." He let his hands fall to his side. "Do you still have it? The camera?"

She shook her head. "It's in good hands."

"It'd be best left dashed to bits and in the hands of Mother Earth."

"I would have destroyed it years ago, but I guess I'd always hoped there was a way to reverse the effects. Is there—"

"—What's done is done."

"What about the pictures? If we destroy the camera, will they lose their power?"

"I suspect not." He turned from the laundry room, working his way back through the wooden pillars in the wine cellar. "But we can take solace in knowing that its legacy ends with us."

"Yes," she lied. "There's that."

Applause reverberated through the upstairs.

"What was that?"

"Maier, most likely, causing the women to swoon through photograph."

Lola rolled her eyes. "God, he was such a pervert."

"I wonder what's become of his photos?"

Lola shook her head. "That's outside of my purview."

Tigerstedt looked up as another round of applause echoed through the basement. "Your time here's almost up. Tell me, how long has it been? How long have I been gone?"

"It's 1987...out there."

"So much has changed, I'm sure." He embraced her. "Promise me you'll come back, regale me with tales of the future."

Tears welled up in her eyes, threatening to spill over onto her makeup. She didn't know if she'd be back, or even survive the next few minutes once she left the image. "Of course."

"Goodbye again, Lola."

She closed her eyes, and clung to him as she felt herself slipping. "Goodbye."

The damp warmth of Tigerstedt's basement then transitioned to Hastings' cool spring breeze. The applause replaced by a cascade of cardboard boxes, and Tigerstedt's embrace replaced by solitude.

She opened her eyes and found herself in her storage unit. She looked down at the boxes, finding she had materialized amidst them. One box lay open, tilted on its side, a cornucopia of random relics spilled onto the cement floor. She bent down to sort through the contents, finding one picture at the base of the pile, a collection of bystanders wooed by Maier's antics. Lola found herself in the midst of the crowd. She picked up the photograph and knocked over neighboring boxes, allowing the contents to spill around her until she found one of her photo albums. She opened the album, tucked the photo behind one of the pages, using her fingers as a placeholder, then flipped back several pages. If Miles was following her, she needed to stall him. Misdirection was all she could muster at the moment.

She held the picture between thumb and forefinger and fell toward the album, through it, and into the past once more.

MIKE

By the time the second shot had fired through the outer wall of Lola's room, Mike was already at the front door of her room with the receptionist in tow. He toggled the doorknob as she caught up. No luck. He turned to see the key already extended in the receptionist's hand. As soon as he took them, she skulked to the nearest exit and watched from the edge of the threshold.

Mike inserted the key, turned the knob, and pushed the door open. It was a reckless move, one that luckily paid off, or at least didn't cost him his life.

The first thing he noticed was the bathroom door. Knocked off the top hinge and warped at the base. He stepped in and lifted the door from atop the toilet. Nobody was there.

He peered around the corner quickly into the deeper area of the room. It also appeared empty. He rounded the corner and checked the wall nearest the bed, then looked over the edge of the bed onto the floor. He kicked the bed frame to make sure there was no opening beneath the bed. It was completely boxed in as he'd remembered from his last stay. "Room's clear," he shouted into the hallway.

The receptionist walked to the doorway. "Is she okay?"

Mike noticed one of Lola's nudes on the floor near the bed. She was mangled, almost unrecognizable save the cropping of her pubic hair, which had been left unscathed. "She's gone."

"I'll call the police." The receptionist ran down the hallway toward the front desk. This was Mike's chance to play cleanup. He started with the photo on the floor, then ran for Lola's coat, rifling through the pockets for any additional bullets she might have had. Inside he found a photograph of Lola, her companion, and several others. No bullets.

He took the photograph and ran to the bathroom, where two more photographs sat on the floor under the broken door. He collected these as well, tucked them into the front of his pants, and headed for the front desk. The receptionist was still on the line.

He pointed toward the exit. "I'm heading to the station to make a statement."

"They're on their—"

Mike was already out the door before she could finish. He turned the stereo down to listen for police sirens and drove down Main Street to the local station. He all but crawled the 2.5 miles, courtesy of three traffic lights that seemed hell-bent on grinding traffic to a halt. He tapped the dashboard anxiously, watching the rearview for flashing lights. As if his stare summoned them, the lights rounded the corner in the distance, sirens still silent. He watched them approach, attempting to coax the light green. "Come on!" he whispered.

The police were close enough now to see the state car colors. Mike rubbed at the photos under his shirt, looked down to make sure they weren't visible. Then the police car turned into the hotel, the light turned green, and Mike relaxed.

The last leg of the short journey found Mike speeding into the department driveway and bolting for the front door.

Spearance stood over the desk with another deputy. "Mike?"

He closed the door behind him. "I need to talk to you."

Spearance excused himself. "Come into the office."

Mike stepped in, waited for Spearance to close the door, and tossed the photos on the table. "Lola's missing. You need to put these in evidence."

Spearance picked up the photos. "What's going on?"

"I think that kid found her. She insisted I wait outside her room, said she'd be fine. I heard a gunshot not ten minutes ago, but by the time I got inside she was gone. Bathroom door was busted off the hinges. There's no way she could have done that herself."

"Jesus." Spearance ran the photos to the neighboring room, handed the photos off to Jim. "Put those in the cold case folder and lock it up."

Jim thumbed through the pictures. "Thought we already had these?"

Spearance headed back to his office. "Lock 'em up." He closed his door and sat down opposite Mike. "Where'd the gun come from?"

"It was hers. She had it in storage, apparently."

"Was there any blood?"

"Just in the picture, like before."

"Nothing on the floor?"

Mike shook his head.

"I hope she's okay."

Mike ran the heel of his palms across his eyes. "I should have stayed in the room with her."

"We should have kept her here." Spearance sat up. "But I still think there's something she's not telling me, something she's too stubborn to let us take care of for her."

"Like what?"

"I think she knows how to find Miles. I don't know if those pictures are like divining rods or what, but she was adamant that I give her the photo...and the gun. If she wanted protection she would have asked you to stay in the room. I think she knew how to find him and wanted to face him alone."

"Fits her stubborn disposition."

"I'll send—"

"John!" Jim called from the neighboring room. "We've got a—uh, a situation over here."

Spearance and Mike ran for the neighboring room, the clatter of evidence boxes compounding their urgency.

Spearance turned the knob and pushed against the door, which was reluctant to give. "What's going on?!"

"Hang on!" Jim shouted. His voice shifted to a milder tone. "Come on. Let's get you up."

Spearance pushed gently against the door and found the source of resistance no longer in place. He and Mike spilled into the room. And there, seated at the table Jim had been occupying, was Lola.

"You've got to be kidding me." Spearance rolled his eyes. "She was in the car with you the whole time." He turned to Mike. "Did you even bother to look in the back seat?"

Jim shook his head. "She just appeared."

Spearance turned to Lola. "How did you get here?"

"It's best that I show you." She pointed toward the evidence box on the floor, fingers trembling. "Can you get my photos for me?"

Spearance brought the box to the table. Lola set them down side by side, closed her eyes, and ran her hand across the image of her and Tigerstedt.

"What are you doing?" Spearance asked.

She ignored him. The slipping came less easy in her weakened state. As such, she needed all of her faculties to make the transition. She felt the pull and relaxed.

Then she was gone.

Spearance took off his hat and rubbed his scalp vigorously. "Jesus." He turned away from the table. "This shit just gets weirder and weirder." When he turned back, Lola was at the table again.

Spearance shook his head. "Out with it. Get me up to speed here."

Lola stacked the photos neatly atop one another. "Remember how we told you the camera reacts differently to everyone?"

"Yes."

"This is how it reacts with me."

"So the pictures make you disappear?"

"I disappear *into* them, yes."

"This is how you ended up at your storage unit a few weeks back?"

Lola nodded.

"This information would have been very helpful."

"I know. I'm sorry."

"Why didn't you tell me?"

"I didn't want to involve you on this level."

"Okay, well, now we have the state police at your motel room, thinking you were kidnapped, or worse, possibly killed, and we have to somehow explain to them how you ended up here."

"I'm not staying." Lola reached for the photos. "That boy—Miles—he was in the room with me. I think he's like me."

"That doesn't explain how he got into your room."

Lola rearranged the photos on the desk. "You can travel through the images chronologically." She pointed to the image of her and Tigerstedt. "Go in here." She pointed to the image of herself, David, Maier, and Tigerstedt. "Come out here."

"So you're going to go back in? Risk him finding you?"

Lola shook her head. "I'm going forward. He's trailing me."

"So eventually he'll end up here."

"Not if you catch him first."

"So where should we check next?"

"My storage unit."

"And then?"

"And then I ended up here."

"Okay." Spearance paced the room. "I just have a few questions."

"Boss?"

Spearance looked up.

Lola was gone.

"Damn it." Spearance squeezed the bridge of his nose with his thumb and forefinger. "Let me think here." He paused in the center of the room. "Jim, you're staying here with Mike and the photos. If Miles 'materializes,' apprehend him. We'll figure out a plausible explanation later."

Bo shrugged. "Why not just put the photos in our cell?"

"Because he'll just dive back into the pictures." Spearance opened the door and peered into the main room. "Bo, I want you watching Molly's place."

Bo grabbed his keys. "All right. Anything I should tell her."

"Just tell her I want you there until we've got Miles in custody."

Bo saluted from the doorway. "Will do."

Jim sat back in his chair, still staring forward at the empty spot where Lola had been. "John?" He continued staring blankly. "What the *fuck* just happened?"

Spearance headed for the door. "That's what I'm going back to my office to try to figure out."

"Lola said we should check the storage area."

"State trooper station number is on Bo's desk. Be my guest." He closed the door behind him. "Give me five, please."

MILES

He'd entered the image to an emptied field, with the doors of Tigerstedt's hotel locked. Just as he began to fade into the present, he'd thought he heard the sound of clapping, but when he opened his eyes, he found himself confined to a place all too familiar. The disheveled contents suggested he had mistaken the clatter of boxes around him for applause.

What a mess.

The room was poorly lit, given approaching dusk, but there was enough light remaining to guide him to the album on the floor, which he must have found his way into the unit through. He knelt down to close the album. He knew this one well. A collection of stills from *Everyman*, and a few old tin photos, none of which appeared to stem from the camera he'd been seeking. He picked up the album and set it atop the undisturbed boxes in the rear of the small unit, noting a photo hanging from the edge of the album, tucked behind another photo.

Lola had been here.

She'd tried to hide the photo from him in case he emerged here like her.

Whatever was happening to him now, she also experienced. She seemed familiar with the phenomenon, familiar enough to know what would happen if he pursued her. Familiar enough to try to obscure her trail, or slow him down. It was a game of cat and mouse in which she hadn't lost hope, and he had grown despondent.

He was tired of chasing her already, and there was a very real possibility she was setting a trap for him. His naiveté would be his undoing if he proceeded.

In lieu of continuing the search—in lieu of pleading with her for the whereabouts of the camera—he'd decided to chip away at her morale, one slice at a time, until she yielded the camera to him or until she bled out, at which point he'd follow the sirens to her hiding place and find her nest of sentimentals.

He just needed to get back to his car.

He rattled the storage door from the inside. It was locked.

Scratch that.

First he needed to get out, preferably as discreetly as possible.

He looked around the room, finding nothing to help him pry his way out, and she'd already secured the pistol. He thought back on his inventory of the room. What would help him get out? She had golf clubs somewhere. The door was aluminum. With some work it might come loose from the casing. It'd be loud though.

With nothing else to work with, Miles settled on the clubs. He struck at the lower corner of the door. The clang reverberated through the room.

He struck again. And again. As many times in rapid succession as he could to hasten his escape.

It was useless.

He was too weak to get out.

He slammed the club against the door again, this time in frustration, then sat back against the far wall and took the picture in his hand. He closed his eyes, submitting to the possibility of being trapped. He was already, in a less ominous capacity.

A knock at the door interrupted him. "Someone in there?"

Miles took the club and dragged it across the floor until reaching the door. He tapped at it gently, trying to emulate the sound of a small rodent.

"Who's there?" he heard from the other side.

He rose to his feet as the sound of keys rang from the other side of the door. He pulled the golf club back in anticipation of the door opening. When it did, he did not wait to see who waited on the other side. He swung downward, again and again. Nathan's skull gave way much faster than the door, and by the time Miles stopped, Nathan's head had begun to meld with the thawing ground, a palette of red, flesh tones, and now, a thick grey with specks of white.

Miles dropped the club beside Nathan and took in the night air, savoring it as much as the kill. This emboldened him. Lola had her years with the camera, but death, that was new to her. He, on the other hand, had become a patron of this fine art, and learned the craft rather quickly. He pocketed the photo from Lola's album, and followed the roadway to the graveyard. The walk was short, the darkness punctuated by the lights on the horizon. As Miles walked up the hill to the graveyard, he already knew what those lights meant, and he confirmed it at the top. The police had found his car.

He turned to walk back down the hill, out of town. As he ambled down the shoulder of the road, he pulled the picture out of his pocket. He took his knife in his other hand and drew it across Lola's face. A light mark, just enough to let her know he was still with her.

CHAPTER FIFTEEN

LOLA

"YOU NEED TO keep your eyes open." Laughter echoed across a vast landscape. "And hold still!"

Lola turned her head to the hand squeezing hers and opened her eyes. She followed the hand up the arm of a navy-blue sport jacket, knowing already it was David. But it was too much to look him in the eyes, knowing that he'd passed only yesterday.

"You okay, Lola?"

"I'm fine."

He put the back of his hand under her chin and tilted her upward to face him. "I mean, out there."

She stopped averting her eyes and faced him, expecting deep wounds echoing those in the real world, hoping for his perfect face, preserved in all its youthful splendor. Instead, she found an ivory mask, a faux skin highlighted with a faint palette of makeup. It made him look even more dead than she remembered.

She recoiled at the mask, struggling against him as he grabbed her gently. "It's just a stage prop."

"Why are you wearing that thing?!"

"What's beneath is far worse." He looked down at Lola's hand in his, ran his fingers across hers. "You're still safe." He hugged her.

She went limp in his arms from shock, unable to reciprocate.

"Have they caught him yet?" he asked, still holding her.

"No." Finally, the shock subsided and the appropriate social courtesy registered. She wrapped her arms around him. "What happened?"

"I went in alone." He stepped away from her, hands still on her waist. "When I got up, he was in the apartment. I tried to wake you. I'm sorry."

"You should have called the police."

"And what if he came back while we waited?" He let his arms fall away from her waist. "Out there, I was weak and emaciated. Here, I'm strong. Here, we have the home advantage."

"He still got you."

"He had one of the pictures with him. I didn't know you could bring them with you."

"You can't." She paused. "I can't."

"How long has it been?"

Lola shook her head. "Everyone keeps asking me that." She met his eyes. "It's only been a day."

"I'm sorry."

"Stop apologizing." She took his hand and guided him toward the house.

"You can't possibly be thinking what I'm thinking."

She closed her eyes and pulled at his hand. "I just want to see myself like this one last time."

He followed her up the stairs, into the house, past the guests, and to her room. She closed the door behind them. She let his hand go as she passed the threshold and walked to the vanity on the right side of the room. She sat down in the chair and stared at herself. "I was beautiful," she said.

David hovered behind her. "You are beautiful."

She smiled. "Here, yes."

"Out there as well." He placed his hand on her shoulder. "You've aged so gracefully, and you're just as headstrong as you ever were."

She placed her hand over his, inviting his warmth.

"I should have asked for your hand in marriage."

"Stop." She slapped at his hand gently. "I know what you're up to. There's no time."

"I've likely lost too much blood for that anyway." He sighed. "I'm speaking directly from the heart."

"Your heart kept me at arm's length for nearly three decades."

"My heart? I believe that was another organ." He bent down and draped his arms over her shoulders. "Now that he's out of the way, or at the very least non-respondent, I see how foolish I had been."

She let her head loll into the crook of his arm. "You're a good man, David. I would have said yes, you know."

"I know."

She remained nestled in his arms, eyes closed, when she felt the skin split in a thin sliver across her cheek. She looked into the mirror. Blood trickled from a small cut.

David looked up, noting her distraction.

Lola wiped away the first layer of blood gathering at the lower edge of the cut.

David tried to pull her to her feet. "You have to go."

Lola squirmed against him. "There's nowhere else to go. This was the last photo."

He loosened his grasp. "There was one more."

Another cut ran across her face. Though deep, they were surprisingly painless. "It never developed properly."

She felt another cut across her abdomen. She looked down to confirm the depth of the wound to find her dress soaked with blood, her entrails tight against the weave of her dress. "You don't imagine they have something in wardrobe for this, do you?"

David gasped.

Tigerstedt knocked on the door, entering without permission. He held the camera up. "May I?"

Lola turned toward him in the chair. David stood behind her, hand on her shoulder. "Go ahead."

Tigerstedt raised the camera and snapped the final photo. The camera attempted to release the image, to no avail. Tigerstedt shook the camera, slapped its side. "That's strange."

Lola looked up at David. "Told you."

David squeezed her shoulder. "Welcome home." He leaned into the back of the chair and bent down to hug her again when she disappeared from his arms.

MOLLY

One more trip. This was the last one. Jolie promised. Molly adjusted the heat and began the trip home *again*. She was tired of driving. It was only a few miles, but time ground to a halt every time she had to go back home.

She was tired of excuses. "It's only a few blocks," only goes so far when your mother is half snapped and you're left making all the trips, carting all of the forgotten items to and fro.

She was just tired, but this time the trip was important. Her mother had forgotten Jolie's EpiPens, and wanted to make stuffed shells for dinner. The egg was almost always undercooked—as it should be in a good recipe for stuffed shells—and Jolie wasn't going to turn them down, even if it meant a bout of full-on anaphylactic shock.

She pulled into the driveway, turning the radio down when she noticed one of the Hastings Police vehicles in the driveway. She pulled up beside it and peered across her car at Bo.

Fucking Bo Durham. Class clown, incessant horn dog...the last person she wanted to see right now.

She rolled her eyes and stepped out of the vehicle. "Getting pretty desperate for a date these days, waiting in my driveway like this."

He rolled down his window. "Very funny." He leaned out of the patrol car. "I suppose I deserve that." He looked her up and down. "You can't blame me though, being as beautiful as you are."

She cocked her head to the side. "You're not really here to ask me out again, are you?"

"Spearance asked me to keep an eye on the house. They think Miles is in town again, and they want to make sure anyone involved in the case is safe."

"I'm just here to pick up some things for my daughter before heading back over to my mother's."

"You want me to come with?"

She looked back. "I'm fine."

Molly unlocked the door, stepped inside, and drew a blank. "What am I here for?" she asked herself. She looked around the room for something to key in her memory; then she noticed Jolie's sky-blue pack on the dining room table. "EpiPens." Once she picked them up, she tried to cycle through the list of potential items Jolie would ask for once the sugar high her mother was sustaining with chocolate cherries wore off. That's what this was all about, after all. Not the EpiPens. Not the stuffed animals from the last trip. It was all about the hidden stock of candy her mother had been feeding her every time Molly left the house.

She cycled through a few items that didn't necessitate another trip, then settled on children's Tylenol and some all-natural cough syrup for toddlers in the event that Jolie ended up with a fever. She threw the Tylenol and cough syrup into her purse, turned, and stopped. What was that sound? She froze, listening for the faucet, or the faint scrape of mice preparing nests in the attic insulation, then shrugged it off.

When she reached the hallway, she heard it again. This heavy scratching, prefigured by a thud. She stopped at the stairs and listened. It was too loud to be a mouse. Maybe a grey squirrel. She remembered her grandfather having a run-in with one of those one particularly cold Pennsylvania winter.

THUD!

That. That was no grey squirrel.

Molly ran down the stairs to the front door and, too afraid to reveal herself in the driveway for fear that someone might be in the attic with a gun—she'd spent a lot of time thinking about home invasion—waved Bo inside.

He stared down at something in his lap.

"Bo!" she shouted in the most hushed tone she could audibly render. "Bo! Goddamn it!"

Finally he looked up, set whatever was in his lap on the passenger seat, and ran to the front door. "What's up?"

She continued in whisper. "I think somebody's upstairs."

He took out his gun, letting it hang at his side. "Stay behind me. I'll enter rooms and round corners before you. You wait for my clear." He started up the stairs. They creaked underfoot, even through carpeting her grandfather had put down years prior. "Damn, that's loud," Bo whispered. "I hope there's no other way for them to get out."

"Only through a window."

Bo continued up the stairs, checking the second floor room-by-room.

There was nothing.

THUD!

"That's what I'm talking about!" Molly pointed toward the ceiling.

"You have an attic?"

Fuck. Not the attic.

Her mind knee-jerked to the impending. *This is it*, she thought, then immediately dismissed the thought. Sure, the attic was a source of bad memories, but it wasn't that general dread that followed her everywhere. She'd built the momentum up to such a degree over the years that there was practically nothing in her mind she could dredge up to match the terror she'd instilled herself with through anxiety accumulated over the years.

Molly nodded and waved him toward the drop stairs. She tugged at the pull cord until the stairs fell into place. "Go ahead."

Bo unfastened his flashlight and handed it to her. "You know the way."

She took it from him and slapped him in the gut with it before taking the first step. "Thanks, Bo."

THUD!

Bo stood behind her. "Maybe we ought to call John. Get a few more men."

Molly pointed to the stairs. "Stop being such a pussy. Come on."

Bo swallowed and took the first step. And the next. When he reached the top, he turned toward the long end of the attic.

Molly had already made her way across the room. "Who's there?!" She waited for a response, then peered into the darkness.

Bo started toward her. "You see anything?"

Molly shined her light across the far end of the room. "It's empty."

THUD!

"Doesn't sound empty." Bo swallowed again. "Got a spare bulb anywhere?"

Molly handed him the flashlight, jogged to her bedroom, unscrewed the bulb from her nightstand lamp, and brought it to him. "Here."

"I don't know where the outlet is."

Molly ascended the stairs again, wondering what the weight limit on the stairs were. "Get on the floor up there."

"All right! All right!" Bo climbed up onto the floor and turned to help Molly up. Once she was on the floor, she dusted herself off and followed the wall to the outlet. "Shine your light over here."

Bo turned the flashlight toward her. She screwed in the new bulb with no effect.

THUD!

"Jesus! Where is that coming from?"

"It sounds like it's in the floorboards."

Bo shined his flashlight along the floor. The light poured into the insulation between the floorboards.

THUD!

"It's by the window," Molly said.

They followed the sound with Bo's flashlight snailing across the floor until movement corresponded with sound.

THUD!

"I see something!" Bo dragged the light across the boards. Molly leaned in.

Shoes...

Clothing...a dress.

"Might have used it for insulation," Bo mused.

"Something's moving down there. Give me the flashlight."

Bo handed Molly the flashlight and she knelt down, shining the flashlight directly into the opening between the boards. As she moved closer she heard the distinct sound of wheezing. "Oh God." She leaned in closer.

"Hair."

"Hair?"

She tilted the flashlight down.

"Eye! Eye! Fucking eye!"

Molly dropped the flashlight. "Holy shit, Bo, someone's down there."

"What?"

"In the floorboards! Oh my god! They're alive!"

Bo picked up the flashlight and shined it into the cracks, and saw the blue-grey eye staring through the thin slit up at him.

"Heeeeeelp," it finally mustered.

Bo handed her the flashlight. "We gotta get them out." He started for one side of the room, then turned for the other. "You got a crowbar?"

"Crowbar?" Molly shook her head. "No."

"We have to get her out of there!"

"I know! I don't have a crowbar though. Sorry."

"Okay. Okay." Bo paced the room. "Hammer. We can pry the boards up, get the nails out with a hammer."

"There's one downstairs." Molly ran for the drop stairs and crawled down, returning moments later with a hammer.

Bo took the hammer from her and knelt. "Shine the flashlight on the floor. We'll find where the boards are nailed in and work from there."

As soon as the light crossed the first set of nails, Bo went to work, rending them up from the floor. He tore the first board up and started on the next.

Molly shined the flashlight on the woman in the floorboards. "There's almost enough room to get her up."

Bo tore another board up and tossed it aside. He crawled to the woman's side and pulled her out of the floor. "Watch the boards over there. Nails are still in them."

"Be careful. She's bleeding."

The woman braced herself against the remaining intact floor and got herself onto her back on the floor.

"It's Lola."

"How did she get in my floorboards?!"

"Fucked if I know!"

Molly knelt down beside her. "What happened?"

Lola looked toward her and smiled.

"We're going to get you out of here. You'll be all right."

Bo drew the flashlight down her body. "She's bleeding bad. We need to call an ambulance."

Molly turned to him. "Then do it!"

"Where's the phone?"

"There's one in my room down the hall."

Bo descended and ran to her bedroom. Molly could hear the muffled urgency in his voice as he begged them to hurry to her house.

"You'll be okay," was all she could say, both to reassure Lola and herself.

In the darkness, Molly saw Lola struggle to reach her. Molly held out her hand to meet Lola's, expecting a cold hand, finding an image. "Help me get back inside," she whispered.

"What?"

Lola tugged at the image. "I need to get back inside." She began sobbing.

"I don't understand."

Lola clutched her then and closed her eyes. Molly felt herself falling. She braced herself against the floor as vertigo took over. "Stop!"

Lola held fast, eyes still closed.

The room began to spin, then recede into a deeper darkness. She closed her eyes involuntarily, still struggling against Lola's grasp.

Finally, she loosened her hold on Molly.

Molly opened her eyes.

Where was she?

Lola tugged gently at her arm. "Come on. Let's get you home."

Molly turned, taking in the waves crashing against the beach, the verdant green fields so full of life, and a large hotel in the distance. "Where are we?"

"Home."

"I need to get back to my daughter."

"Relax." Lola turned to face her. The voice emanating from the visage was familiar, but it was a younger face now, still adorned with cuts and abrasions rendering only her relative youth recognizable. "We can help you."

Molly pulled away and ran for the hotel. Inside, a crowd had gathered at the base of the stairs. They watched a man in the center, Molly's camera in hand. She bumped into a man at the outer perimeter. "I'm sorry."

He turned, revealing another mutilated visage.

Molly backed away, taking in the surrounding guests now. Some appeared unharmed. More appeared disfigured in multiple capacities. Burn victims dotted the crowd. Others had heads that lolled at the neck as they turned to face her. Yet more gazed upon her with mutilated faces, or cradled their innards to keep them from spilling outward.

"Young lady."

Molly recognized the voice. It was Lola. She closed her eyes. "Get me out of here."

"That's what I'm trying to do."

"What is this place?"

Lola grabbed her hand and led her up the stairs. "Just keep your eyes closed. We'll get you out." She guided her to her bedroom. "You can open your eyes now."

Molly let her eyes adjust to the relative darkness.

"Lie down on the bed."

Molly continued staring at the room. "It's beautiful."

"We don't have much time. Please lie down."

Molly let herself fall into the soft mattress.

"I need you to concentrate."

"On what?"

Lola grabbed her hand. "Your home."

"Where are we?"

"Inside one of the photographs, from the camera."

"What?!"

Another man entered the room. "What happened?!"

Lola looked up at him. "She tried to save me." She turned her gaze to Molly. "This is Eric Tigerstedt. He invented the camera."

He knelt beside her. "Her clothes, so garish. If this is what style has become, I'll gladly spend eternity here."

Lola glared at him. "We need to help her get out, and if necessary, get back in."

"Why would you create something like that? Something that has caused so much pain?"

"That was never my intention." Tigerstedt tightened the scarf around his neck. "The camera was a gift, a way to feign immortality." He looked around the room. "And I'd say, for all intents and purposes, in that aspect I succeeded." He smiled at Molly. "Even though we're gone out there, in here we can stay forever."

Lola jumped in. "But there's someone else out there who knows about the camera. He was chasing me. Through the photos. He can enter them and leave them at will, like me. He'll come for you too. You must find somewhere to hide any photographs taken by the camera. If you know where the camera is, you need to destroy it. Do you know where the camera is?"

Molly nodded. "My grandfather had it. I don't know how he got it. His name was Barry Richards. It's with the chief of police now."

"Spearance told me about your grandfather. It's possible someone stole it and sold it to him. Perhaps he stumbled upon it, or stole it himself. Let bygones be bygones. What's important is that we get you out of here."

"How do I destroy the camera?"

Lola looked at Tigerstedt. He spoke. "Just smash the damned thing."

"That's it?"

Tigerstedt shrugged. "Should do the trick. It's older than dirt. I'm surprised it hasn't fallen apart by now. What, fifty years have transpired, haven't they?"

"Will it hurt you?" Molly asked.

"Does it really matter at this point? Like all art, my intentions when creating the camera don't figure into how the camera is used, or what it means to others. It needs to be destroyed, regardless of what happens to us." He placed his hand on Lola's back. "We've lived long enough."

"Okay." Lola folded Molly's hands over her chest. "I need you to concentrate. If we manage to get you out of here, whatever you feel during the transition, that's how you'll get back in as well. We'll try to guide you through it."

"Okay." Molly closed her eyes again once more, thought about the attic where she had found the camera, worked her way down to the second floor, where she and her husband had slept and, at the beginning of their relationship, made love.

"Think about what most draws you back."

She thought about her mother. Then Jolie, the girl who had worked her way under her skin and into her heart from the day she'd first felt her kick inside her. "My baby."

Lola gripped Molly's hand. "Tell me about her."

"She's—" Molly felt herself slipping.

Lola's grip grew tighter. Tighter still, until intense pain radiated through Molly's hand and up her arm. "You're hurting me!" Molly dug her heels into the floor and kicked herself out of Lola's grasp, taking the image with her.

Lola's arms reached out for her, then fell limp. She wheezed against the weight of her body. She'd only wanted to go back—stay back—but she didn't have the strength to make this young woman understand. Now she watched the room recede into darkness, a deeper darkness than she'd ever encountered before. Then the slipping began, and she felt herself falling.

And falling.

And falling.

"They're on their way." Bo looked into the attic from the drop stairs just in time to see Molly materialize in the corner. He blinked. "What—?" He shook his head. "You okay?"

"She's gone."

Bo stepped into the attic and helped Molly to her feet. "Come on."

Molly shook her head. "I can't leave her alone up here."

"She'll be fine."

"No. We should stay with her."

"You don't even know her."

Molly looked up at him. "I don't care who she is. Nobody deserves to die like this. Alone. In the dark. In some old house you've never seen." She backed away from him and slid down the wall.

Bo sighed in resignation and sat beside her. "You leave the front door unlocked?"

"Yeah."

"All right. We'll stay with her, then."

Molly clutched the photograph in her hand, refusing to look away from the wide-eyed death stare of this old woman she'd heard much about, but knew little of. She took inventory of what needed to be done. She needed to find the remaining photos, lock them away somewhere safely, and destroy the camera. But first, she was going to make sure Lola's remains were taken care of properly.

Bo tucked his flashlight away. "Did I see what I...What did I just see?"

Molly stared at the body. "What did you think you saw?"

"Never mind." Bo put his arm around her. "We'll be all right."

His words barely registered. Molly still felt like she was falling backward. But beyond the lingering disorientation she felt when Lola had touched her, a sliver of hope permeated the tragedy. Once again, that constant undercurrent of dread that had haunted her for years had left her for a brief interlude. She realized then that, for her, it was better to feel pain than fear it. Though she knew she'd fluctuate between those two extremes for the rest of her life, she at least knew now where she preferred to be. It was here, in the midst of tragedy.

The sound of approaching sirens carried through the evening until finally reaching her driveway. Bo stood and helped her to her feet. "We should go down."

Molly followed him to the front door, lagging at her bedroom to place the photo Lola had given her in her nightstand. She'd save that for Spearance.

She ran to catch Bo, who already waited at the doorway below. He tipped his hat at the first responder before letting him in. "She's passed."

He nodded. "Where is she?"

Bo pointed to the stairs. "Attic. Ladder's already down."

The EMT nodded and walked up the stairs. The second closed the ambulance door and approached the house. "Hi, Molly."

"Greg?"

"I still fill in when they need me." He watched his colleague take the stairs. "Can I come in?"

Molly moved out of the way, allowing him to pass.

Bo turned to the stairs. "Might as well get the play-by-play."

Molly closed the door and followed.

"So..." Bo sighed. "He an old friend?"

"In a manner of speaking, I suppose."

At the base of the drop stairs, Molly and Bo waited for Greg and his colleague to bring Lola down.

"What the hell happened?" Greg asked.

"We found her in the floorboards," Bo called up. "Ergo, I don't know what the hell happened."

"Just keeps getting stranger and stranger," the other man observed as he stepped down the drop stairs. "All right, send her down."

The front end of the stretcher slid into view. Greg steered it from the top, sloping it downward until his colleague had the front handles. "Bring it down slowly." Greg pushed from the attic until the back of the stretcher was resting on the stairs. Greg poked his head over the edge of the attic floor. "Give us a hand?"

Bo stepped in to help them get the stretcher on the floor as Greg stepped down. Together they carried Lola to the ambulance with Bo and Molly in tow.

When they got to the door, Spearance was exiting his car. He stopped Greg at the edge of the ambulance. "It really her?"

Greg nodded and continued toward the back of the ambulance.

Spearance came to the front door. "You two all right?"

"We're fine."

He turned to Molly. "You?"

She only nodded.

"Care to take me through it, or would you rather wait a day or two?"

Molly waved him inside. "I'll talk."

Spearance nodded outside. "You want to give those two a hand?"

"Sure." Bo reluctantly made his way to the ambulance.

Spearance shut the door behind him. "What happened?"

Molly sat at the table. "That's what I'm trying to figure out."

"Well, start with the senses." Spearance pulled out a chair and sat beside her. "What'd you see?"

"We found her in the floorboards, completely sealed in. She was covered with cuts; blood obscured any bruising that may have been there."

"My god." Spearance nodded. "You find a picture down there with her?"

Molly nodded.

"You show it to Bo?"

"I put it in my bedroom. I don't think he saw it."

"All right." Spearance stood. "Let's have a look at it."

Molly guided him upstairs to her bedroom and closed the door. "When Lola died, something weird happened."

"I'm all ears. Going to be hard to shock me at this point."

"She took me inside the photo, or into the past or something."

"Okay, you've shocked me." He smiled. "Might as well keep going."

She went to her nightstand and retrieved the photo. "There was another man there, Eric something."

"Tigerstedt."

"Yeah." She handed Spearance the photo. "They want the camera destroyed, and the pictures locked away. They said others can travel through them and could put us in danger."

"It's Miles." Spearance stared at the photo as he took Molly's story in. "I've seen one like this. We have it at the station." He waved it. "I'll make sure the photos are stored safely." He tucked the photo into his jacket. "I don't have time to go into the details, but a few incidents over the last twenty-four hours have given me a pretty good understanding of how and why Lola ended up here." He turned for the door. "I'm pretty sure Miles is following her." He opened the door and peered out to one side, then the other. "Do you have any more photos from the camera?"

Molly shook her head. "No. My grandfather only had one. The rest of mine burned in the fire."

"You sure nobody else is in the house?"

"Bo checked the top floor and the attic. I went through the bottom floor to get Jolie's things." She rubbed her forehead in frustration. "Shit. I gotta get her EpiPens over there."

"I can run them over for you."

"You sure?"

"State police will be here shortly. They're going to want to ask you about what happened. They've got a lot on their hands, so I don't think they'll hold you up all night, but you're stuck here until they're finished with you."

"Shit."

"You'll be safer with them in the house anyway." He walked through the bedroom door, turning before going to the stairs. "You okay keeping this between us?"

"Yeah." Molly closed her bedroom door behind her. "Jolie's stuff's downstairs."

Molly let her hand run down the staircase as she descended.

Spearance shook his head. "Try not to touch anything else. This is a crime scene." He smiled.

"Got you." She took her hand off the railing. "You still have the camera?"

"It's in the car." He read the look of concern on her face. "Don't worry, it's locked."

"We need to destroy it."

"It's the only collateral we have left if Miles catches us with our pants down. I think we should keep it for the time being."

"Can't we just forget about him? Let the state troopers track him down."

"Lola said there are other pictures out there, like the one in your attic. We let him get away and everyone in those pictures is in danger.

Now that she's gone, we have no idea how many photos, or where they are."

Molly walked him to the front door and opened it. A flurry of lights cascaded across the lawn from two state trooper vehicles parked beside the ambulance. "Right on cue."

Greg stepped up to meet Molly and Spearance. "I, uh—I have to go once they're done with me." He leaned in. "Is there anything you want me to say?"

Spearance shook his head. "Just be honest."

Greg nodded. "Are you okay?"

"I'm fine." Molly cradled herself to stave off the cold. "A little chilly."

"I'd like to come back."

"I don't think that's such a good idea."

"I just want to make sure you're safe. I'll come under whatever conditions you want. I could stay in my car, handcuffed to the mailbox, whatever."

Molly looked at Spearance.

He shrugged.

"All right."

"I'll be back soon." Greg walked back to the ambulance.

"He is so getting handcuffed to that mailbox."

Spearance laughed. "I'm going to have Bo stick around too. I think you ought to have both of them accompany you to your mom's once you're done here. I'm going back to the office to lock this damned thing up."

"All right."

Spearance reached out to shake her hand. "You take care of yourself."

Molly wrapped her arms around him. "You too."

He raised his arms to pat her on the back. "All right. Come on."

She let go and stepped back. "Thanks."

"Any time." He took the first step. "I mean that."

Molly nodded.

MILES

Miles watched Spearance raise his arms to greet the state troopers approaching Molly's house. "She's all yours, gentlemen."

He watched Spearance get into his car, toss a small assortment of items on his passenger seat.

Children's Tylenol.

A sky-blue package.

Spearance buckled himself into the car and reached for his keys. He patted himself down, opened the car door, and noticed them on the ground beside the car. He struggled to pick them up. A decade of overeating had made such gymnastics difficult.

Spearance struggled to catch his breath as he started the car and pulled out of the driveway.

Miles rocked on the floorboards as the car backed over the curb at the end of Molly's driveway. He angled himself so he could see just below the tree line on the right side of the road, once the tree line finally appeared. He waited for the birches. He knew the small birch forest was the most remote area on this end of the road, with a small cluster of blue spruce marking the most desolate at the other end. The forest began with a light peppering of white birch between the other trees, eventually transitioning into a full forest of birch, mostly bent and broken from an ice storm during the winter. Miles noted the birch dotting the forest and sat up. He set the camera down, hard as it was to do so, and took the three short bungee cords from under the back seat.

White birch stretched as far as the eye could see.

Miles wrapped the first cable around Spearance's neck. "Pull over."

Spearance spun out on the road, reaching for the cord with his other hand.

Miles pulled tighter. "Pull. Over."

Spearance grabbed the wheel with both hands and pulled to the side of the road.

Miles dragged the cord down Spearance's body and locked the ends together behind the seat. "Cross your forearms over your chest."

Spearance did as asked, waiting for the cord to slide down over his hands. Once they reached the last knuckles on his fingers, he turned his hands and pulled the cord toward the steering wheel. He dropped his right hand to his holster, drew his gun, and raised it to the side of his head, firing into the back seat. The blast immediately deafening.

Ears ringing, Spearance felt the cable slacken and bolted from the car, pistol drawn on the back seat.

Miles was gone.

The door was still closed.

Spearance circled the car first, then knelt down to look under the vehicle, eliminating the most plausible options first.

He had to be in one of the photos.

Spearance opened the back door slowly, scanning the seat and then the floorboards for one of the photographs.

That's when he remembered the photograph in his pocket.

He turned quickly, reaching for the photo.

It was too late.

Miles stood behind him, grabbing the gun before Spearance could turn fully. He wrenched it from his hand and turned it on him. "You're smart, but that photo in your pocket..." Miles shook his head.

Spearance raised his hands in the air. "Miles, you've got to stop."

Miles backed toward the front seat and reached in for the camera. "This it?" He kept the gun on Spearance as he looked the camera over. "Pretty unspectacular."

Miles raised the camera to his face. "Hold still." He clicked the button at the side of the camera as Spearance charged him.

Miles cradled the camera as he fell to the pavement, dropping the gun.

Spearance tore at the camera in his hands. The gun was forfeit. He needed to destroy the camera.

When it became apparent that Miles was not going to let go, Spearance began tearing at the camera, at any mechanism on the camera's surface he could find. It was surprisingly sturdy, but as Spearance gripped tighter, pieces of the camera began to give way.

The camera moaned under the mechanical duress of gear upon gear within until it began to eject a grainy image.

Spearance saw himself looking back at him in the photo. His eyes grew wide. He reached then for the gun, barely feeling the handle in his fingers when he felt the first jolt of pain surge through his body. He rolled onto his back as the gun fell from his fingers. He was bleeding from the torso.

Miles stood, partially torn photo in hand. "How'd Lola end up in Molly's house?"

Spearance cupped the wound as best he could. "I have no idea."

"You know."

Miles folded the lower corner of the photo. Spearance lurched over the hood of the car. "How'd she end up there?"

"I..." He gasped in pain. "Don't know."

Miles folded the next corner. "I bet she has an idea."

Spearance drove his fist into the hood of the car. "She doesn't know anything. None of us do."

Miles watched him squirm across the front end of the vehicle and looked both ways. "Into the ditch."

Spearance stopped.

Miles bent another corner of the photo. A sharp crunch coincided with the act, and Spearance fell to his knees. "Into the ditch."

Spearance shook his head. "You're going to kill me either way. You want me in the ditch. You put me there."

Miles bent the photo again. Spearance's right arm hung from the socket. He fell onto his other side and rolled toward the road.

Miles kicked him, but didn't have the strength to move Spearance's body down the hill.

"That camera's not the silver bullet you think it is. It isn't going to solve your problems." Spearance laughed, delusional now from the pain. "You can't even move a fat old man downhill."

Miles bent the photo again, causing Spearance to shriek.

Both arms broken, Spearance dared not roll. He lay on his back, waiting for it to be over. "Come on then!" he shouted. "If you're going to do it, do it. I never gave you any reason to make me suffer."

Miles stood over Spearance and turned his own photo toward him. He pinched Spearance's head in the photo and turned slowly. Spearance screamed as Miles crushed the bottom half of the photo and twisted in the opposite direction. Screams transitioned to snapping bone and gurgling as Miles twisted further, Spearance's neck warped like taffy on the ground below until only a thin strand of the photograph connected head and body. The last remaining threads of life connecting heart to brain pumped enough blood into his skull to conjure up a series of images, photographic flashes of his life. The memories blotted out the pain, erased his visual input, housing him comfortably inside the past. In his final moment, he returned to the picture on his nightstand.

No regrets.

No sorrows.

Only love.

When the life all but left Spearance's eyes, Miles tore the head from the lower half of the photograph, sending Spearance's head rolling into the ditch. Miles stuffed the two ends of the photograph into his pocket and pushed Spearance's body into the ditch beside his head. He overturned a pile of mud on the shoulder of the road to cover the blood, and left the body there as he drove away. He rolled down the windows to get rid of the stink of Spearance's cologne and headed toward the dump to ditch the car. They'd find it there eventually, but he only had a few loose ends to tie up before he could leave Hastings for good, find somewhere more desirable to perch while he watched the world burn.

CHAPTER SIXTEEN

MILES

MILES WAITED JUST outside the purview of the street light in front of Molly's mother's house, watching the lights switch off room by room. First, the living room lights dimmed. An hour later, they shut off completely, replaced by a lamp on the second floor. It took another hour for that light to turn off.

Around 1am, the man parked in the front yard turned his car off, stretched his arms to the degree the interior dimensions of his car would allow, and, presumably, fell asleep.

Miles waited another hour to be safe, following the fence line into the back yard. There was a screened-in porch on the second floor, but no way to get up.

The basement doors were locked, but a modest light splashed across the floor. The camera had no flash, but the light might be just enough to pick up the doors. Miles wondered if it would even matter. If whatever was photographed wasn't visible in the image, could it still be manipulated? Moreover, to what degree could inanimate objects be manipulated via photography?

He raised the camera and shot the lock on the basement doors. Minutes later the image slowly reeled out of the camera. He took it in hand and twisted the photo, watching the lock warp to the contours of the image in his hand.

When the image had been bent beyond recognition, Miles reached down for the warped lock. It was hot to the touch. He recoiled, then stepped on the lock with his foot. It burned into the sole of his shoe as he pulled, watching the last strands of hot metal give. What resistance remained immediately ceased once Miles popped the door open via the handles.

He was in.

He took the stairs to the ground floor and entered the house. From there he crept room to room, looking for signs of life. Molly's mother slept in a bedroom on the ground floor, Jolie nestled up beside her. Miles walked around the edge of the bed and rolled Jolie onto her back. She fussed only briefly, then settled against the comforter. Miles raised the camera to his face and caught Jolie through the lens. He paused, transfixed by her innocence. No, her vulnerability. For a brief moment he despised her for it, and in that moment he took the photo and left the room as it ejected from the bottom of the camera. He took it in his hand and continued exploring the house.

He found Molly on the second floor, in her old bedroom. She lay in fetal position, facing the window. Considering what she'd been through, Miles didn't want to risk waking her by shifting her to one side, so he walked to the window, knelt before Molly, and raised the camera to his face. As the camera's inner mechanisms went to work processing the photo, Molly's eyes opened. She sat up.

"Ah ah ah." Miles smiled as Molly's image ejected from the camera. "You can't afford to do anything rash."

The immediate threat of her life distracted her from a realization that came only seconds later. Miles had the camera, or *a* camera, just like the original. Even in the dark she could recognize its odd construction. "Where did you get that?"

"From our mutual friend, Mr. Spearance." He reached into his pocket and scattered the remains of the cellar door and Spearance's image across the bed. "He's no longer with us, though, I'm afraid."

Molly pulled back from the images.

"I wish I hadn't had to take my work to such extremes. I'd wanted to revisit him in the future." He reached down and pieced Spearance together in the photo. "Do you think it's salvageable?" He looked up at her and smiled. "No?" Miles scattered the pieces on the floor and stood above her. "I suppose he'll live on in some capacity. There'll be case photos tucked away in evidence. His body will serve as testament to my work." He set the camera down on the windowsill and sat down on the bed beside her, holding her picture in his hand. He pinched the photo at the edges, and he knew from the look on her face that she understood he held her life in his hands. She was his captive audience, and her beauty made her worthy of what he had to profess. "The corpse is a text, a testament to the deceased's life. The scars, the genetics, the dress, if still present, all contribute to a discourse, a clamor of voices shouting from a single conduit. But if the corpse is the result of murder, it becomes the transcript of not one but two." He smiled at her tenderly, which made his words all the more unnerving. "The human body really is the most versatile canvas. The temporal versatility of the corpse—in relation to discourse—is amazing. At any time, the corpse can enter into discourse with the living. Thousands of years after their burial, Egyptian pharaohs continue discourse with mankind. But only the living can engage such an opportunity for the short time they are here: a pseudo immortality for the dead, centered around the living." He reached for her leg, letting his fingers graze her inner thigh as he patted her. "In a manner of speaking, I've done Mr. Spearance a great service, a service his life was unworthy of. I've made him timeless."

Molly squirmed against his touch. He withdrew his hand and sighed. "The several mediums through which one may immortalize the self—generating corpses, engaging in discourse with corpses, i.e., tabulating body and bone—hinge upon the living and their reactions. I suppose I shouldn't be surprised by your reaction now. I came expecting something different though." He rose, holding the photos behind his back as he turned to the window. "Your admiration, perhaps. Your affection, ideally."

"You're insane," she muttered.

"And you are still alive, at my discretion." He turned back to her.

"You have the camera," Molly sobbed. "Why are you here?"

"I came to make you mine again."

"I'd rather die."

Miles held up the photos in his hands, revealed the image behind Molly's.

"What about her? Does she serve as some sort of collateral?"

Jolie.

Molly gasped. "You sonofabitch!" She sat up and uncovered herself, ready to jump at him.

Miles stepped back and shuffled the photo of Jolie to the top of the stack in his hands. "I see I have your attention." He held the photo as he had held hers, pinched at opposite ends, ready to tear. "Listen, I think you'll accept my offer."

"Fuck. You!"

He cocked his head, processing her reply. "I'm fine with you keeping me at arm's length. I prefer it, in fact." He reached for the camera and tucked it under his arm, returning the photo of Jolie to its vulnerable position between his fingers. "My muse is dead, and I'm in the market for another. You, preferably."

"What do I have to do?" She spoke through gritted teeth.

"Just know, every day, that I hold your and your daughter's lives in my hands." He smiled. "Know that I'll be watching."

Molly shook her head. "I can't live like that."

"You don't have a choice." He turned for the door. "Oh, and one more thing."

"What?"

He held the photo up. "I need to know who else knows about the camera."

"Nobody."

He warped Jolie's photo ever so slightly.

"Stop!" she shouted.

From downstairs, the pitter-patter of tiny feet echoed through the living room and stopped at the base of the stairs. "Mommy."

"I'm fine, honey. Go back to sleep."

Molly closed her eyes, the drying tears now streaming once more as the sound of Jolie's tiny feet hopped up the stairs. "Mommy?"

"Honey, please go back downstairs."

"Who's he?"

Miles knelt down in front of her. "I'm a friend of your mother's."

"Don't touch her."

"Tell me who else knows."

Molly shook her head. "No one else knows."

"Are you sure?"

"There's nobody else!"

He cradled Jolie's chin and ran his thumb along her soft cheeks. "You be good for your mommy."

She stared at him, frozen.

He rose. "Remember, I'm watching you." He took the first step and stopped. "Something to remember me by." He cradled the images in front of him, outside of Jolie's sight, checked the image, and bent the lower quarter of her photo. Her legs buckled and she collapsed on the floor. "Mommy!"

"What did you do to her?!" Molly ran for her daughter.

He descended the stairs. "She'll live."

Molly's mother met him at the bottom of the stairs. "What's going on?"

Miles walked toward the door, looking forward. "Your granddaughter's been injured."

Jennifer ran up the stairs. "What happened?!"

Miles savored the moment as he opened the front door. The

porch light revealed Greg, still asleep in his vehicle. Miles walked to the driver-side door and snapped a photo of Greg.

Greg woke, dazed. As soon as he recognized Miles, he unlocked his door and slammed it into Miles.

Seconds. He had seconds before that old camera would eject the photo. He knew the timing well.

Greg slid out of the vehicle and knocked the camera out of Miles' hands.

It dashed on the pavement in the driveway, surreptitiously expelling Greg's picture.

Miles dove for it.

Greg followed, pinning Miles to the ground.

The photo was just out of Miles' grasp. Hand outstretched, he could feel his lungs burning for air. Just a little bit further.

The photo mocked him.

Greg drew his fist back and landed the first blow on the back of Miles' head.

With each blow, Miles could feel the photograph traipsing across his fingers.

As Greg tugged at his outstretched arm to restrain him, the camera let loose the image. It all but fell into Miles' hand. He clasped it against the pavement as Greg dragged his arm back. He stopped mid-action as the pavement scoured his picture and body alike.

Sensing the opportunity, Miles drew the photo into his palm and crumpled it as quickly as he could.

No time to savor the kill.

Greg fell to the pavement, a mangled heap that mirrored the striations in the photo.

Miles watched as the last intimations of life left Greg's body. Then he became still like one of the photos Miles had become so accustomed to.

He took the photo in each hand and tore, watching as the body seemingly rended itself from the core outward until Greg's innards lay splayed open, a warning to anyone who tried to enter or leave the house.

Then, as quietly as he had arrived, he stepped into Greg's vehicle and pulled out of the driveway.

MOLLY

Jolie lay on the floor, reaching for her legs. "It hurts, Mommy!"

Molly stroked her forehead dry, watched as another layer of sweat beaded on the surface. "You'll be okay."

Molly's mother ran back down the stairs. "I'll call an ambulance."

"Call the police! They need to find him!"

"Am I going to die, Mommy?" Jolie asked.

"You'll be fine." She stroked her forehead again. "It only hurts in your legs, right?"

Jolie nodded. "Really bad."

"You'll be okay," Molly lied. She knew Jolie would live, but how extensive the damage was, she couldn't say. Would she be able to walk again? And if so, would she be able to run and play with her friends at school? Molly thought of all the times she'd scolded Jolie for running through the house, slipping on their hardwood floors, jumping on the couch. She thought of how quiet the house would become if all the sounds she'd cursed and rolled her eyes over while studying were replaced by silence and the faint squeak of a wheelchair. It was too much. Molly picked her daughter up and held her. "I'm so sorry." She ran her downstairs and to the living room. She set Jolie on the couch as gently as possible.

Her mother ran into the room. "They'll be here in fifteen." She knelt beside Jolie. "You okay, sweetie?"

Jolie nodded. She was being so brave in the face of all that had happened.

Molly shook her head. "We can take her now."

"I already called the ambulance."

"There's no time!"

Molly picked Jolie up and headed for the door.

Jennifer followed. "Shit, my purse." She ran back to the kitchen to grab her purse and keys and ran to the door.

They stepped out to Greg, lying on the blood-soaked pavement.

"Oh Jesus!" Jennifer turned and covered her eyes.

Still in shock from the past half hour, Molly turned Jolie away from the body. "Close your eyes, honey."

Jennifer ran back inside and closed the door behind her.

Molly knocked on the door. "Mom."

"I can't do this."

"Mom, Jolie needs to go to the hospital."

"There's a dead man in our driveway!"

Jolie looked up. "What?"

Molly turned her away from Greg's body again. "Honey, eyes closed."

Jennifer leaned against the door and began sobbing. "Oh god."

Molly leaned in to talk through the door. "Mom. Please."

Jennifer nodded to herself. "Okay. Okay." She took a deep breath and opened the door. Eyes down, she darted for her vehicle. "Okay. Come on."

Molly followed her to the vehicle, lay Jolie in the back seat, and sat in the passenger seat beside her mother.

Jennifer paused to take it all in, took too much in, and began hyperventilating. She let her head fall onto the steering wheel and began sobbing uncontrollably.

"Do you want me to drive?"

Jennifer nodded, stepped out of the car, and traded places with her daughter.

Molly started the car, turning off the headlights until they pulled into the road. She couldn't see Greg like that again. Not tonight. Not ever.

***

Jolie had passed out from shock by the time they reached the hospital. Molly carried her into the ER while her mother registered them at the front desk. Once Jolie was in a room resting comfortably, Molly ran to the front desk to find her mother. "She's in."

"Thank god."

"Look, I need to go get something at the police station. Can you stay with Jolie?"

"You sure you're okay?"

Molly nodded. "I'm fine."

"That guy's still out there. You should wait with us until they catch him."

"This is important."

"Fine," Jennifer resigned, handing over her keys.

Molly headed for the door.

"Molly."

Molly turned. "Yeah?"

"Stay safe."

Molly nodded.

***

The lights were still on at the station when Molly arrived, but the door was locked. She toggled the door knob and began banging on the large-panel glass in the door. "John!" She hammered the door again. "Jim!"

Jim ambled out of the evidence room and unlocked the door. "What's going on?"

Molly ran past him. "I need my photo."

Jim followed her into evidence. Molly was already digging through the box on the table. "Is it in here?"

"Hold up." Jim put a hand on her shoulder, gripped firmly. "What's going on?"

"Miles was just at my house."

"I heard on the scanner. They sent an ambulance to your mother's. What're you doing here?"

"My mother's at the ER with Jolie." She stopped to catch her breath. "Look, I really need that picture." She started for the nearest evidence box and began rifling through it. "Have you seen Spearance?"

"I thought he was with the state boys."

Molly shook her head. "He's in trouble. We're all in trouble. Miles has the camera." She continued shuffling through the papers. "I need the goddamned photo!"

Jim unlatched his keys, stepped to the evidence box, and opened it. "Which one you looking for?"

"The one they took of me, the night of the fire!"

Jim dumped the photos, turned them over, and spread them across the table.

Molly scattered them until she found herself staring back at her. There she was.

The girl she used to be. "Thanks."

"I can't let you take it."

"That's fine." Molly sat at the table. "Can I have a minute alone?"

"I don't feel comfortable leaving you alone."

She glared at him. "Leave the room, Jim."

He raised his hands. "Okay." He looked at her quizzically, then swept the other photos into the evidence box and took it into the neighboring room.

Molly held the photo in her hands and closed her eyes. She tried to remember how it felt, the slipping away from consciousness that accompanied her transition with Lola. She tried hard to replicate that feeling, to little effect.

She opened her eyes, then sat back in the chair and tried again.

No luck.

She began to panic. She *had* to go back.

She closed her eyes again, tried letting them roll back into her head behind her eyelids, tried to emulate sleep. She couldn't do it.

She fell onto her arms on the table and began to cry again. The shock was beginning to wear off, and her mind was all but forcing her to process the evening's incidents. It needed desperately to process the last decade or so, in all honesty. Though she'd been keying in and re-living the better part of that decade on a daily basis, she'd never really taken the time to reflect on it and grow from it. She pushed them out of her head, trying to remain empty.

It occurred to her that it was around this time, on this date, six years ago that she was finally released from the hospital and allowed to go home. They had returned some of her belongings to her that night, and the faint smell of smoke took her back to the night of the fire. She hadn't escaped that for years. Burnt toast took her back. The winter's first stove fire took her back. The time she left her curler on the bathroom sink and it started to smolder took her back. Everything reminded her of that night.

She looked into the photo, inhaled the charred edges through her nose, and closed her eyes.

And she was back.

Sam held up Molly's camera and took a picture of her. "Welcome to the party!"

The image fell out of the bottom of the camera. Molly bent down to pick it up, and noticed a stack of grainy photos on the desktop. When she rose, Sam fell into her.

Molly pushed Sam away.

"What's your problem, pledge?"

"Give me my camera back. Please."

"I just wanted to see if it still worked. We got some great pictures." Sam reached for the stack of photos and held them up. "They're a little fuzzy, but you can still see the penis we drew on Bev's forehead, right?" She laughed. "Where'd you get this old thing anyway? You pick it up at the thrift store?"

"It was my grandfather's."

"Tell you what, you find me another camera and I'll give this one back."

"Please. You don't understand," Molly pleaded.

But nothing changed, and the night ended as it had six years ago, with Sam's blackened body rolling on the front lawn as PXO went up in flames behind her.

The only difference was, this time as Molly watched, she also thought about Jolie, and whether or not she'd be okay between then and now, even though she hadn't even been born yet.

Again, Molly lived through the initial investigation, the court cases, and more interviews. She tried to change her answers, but the transcripts never captured any of it. She was a passive observer, only able to change the things that she thought at the time, and that turned out to be a special hell in itself, because through it all—through her marriage, the extramarital affairs, the birth of her daughter—all she could think about were Jolie's broken legs, and the uncertainty they carried with them.

For a second time, she watched her husband die. She tried to prevent it, but agency was only illusory. She could step outside herself during the painful interludes, but what had happened was burned in celluloid, eternal. These images she and Lola had dove into, they were not actual history. They were recorded history as it had transpired. Nothing could be changed, and nothing was a stronger indication of that reality than her times with Miles, watching the soon-to-be killer pump awkwardly between her thighs. Even with her eyes closed, she could see the images she'd retained from the original experience, wishing there were some way to fast forward past the gooseflesh-inducing thrusts, his hot breath in her face.

For a second time, she let the tall, shaggy-haired man named Greg into her life, and almost into her bed. Knowing what she did, she was glad she hadn't been so liberal with her desires. For a second time, he lied to her, only this time she let him lie to her. She let him reveal his secrets on his terms, in his own time, and she hated him less for it.

For a second time, she found a forlorn and forgotten silent-film actress dying beneath her attic floorboards. For a second time, she had been taken back to a life before hers. She watched Lola carefully this time, held fast to every nuance of the experience. If she ever had to go back again, she'd do it with the speed and efficiency of that old woman. She'd do it like she had years of experience.

And as the night her picture was taken again with that camera approached, Molly braced herself for the inevitable: that all of this would be for naught, that she had just re-lived the most painful years of her life for nothing.

She opened her eyes in the darkness as Miles snapped the photo of her, and when she did, she found herself in the passenger seat of Greg's car, Miles at the helm. This was one of many scenarios she'd imagined when she thought about how she'd return—and she'd thought about it often.

Molly reached for the steering wheel and pulled toward the roadside. Miles let go of the steering wheel in shock and she drove her fist into his face, then opened her hand and gouged at his eyes. Miles hit the brakes, sending Molly onto the dash. Her head slammed into the windshield, and she felt the same sense of slipping she'd felt when entering her photo. She shook it off, pushed the car into park, pulled herself over the steering wheel, and clawed at his eyes again.

Miles brought his fists down over her head, always with the soft base of his hand. He was weak, and his weakness emboldened her. She raked his eyes with her nails as he struggled to open his door. She pulled herself down onto the passenger seat, raised her knee as she prepared to top him, then dropped it into his crotch. He screamed, his struggle with the door handle growing more fervent. His other hand cradled the ache between his legs as he finally opened the door. As he fell to the roadside, Molly grabbed his coat and pulled as he slipped out of it clumsily. "Where's the pictures?!" she shouted, shaking the coat out. She draped it over her shoulder and jumped out the driver side door. Miles reached for her foot. She raised it and stomped down on his open palm. "Where are they?!"

He screamed in agony as she rifled through the coat, pressing harder on his hand with the heel of her shoe.

"Stop!"

Her hand grazed something glossy. She found the edge and pulled it out. Jolie's photo. She reached for the other pocket as Miles reached for her foot with his other arm. She stepped back and kicked at his hand. He flailed on the ground, desperately trying to grab her leg. But Molly was faster than him. Fresher. She had been waiting for this moment for six years.

She reached into his other pocket and felt another photo. She pulled it out and tossed the jacket over his flailing body and stomped indiscriminately, relishing every time her foot made contact with flesh. She had both photos, and he had nothing.

When his frantic movements slowed, Molly left him moaning on the roadway. She rounded the front of the vehicle, took the camera out of the passenger seat, and went back to Miles.

She uncovered him.

His eyes widened as they focused on the camera held to her face.

Molly's finger hovered above the button. "Smile, motherfucker." Molly took the photograph and stepped back as it ejected from the bottom of the camera.

"No." Rolling onto his hands and knees, he begged her. "Don't destroy it. Please."

She pulled his photo from the mechanism beneath the camera and looked it over. The interior lights of the car had rendered him visible in the image. She tucked the camera under her arm and bent the bottom of the photo.

Miles' legs twisted to conform to the photo.

"That's for my daughter."

She folded the image in half. Miles' back snapped. Ligaments tore from bone, and flesh separated from flesh. Miles gasped.

"That's for John."

He reached out to her, pupils dilated from the pain.

Only now did she feel safe.

She zipped the photos of herself and Jolie into her jacket. Tears streamed down her face. "Six years!" she screamed at him. "I had to re-live six years of my life to get to you!" She held the camera above her head. "I had to watch the husband I betrayed die. I had to work with you at that fucking grocery store. I couldn't say anything! Any time I tried to deviate from my horribly scripted life, it would just continue around me, like I wasn't there. I had to watch everything unfold like I knew nothing!"

He lowered his hand and fell onto the road. He was dying.

"Fuck you!" she shouted.

Miles stopped moving, but she hoped he could still see.

It was over. It was finally over.

She threw the camera against the pavement with the last of her strength. It smashed to pieces.

Molly noticed Miles' eyes shift to the camera's remains as she kicked the smaller bits to the side of the road. He had focused on the larger portion that remained intact, the inner mechanisms, a matrix of gears, bone, and flesh.

At the center of the piece, something throbbed.

A heart, distended from the mechanisms within it, pumped. With each beat, the matrix of gears surrounding it churned, as if trying to develop one final image.

Miles smiled. Tears streamed down his face.

Molly raised her foot and brought it down on the camera.

Whatever throbbed at the center, it throbbed no longer. A thick viscous yellow oozed from under her foot.

Molly stood over Miles with his photo in her hand. "This is for Lola." She folded his image at the neckline, watching as his body contorted.

And with that, the next great innovator was dead.

Molly took in her surroundings, noted the faint orange glow on the horizon in the east. She wasn't far from Hastings. She felt the images in her coat, grabbed the largest remnant of the camera on the curb, and followed the roadway toward the soft light just above the tree line.

EPILOGUE

MOLLY WALKED TWELVE miles that night back to Hastings.

Twelve miles walked.

Six years re-lived.

Eight weeks until Jolie could put weight on her legs again.

And in a handful of hours, six feet below the surface of Saint Bernard Cemetery, she'd be laying her professor, and her sheriff, to rest.

All because of some goddamned camera.

Molly waited in the modest line that had gathered at the service of John L. Spearance, sheriff of Hastings, PA. It was an open-casket ceremony, at his sister's request. Molly had settled on closed-casket for her husband. Twice. It was one of the few decisions she didn't regret from the past six years.

As she approached the casket, Jim stepped back and ushered her forward. "You going to bury the pictures with him?"

Silence.

"John's family paid for a concrete vault. Waterproofed. They'd be safe. John's nephew stuffed a few cigars in the lining. Nobody'd think anything of it if you added something."

"I worry about mold, or how decomposition might affect them. Bo said I could keep them in the fireproof safe at the station. I think they'll be safer there."

Jim nodded.

"I do have something for him, though." Molly took three loosely connected gears from the camera out of her purse and tucked them into the lining of the casket.

Molly drove to the cemetery alone. She hovered outside the centrally gathered throng awaiting Spearance's arrival. Then the hearse pulled in, with a squad car following. A third state vehicle followed. Once the hearse parked, Jim and Bo stepped out of the squad car and took the left side of the casket. Two state troopers and John's brother-in-law took the other. They disappeared into the crowd, and this was, for Molly, the proverbial lowering of the casket. She did not see the ground cast over his casket as it descended. John Spearance disappeared into a group of his loved ones, carried by his colleagues. It was as honorable as Hastings could muster. It was good, and in this circumstance, good was good enough.

She had refused to hear the details of Spearance's death. Greg, on the other hand, she had seen in full view. That funeral was a city and a day away. Molly'd make it if she could, if for no reason other than to be sure his niece and nephew were still okay. That, and she still held a small place in her heart open for him, even after he lied. He'd died trying to protect her. She'd forgiven herself for that. She had six years to do so. But she hadn't forgotten.

After the casket had been lowered, Bo handed Jim his keys to the squad car. "You take it back into town for me?"

Jim nodded, a faint glow emanating from his bloodshot eyes.

Bo walked toward Molly, hands in his pockets. "Can I catch a ride back to the station with you?"

"Sure."

They walked between the stones, noting the reverse chronology apparent in the disappearing names eroded by time as they approached the roadside.

"Amazing how much heartache exists in these places, isn't it?"

Molly nodded. "I think I'm going to be cremated."

"It shouldn't be up to you."

"It's my body."

"And it's yours to die how you please with." Bo stopped at the edge of the cemetery and looked down at the first row of graves. "But all of this." He stared down the length of the row. "This isn't for the dead. This is for the dying."

"Deep." Molly smiled.

"Whatever." Bo smiled at her. "Where's your car, woman?"

"Just over the hill."

Once inside, Molly pulled into gear. "You hear anything about the investigation?"

"I think we'll be all right." Bo looked out the window. "They've traced everything back to Miles. Fingerprints just about everywhere a body was found, except Lola's house. Even Maier up in New York. He was sloppy."

"Any word on when I'll be able to go back home?"

Bo shook his head. "They ought to be just about cleaned up at this point."

"You don't think they're going to give me a hard time about..." She drifted.

"You acted in self-defense." He turned to her. "Remember?"

Molly pulled into the station.

"Don't mean they won't have more questions." He turned back to the window. "Just remember. Car went off the road and he was rendered nearly unconscious. You made sure he stayed that way and escaped."

"Shit." Bo stepped out of the car and patted himself down. "Keys."

"Seriously?"

"Close your eyes and turn around."

Molly closed her eyes and heard Bo walk to the corner of the building.

"All right." Bo shook the keys. "We got 'em."

Once inside, Molly handed off the two photographs to Bo. He walked them into the evidence room. "Fire safe is pretty dry. Temperature's always a steady 72 throughout the building. These ought to be fine."

"Thanks." She watched Bo seal the fire safe. "You really think they'll have more questions for me?"

"Probably, unfortunately."

She sighed. "Spearance promised me I wouldn't get wrapped up in this."

"Maybe this is it. The last time you'll have to deal with anything like this. If karma's real, you've cleared your bill and then some, right?"

"One can hope."

"One can."

"So, ah, hey. This might not be the best time to ask, but—"

Molly turned for the door. "No, Bo."

"All right." He laughed. "I won't ask again. Offer's always open."

"Oh, I know." She smiled. "Thanks, Bo."

"My pleasure!"

Molly met Jim at the door. Jim tipped his hat. "Bo ask you out again?"

"Yeah."

Jim laughed. "Looks like Spearance owes me five bucks after all."

"You guys seriously started a betting pool on Bo's love life?"

"Or lack thereof," Jim chided. "Got one hundred riding on

whether or not you'll ever say yes, too."

Molly turned just outside the door. "How's Saturday night at 6:00 sound?"

Bo's eyes widened. "Really?"

"Why not."

"Got any place in mind?"

"Burning Fields is this weekend."

Molly held out her hand. "So, about that $100 you owe Spearance."

"Well, shit." Jim pulled his wallet out of his pocket and opened it.

Molly stepped up and took the bill out of Jim's wallet. "Thanks for paying, Jim." She pocketed the bill and stepped out the door. "And if you're thinking of starting a betting pool on whether or not Bo's getting lucky, he's not. We're just going as friends."

"Can't win 'em all." Bo sat down at his desk, still beaming. He grabbed the letter opener and found some semblance of comfort in the routine of opening his mail.

Jim closed the door behind Molly. "Things aren't going to be the same around here without John."

Bo set the letter opener on his desk. "No, they aren't."

"Next time we're off duty together, let's grab a beer. What do you say?"

Bo picked the letter opener up and started on the next envelope. "We're the only two officers left. Something tells me there's not going to be an 'off duty' for a while."

Jim nodded. "You're probably right."

Bo dropped the letter opener again, grinning from ear to ear. "You can't win 'em all, but that doesn't mean you can't ever win."

Jim looked up from the stack of paperwork on his desk. "What now?"

Bo waved the letter above his head. "Publisher's Clearing House." He opened the letter frantically. "Oooh, there's a check for..."

He flipped the letter over and back again.

"One dollar?! Son of a bitch!"

***

The Burning Fields Festival always kicked off at the Moore farm just outside of town. They had eighty acres—mostly grains—and, as one of the larger farms in town, had the luxury of being first on the list each year. Following that first day, the fire department would make their way through the farmland, staggering properties two to three a day, so everyone was done by the time planting started.

The Moores decided to start the tradition after buying a vendor trailer for the dairy princess parade. Each year since its inception it grew a little more, now involving the full fire department, bouncy castles for the kids, outdoor readings in coordination with the library, and more. And though most residents could get past the thick plumes of smoke carrying through town, the first fire was always lit *after* the festivities.

Bo and Molly arrived at dusk, just an hour before the lighting of Moore's field. Normally Molly could make a full day of it, but with Jolie wheelchair-bound for the next six weeks, there wouldn't be much for her to do. As they wheeled her in, her eyes darted from one activity to the next, almost all of them involving legs in some capacity.

Molly frowned, looked at Bo for ideas.

"I'll take her over to get some cotton candy." He took the handles of the chair and leaned down. "What do you say, cotton candy?"

"Do they have different flavors?!"

"I'm sure they do."

"Let's go!"

Bo started toward the cotton candy booth when one of the Moore kids, Christopher, walked up to the edge of Jolie's wheelchair. "That's a nice chair you have."

Jolie smiled. "Thanks."

"They wouldn't give me a chair when I broke my leg. Fell off the merry-go-round up at the school playground. Just crutches for me."

"I broke both my legs."

The Moore boy looked to the right, toward the swings, then toward the dunk tank. "Your arms okay?"

Jolie nodded.

"I bet you could dunk my aunt. They'd probably let you get a bit closer on account of your chair, too. It's only fifty cents for three balls."

Jolie turned her head to Molly. "Can I try it, Mom?"

Molly dug through her purse and handed a few quarters to Jolie. "Sure, I've got some change."

The Moore kid edged Bo out of the way. "I can take her."

Bo raised his hands. "Be my guest."

Molly zipped her purse. "That was awfully nice of him."

Bo rolled his eyes. "They got those damned kids working the

crowd every year."

"They're a good family."

"They're money hungry."

"You afraid they're going to take your Publisher's Clearing House winnings?"

Bo slid his arm around her waist. "They aren't getting my dollar."

"You'll spend more than a dollar before the night's over."

"All right, well, they aren't getting *that* dollar."

The fire trucks began the slow roundabout trip to the edge of Moore's field. Their lights flashed rhythmically, conjuring up a thread of blaring sirens and strobing lights in Molly's memory. She didn't want to remember. Not today. She closed her eyes. "They light it yet?"

"Hang on." Bo held her closer. "All right. She's lit."

He watched as the fire began to spread across the field. "Spearance hated this time of year." Bo laughed. "Ever since I've been on the force, he'd burn through his vacation time upstate, get as far away from the festival as he could."

"Can't say I blame him." Molly opened her eyes again to the fire, and watched as the black clouds blotted out the last rays of sun on the horizon. This, too, brought back memories, memories of campfires by the river with her cousins, of state parks with her husband, Tom, of the starless sky in Johnstown rehabilitation. Now she could smell the sterilized rooms, the thin layer of fresh plastic under the bedspread...

She shook that last memory off, forced herself back into the moment. Nearly everything in her life—every experience, every sense—brought back a cocktail of pleasant and unpleasant memories alike.

Except fire.

Even after Sam and the others had passed, it was always photographs, sirens, men in uniform, even flapper-era attire, that reminded her of that night. Somehow the fire itself had taken on a different role. While everything else orbited and fed her almost perpetual sense of dread, fire rested at the epicenter, the quiet eye of a tornado where she could see the cacophony of anxiety swirling around her. When things were at their worst, when her life was in flames and burning at the highest temperature possible, that's when she felt her resilience return to her. That burning—fear ablaze in her chest, guilt alight in her mind, in the very core of her being—that was the worst things could ever get.

She'd survived it, and knew she could survive it again.

"You think Hastings is ready for a lady on the force?"

"Does it matter if they're ready?"

Molly smiled.

"Didn't think so."

ACKNOWLEDGMENTS

I HAVE THANKED a lot of people over the years for their help and dedication. This time around I'd like to focus on a few who really helped keep me going. First, I'd like to thank Shawn Tiernan, colleague, friend, and infinitely helpful reader of all my manuscripts. I'd like to say we equally share the responsibility of reviewing one another's work, but he's always put in more time than me, and that hasn't gone unnoticed. Second, I'd like to thank my fellow authors who paved the way for our previous subgenre at JournalStone, in particular Karl Fischer and John Bruni, whom I have had the opportunity to work with in the past. Finally, I'd like to thank my previous publishers and editors, Andersen Prunty and C.V. Hunt of Grindhouse, and Jason Sizemore and Lesley Connor at Apex Publications.

ABOUT THE AUTHOR

Kirk Jones (kɜrk Dʒoʊnz): 1. English Director of *Nanny McPhee* 2. "Sticky Fingaz," rap artist and actor who played Blade for the television series. 3. Canadian who survived a dive over Niagara Falls...only to return and pass upon his second attempt. 4. Boring author of *Die Empty* (Atlatl, 2017), *Aetherchrist* (Apex, 2018), who often gets mistaken for the other, arguably more notable, Kirk Jones fellows. 5. Also not Kirk Byron Jones.